CORY'S FLIGHT

FACING THE MUSIC

SUSPENSEFUL SECRETS
BOOK 2

DAN PETROSINI

Print ISBN: 978-1-960286-17-8
Naples, FL
Library of Congress Control Number: 2023903466

OTHER BOOKS BY DAN

Complicit Witness

Push Back

Ambition Cliff

PROLOGUE

Lew Stein trudged up the steps of his brownstone near the Brooklyn Heights Promenade. He was coming home from a bar where he'd watched the Knicks beat the spread. Stein couldn't remember if they'd won or lost, just that they'd beaten the spread. He had bet they wouldn't. Big. Stein shook his head; he'd make it back tomorrow. From his rooftop he had a good view of Lower Manhattan. He decided to head up there with a brew and roll around the next day's games.

He put the key in his front door, and the thick, hundred-year-old door swung smoothly on its well-oiled hinges. As he tossed his keys on the foyer settee, a bag went over his head, and he was pinned against the wall. As the bag tightened around his neck, Stein struggled to claw at it. The killer pressed his forearms across Stein's shoulders, blocking his attempt. Stein sucked in the last remaining air as the killer wrestled him to the floor, putting both knees on Stein's back.

Stein turned his head, eyeing his prized recliner with the built-in cooler, when his vision went white. He couldn't make anything out. The white light that people remembered when they came back from near-death was usually their vision going from low blood pressure. But Stein wasn't having a near-death experience. He had just crashed through its door.

The killer took the bag off Stein's head, putting it back with the collection under the sink. He rummaged through the rest of the kitchen, disgusted the compulsive gambler hadn't stashed any cash.

The killer stepped over Stein, cracking open the heavy door. Coast clear, he slipped away.

1

____

A YELLOW CAB BEEPED ITS HORN AS CORY DODGED TRAFFIC on Madison Avenue. He waved, believing the driver recognized him, but the cabbie gave him the finger.

Life was different now, but he didn't miss the celebrity or the money.

Cory was more grateful. He'd almost self-destructed but had held on during the ride up and during the fall from grace. Surviving felt good, but he knew there was still one thing to conquer as he weaved through the crowded sidewalk.

Cory walked into Mt. Sinai fingering the vial in his pocket. He needed a lift.

Jane Santo, the hospital's PR woman, met him in the lobby. The pair headed to the children's wing, walking down a balloon-filled corridor that smelled of flowers.

Santo said, "We're thrilled you agreed to do this."

"Anything for the kids. I would've done it sooner, but uh, life got in the way."

"You're here now, and they're excited beyond belief."

"Let's hope I don't disappoint them."

"They love you. I saw you teaching them at Cornell."

Cory smiled. "That was fun. I wish I could've gotten guitars for everyone, but . . ."

"No problem. A donor came through."

"Good for them. Did you get the numbers on transplants?"

"I was surprised with the numbers on pediatric transplants. The most common are liver and kidney, and we performed twenty last year."

"That's super low."

"We're having a difficult time with the donor pool."

"What about waiting times?"

"After three years on the list, about forty percent of patients receive a liver."

"That's worse than the national average. What about kidneys?"

"I'm afraid the numbers are lower. After a three-year wait, it's sixteen percent."

"That's terrible. We got to do a lot better than that for our kids."

"We're working on it." Santo pointed to a door. "We're in here."

Cory peered in the door's window. The room was full of kids. In front, children in wheelchairs were chatting, and behind them it looked like a playground. He slipped out of the backpack holding his guitar and handed it to Santo. "I'm going to hit the boy's room."

"I'll hand out the guitars."

He locked the bathroom door, catching a glimpse of himself in the mirror. It felt good seeing the kids so animated.

Cory patted the vial and shook his head. Should he go without it? He took the vial out and stared at it. He opened it, considering a quick hit.

He wagged his head, poured the powder down the sink, and threw away the container.

The volume in the room rose when Cory stepped in. "Hey everybody. How we doing today?"

The room erupted. "Super. Who wants to learn to play the guitar?"

A cacophony of we dos sounded as guitars were handed out.

"Fantastic. Now, remember, everyone is going to get a chance today. Some of you I'll bring up here as an example, but don't worry, I'll walk around and help everyone."

Cory slipped the strap over his shoulder, attaching his Martin. "For the righties in the room, put your left hand on the skinny part. It's called the neck—"

The door to the room burst open, and four New York City cops rushed in. "Mr. Lupinski, you're under arrest for murder. Put the guitar down."

"Me? I didn't kill anybody."

An officer unhooked the strap and the other slapped a cuff on his wrist.

"Hey, what are you doing? There's been a mistake. I didn't do anything!"

As a cop read him his rights, Santo tried to calm the children.

"LINDA, THEY ARRESTED ME."

"For what? Don't tell me it's for drugs."

"No, they said I killed Lew Stein."

"Lew Stein? Your old manager?"

"Yeah."

"Did . . . did you?"

"Of course not."

"I don't understand what's going on."

"Me either. I need a lawyer, fast."

"Who we gonna use?"

"I don't know. Call the label, see if they can help. No, call Tracy instead."

"Tracy? She used you—"

"She's got a lot of contacts. The label didn't give two shits about me when I was on top, now they'll give me some corporate hack."

"Okay. When are you getting out?"

"I don't know. I got to be arraigned and hopefully get out on bail."

"Where are you?"

"Manhattan Detention Center, downtown, on White Street."

"The Tombs?"

"Yeah."

"Oh, Cory. I'm scared."

"It's going to be all right."

"What do I tell the kids?"

"Tell them the truth. I didn't do anything, it's some kind of mistake."

"I don't understand how—"

"They're telling me I gotta go."

"Be careful, Cory. I love you."

"Love you too."

2

Cory had one arm chained to the steel table. He put his free hand in front of his mouth. The smell of his breath was enough to quell his hunger. As Cory yawned, the door opened.

Stephen Worth marched in. "Mr. Lupinski. How was your night?"

Worth used the sleeve of his jacket to move the chair out and sat.

Cory shook his head. "Terrible. The place is filled with lunatics. They never stop shouting. It's worse than in the movies."

"Let's see if we can get you out of here."

"If? I gotta get out, today."

"We'll do our best, but ultimately it's up to the judge."

"But I'll get out, right?"

Worth kept his hands in his lap. "I've had a discussion with the assistant district attorney handling the case. We debated the bail issue."

"How much do they want?"

"It's complicated . . ."

"What's so difficult? They let crooks out with nothing these days, and I didn't do anything."

"You've touched upon one of the factors. New York revised its rules, and most accused are released without posting bail. However, many of those released don't appear in court as promised, and many commit crimes while released."

"What's all this got to do with me?"

"There is a lot of pushback from law enforcement and citizen groups over the change, and as a result, they're being especially hard on violent crimes."

"I didn't kill him or anyone."

"Whether you did or not is not material—"

"Not material? How can that be?"

"This is a bail hearing, not a trial. The proceedings are limited to the threat you pose to the community and the likelihood you would flee."

"This is crazy. I'm not a threat to anybody."

"You have to keep in mind the court doesn't know you or anything about this case. However, you do have a history with the victim."

"That was long ago. The degenerate gambler ripped me off, stole all my money."

"We'll have to discuss that incident in detail."

"It has nothing to do with anything. How can they say I killed him? I haven't seen him since then."

"The DA has witnesses who claims you were at the victim's house and—"

"That's bullshit! I wasn't there."

Worth threw a palm up. "We'll have plenty of time during discovery to examine any witness or evidence they have. But at this time, we must concentrate our resources on the bail hearing."

Cory exhaled. "Okay, okay. What can we do?"

"The DA is recommending a five-million-dollar bail."

"Five million? That's crazy. I don't have that kind of money."

"We could work with a bail bondsman. They'd post a bond guaranteeing the court the money in full."

"How much do they want?"

"They usually demand collateral. Maybe a lien on your home or other assets."

"I don't have other assets."

"You do receive royalties from your recordings, correct?"

"Yeah, but I give most of it to a children's charity to fight cancer."

"I've been made aware of that. It's a very commendable thing to do, but we're going to need to access those funds if you're going to make bail."

"How can I do that? It's in a trust."

"You're the trustee, I assume."

"Yeah, I think so."

"We can enter into a loan agreement with the trust."

"I don't understand."

"You'll borrow the money from the trust and pledge the revenue stream to a bail bondsman. You'll have to supplement it with other liens, say on your home and any savings if the stream comes up short."

"Okay, that sounds good, but do the kids still get the money to fight cancer?"

"I'm afraid not."

"I can't do that. It's too important to them and me."

"If you don't have the cash or have enough assets to pledge, I don't see another way to make bail."

"Can't we ask the judge? I mean, it's for the kids. They need it."

"We can present this unusual effort to achieve bail and

perhaps the judge may reduce the amount, but given the environment, I'm not hopeful."

"How much do you think it could be lowered?"

"A million-dollar reduction would be on the high side."

"Isn't there any other way to get me out?"

"Unless the charges are dropped, this is your only opportunity. I recommend you take advantage of it while it's available."

"I want out of here, but I'd just hate it if even one kid had to suffer because of it."

"If you get this behind you, you can resume your philanthropic efforts. Also, mounting a defense will be easier if you're released."

"Okay, okay. Get it done. How soon can I get out?"

"These things take time."

"I can't stay in here. You gotta get me out."

"I'll have the documents drafted and ask the DA to expedite the hearing."

3

―――――

Linda threw open the door. "Daddy's home!"

The apartment was quiet. Cory asked, "Where is everybody?"

"Mrs. Baker is watching Tommy."

"Ava?"

They went into the family room. Their daughter was sitting in front of the TV.

"Hey, Ava!"

She didn't move her head. "Hi."

"Get up, Ava. You haven't seen your father for five days."

Cory said, "It's okay, honey. I'm going to jump in the shower."

"No, it's not okay. Say hello to your father."

Eyes rolling, Ava got on her feet. "How was jail, Dad?"

"Go to your room!"

"It's okay. Listen, honey, this is all one big mistake. I didn't hurt that man."

"That man was your manager."

"Yes, a long time ago. But that has nothing to do with anything."

Another eye roll. "The news said you stabbed him a couple of years ago."

"That's true. It was wrong to do that, and I'm not making excuses, but believe me, I had nothing to do with whatever happened to him."

"Then why were you arrested?"

"I really don't know, but I'm sure the incident you mentioned played a part in it. I kind of get it, but it's a big mistake, and we're gonna straighten it out."

"It's so embarrassing. I can't go anywhere without some-body saying something."

"I'm sorry, honey, I really am. But I'm gonna get it taken care of."

Ava walked away. "If you say so."

"What did you say?"

"Forget it, Linda, let her go."

"You have no idea how difficult Ava's been."

"It's hard on her, plus she's a teenager. I have to take a shower, or I'll be late."

<hr>

CORY BUTTONED his jacket as he emerged from the Lexington Avenue subway station. Leaves and papers swirling, Cory put his head down and walked into the wind.

It'd taken his lawyer too long to get him out of jail, but Stephen Worth seemed like a pro. Cory was pissed he had to tap the trust set up for kids with cancer, but the lawyer had come up with the idea and he was free, for now.

Cory stepped off the elevator into the wood-paneled lobby of the Worth and Colby Law Firm. It was stuffy and conservative, but Cory had had his fill of slick entertainment lawyers. This lawyer wasn't cheap, but Cory joked to himself, maybe Worth was worth it.

Shown into his attorney's office, Cory was concerned that Worth was seated wearing his suit jacket. This guy was a stiff. How would this guy believe him if he couldn't connect with him?

Worth rose, buttoning his jacket. "Mr. Lupinski, how are you?"

"Okay."

"I heard the release went as planned."

"I thought you would be there."

"My associates are very capable. Sit. Can we get you anything?"

"No. I'm good."

"We'll get started then."

"I can't wait to straighten this out. It's some kind of a misunderstanding."

"The DA views it otherwise."

"But we'll explain I had nothing to do with it. They need evidence, don't they?"

"Yes. The burden of proof lies with the state; however, I must advise you that the allegations are supported by two witnesses that place you at the scene of—"

"How can that be? I wasn't near his house. Who said they saw me?"

"Yes, we examined their sworn statements, and they're ironclad."

"How can that be?"

"We'll take a further look at the witnesses, but—"

"Who are these guys?"

"Their names are Thomas Rizer and Robert Ford. Both men work in the area. We're looking into them, and we'll write up their biographical profiles."

"This is all one big misunderstanding or something. How long is this going to take to clear this up?"

"It's difficult to predict the nature of a case. If a plea can be negotiated, it would dramatically shorten the process."

"What kind of deal?"

"You're charged with the first-degree murder of Mr. Stein, meaning it was premeditated."

"That's frigging ridiculous."

"That may be. However, your prior, uh, encounter and business relationship with the victim support the charge."

"Just because I confronted the bastard about the money he stole from me, I'm the guy they think killed him?"

"I should add that the DA mentioned a blood sample that was collected at the crime scene and which did not match the victim's."

"That's super! Why didn't you tell me?"

"They're running DNA testing and will compare the sample taken when you were processed, to the blood collected at the crime scene."

"Go for it, man! That's it. They're gonna drop the charges."

"Not necessarily."

"What do you mean?"

"A nonmatch would be good news, but in and of itself, it's not proof you're innocent."

"But whoever's blood it is, he's the killer."

"Not necessarily."

"Well, then whose is it?"

"It serves no purpose to speculate. Why don't we firm up your whereabouts during the time the murder took place?"

"Okay. What do you want to know?"

"Where you were during the day of October 9th?"

"I got up around seven, and you know, we have two kids.

I made Tommy, he's six, breakfast and we played a little. Then I worked on a new song. I had to go to Quad Recording Studio, on Seventh Avenue. They hired me to lay down a track on a Willow Man tune. I thought the other player sounded good, but I was glad to get the gig."

"What time was that?"

"I got out of there about one."

"Where did you go?"

"I headed back to Brooklyn to teach. I give lessons seven days a week and have quite a few students. It helps pay the bills."

"I'll need their names and addresses."

"Sure."

"Where in Brooklyn do you teach?"

"All over. I go to their houses. Most of them are kids, but I have five or six adults I teach."

"What parts of Brooklyn were the lessons on the nineteenth?"

"Um, I started out in Bay Ridge, and you know, then went to Bensonhurst. This kid Billy is going to be something, and um, yeah, I went to Fort Hamilton and, uh, then finished up downtown."

"Downtown Brooklyn?"

"Yeah."

"What time was this?"

"About four p.m."

"Near Brooklyn Heights?"

"Uh, I guess so."

"I'm sure you know Mr. Stein lived there, right off the Promenade, and the time of death was established between the hours of three and five p.m."

4

Cory came into the apartment. "Hey, guys."

"Daddy!"

Linda was playing Trouble with Tommy at the kitchen table.

Cory kissed the top of his son's head. "Hi, little man."

Pushing the game's bubble, Linda saw her husband's face. "What's the matter?"

"Nothing."

"Tommy, I need to talk to your father. Can we finish this later?"

"Okay." The kid picked up his iPad and went into the living room.

"What did the lawyer say?"

"I don't know about this guy."

"You said he was good, that you liked him."

"I know, but it's like he sees the bad in everything."

"That's what lawyers do. What did he say?"

"He said they have two witnesses. Somebody said I was by Stein's house."

"But you weren't, you can prove that."

"But I was close by. That kid Freddo I teach, he lives on Remsen Street by Borough Hall. Stein is on Hicks Street, a couple of blocks away."

"But that's okay. Don't worry. You didn't go there, right?"

"No, I didn't. You believe me, don't you?"

Linda grabbed Cory's hand. "Of course, I do. We'll get through this. What else did he say?"

"That they found blood at the crime scene and it wasn't Stein's."

"It's got to be the killer's!"

"That's what I said, but Worth said it wouldn't prove anything."

"How can that be?"

"He's got a negative vibe. It's like if the blood matches my DNA, it's a problem, but if it doesn't, it don't mean anything."

"You don't have any cuts, right?"

"No."

"Are you sure?"

Cory jumped off the couch and rolled the sleeves of his sweater up. "No! See?"

"I'm sorry, I didn't mean anything by it."

"Nobody believes me."

Linda put her arms around Cory. "I believe you. I know you'd never do anything like that."

Cory shrugged. "I can't believe this is happening."

"I know. By the way, how was Stein killed?"

"He was suffocated."

"Oh my God."

"He got what he had coming to him."

"Cory, don't say that. The poor man is dead."

"He screwed me when he was alive, and now the bastard is haunting me from the grave."

Cory opened the door to a cabinet and Linda said, "Cory, please don't start."

"I'm just gonna have one."

"You're doing so good, and it's only four o'clock."

"I'm too wound up to think straight."

"Promise me you'll only have one."

"Don't worry."

"I am. You're under a ton of pressure, and you can't go back to hiding behind a bottle."

Cory poured a glass of bourbon. "I'm okay."

"Why don't you get some help, at least until all this blows over."

"I don't need it."

"Maybe some group therapy."

"I'm not going to some AA thing. I can handle it on my own."

"I didn't mean AA. Just that everybody needs help."

Cory sat down with his drink. "I'm not everybody."

"Come on, Cory, an attitude like that is going to get you in trouble."

"Yeah, well, I can't be in any deeper shit than what I'm in."

Linda sat beside her husband. "I know you're upset. We all are. Just don't make things worse than they are, okay? Can you promise me?"

"Okay, okay already."

"Why don't you call Donny? It'd be good for you."

"Yeah, he left me a couple of messages."

Cory took out his phone, and as he was dialing, a call came in. "Hello?"

"Cory Loop?"

"Yeah?"

"It's Mish from *Rolling Stone*. How you doing, man?"

"What do you want?"

"We'd love to talk to you, get your side of the charges against you."

"Look, I didn't do anything, it's one big mix-up."

"Are you saying you didn't kill Lew Stein?"

"Of course, I had nothing to do with it."

"Our sources tell us that witnesses, maybe two, put you at the scene."

"That's bullshit."

"Is it true that you had to dip into the assets of the Reach for the Stars Trust to make bail?"

"I had no choice; the bail was set too high."

"That's because you're charged with murder."

"And I'll be exonerated."

"Will you claim it was in self-defense?"

"No, I didn't kill Lew Stein. I had nothing to do with it."

"We've heard rumors that your record label, Dream Weavers, is going to drop you."

"That's ridiculous. I haven't done anything wrong. Just wait till this gets cleared up, you'll see."

"We'd love to do a long-format interview. It'll give you an opportunity to get your side of the story out. What do you say?"

"Look, I got to go, but I have your number. I'll think about it."

Cory tossed his phone on the table. "That was *Rolling Stone*, they said Dream Weaver is gonna dump me."

"How could they?"

"Oh no. Is this going to screw up my bail thing?"

"You think so?"

Cory reached for his phone. "I have no clue. I gotta call Baffa."

"He'd know what to do." A loud sound came from the

other side of the apartment. "Call him, I gotta check on Tommy."

Linda came in holding her son's hand as Cory finished the call with his manager. Cory hung up, saying, "Hey, little man. What did you do in there"

"I tried to get a book, but it fell over."

"He stepped on the shelf and it tipped over."

"Me and Mommy cleaned it up."

"Good."

"What did Baffa say?"

"He said there's a clause in the contract, some morality thing, and they can drop me."

"That's so unfair. Did he hear from them?"

"Not yet." Cory reached for his phone. "It's Worth."

"Hello . . . Yes, I'm free, what's going on? . . . What? That can't be."

5

———

Cory hung up and collapsed onto the couch.

"What's going on?"

Cory pulled a pillow over his head.

"Daddy's playing hide-and-seek. Come on, Mommy, let's hide."

"Tommy, go hide in the bedroom. Mommy needs to do something first."

The kid scampered off, and Linda sat on the edge of the couch. "Cory, tell me what's going on?"

"The blood . . . they found at Stein's house."

"Yeah, what about it?"

"They said it matches mine."

"What are you talking about?"

"The blood, they say it's mine."

Linda put a hand to her mouth. "Oh my God."

"It's bullshit."

"What does this mean? I mean, how can it be?"

"They're trying to frame me."

"Who? Who's framing you?"

"I don't know."

"Are you sure about that?"

"What's that supposed to mean?"

"Just that, are you sure you weren't there? I'm not saying you did anything but how—"

"Jesus, if you don't believe me . . ." Cory got off the couch.

"I believe you. I'm just trying to understand all this. Who could have framed you?"

"I don't know."

"You have to have some idea, no?"

"I never hurt anybody. I mean, I screwed up big time with stealing the songs from Jay Bird, but that was a couple of years ago."

"Could it be that? You think somebody went nuts?"

"You mean a fan or something?"

"I don't know. People are crazy these days. Or maybe somebody who believes you screwed them out of royalties."

"I've been thinking about that, but he had no family to leave money to."

"But what about somebody who made money off him? Like a manager or agent? Or even a band member."

"Yeah, I've been thinking about that. What about Riley?"

"The guy who played with you?"

"Yeah, he played rhythm guitar. I never trusted him. He played with Jay Bird for years."

"He replaced somebody, right?"

"Kind of. I wanted Vince, but he was touring with the Pinkletons, and Dave got Riley."

"What would he have lost? Jay Bird was dead. You gave him a slot in the band."

"I know, he made some money when we were hot."

"You think he could be mad that you moved into children's music?"

Cory shrugged. "I haven't used him for anything."

"Has he been gigging a lot?"

"I kind of lost touch. Let me call Donny, he'd know."

"Good idea, let me play with Tommy while you talk to him."

Drink in hand, Cory was on the couch when Linda came in. "What did he say?"

"I left him a message."

"Cory, please don't drink too much. It's going to make things worse."

"Worse? Do you think it could get any more fucked up?"

"Shush. Look, I know you're upset, and you have every right to be, but cursing and drinking aren't going to help. I won't have the kids exposed to that. I'm telling you."

"Okay, okay. I'm sorry, all right? This isn't easy to deal with."

Cory's phone rang. "Hey, Donny."

"Man, are you all right?"

"Yeah, got out this morning."

"I can't believe it."

"You? It's a frigging nightmare."

"You didn't do it, right?"

"No. It's either one giant mistake, or somebody is framing me."

"Framing you?"

"Yeah. What's Riley been up to?"

"Riley? You think he has something to do with this?"

"I don't know what to think."

"He got along good with Stein when he was managed by him."

"Stein worked for Riley?"

"Yeah, you didn't know?"

"No, this is huge."

"Hold on, I can't see Riley doing it. Why would he kill Stein?"

"I don't know. Maybe they had an argument or something. I got to call my lawyer. I'll get back to you."

"Linda!"

"What's the matter?"

"Stein used to manage Riley. It's got to be him."

"But why frame you for it?"

"I don't know, they probably had a fight and it got out of hand. He figured he'd pin it on me."

"I guess it could be, but how did your blood get in Stein's house?"

"I don't know. I'm going to call Worth and let him know."

"Okay. I'm taking Tommy to gymnastics. We'll be back in two hours or so. I have to stop at Shoprite."

"All right. When is Ava getting home?"

"She's got dance after school. We'll see you later."

———

"CORY. WAKE UP!"

Cory rolled over. "Uh, what time is it?"

"Six fifteen." She turned to Tommy. "Go put your stuff in the hamper and wash up."

Linda picked an empty bottle of bourbon off the table. "You can't be doing this."

"I'm sorry. Everything just overwhelmed me."

"I know it's hard, but I'm warning you, I won't stand for it. I'm not putting this family through that again."

"Okay, okay."

"What did Mr. Worth have to say?"

"He never got on the phone. I have an appointment tomorrow morning at ten."

"That's good, I think. He should know about Riley."

"Yeah, and you know, it hit me—what about Bonner? He had it in for me from day one, blackmailing me over the songs."

"You think he set you up as revenge for shooting him?"

"Hell yeah. I mean, I should have fingered him first."

"Did he know Stein?"

"I have no idea, but he's been in and out of every recording studio in the city. But it doesn't matter if he knew him, he knew about me and Stein."

"Yeah, Bonner makes more sense than Riley to me. Bonner's an evil man."

"The fact he wouldn't stop with the extortion shows he doesn't know where to draw the line."

6

———————

Cory stopped at the corner newsstand and bought a bottle of water. He popped two Excedrins and guzzled the water. Crushing the empty bottle, he tossed it in a can and pushed through the doors of his lawyer's building.

The elevator's rise upped the pounding in his head. A wave of nerves swirled in his belly as he announced himself to the receptionist.

Worth, in a dark blue suit and red tie, was writing on a legal pad. The attorney was seated at a round table in the corner of his office. He lifted his head, picked up a Dictaphone, and spoke a note before saying, "Please, have a seat. I've been reviewing your case."

"I've got some information on who could be behind this."

"I'm not sure I understand."

"I'm being framed. There's no other explanation."

Worth clasped his hands. "I'm listening."

"There are two people, Gerry Riley and Joe Bonner. It's a long story, but Bonner was the one blackmailing me, and he's the one I, you know, shot in the leg, so he has plenty of reasons for revenge."

"To avenge the shooting?"

"Yeah, and I stopped paying him."

"And the other gentleman?"

"He used to play in my band, and we don't get along. He was managed by Lew Stein, and them two didn't get along."

"Do you have details on how the plot was carried out?"

"No, but we can hire an investigator to dig into this, right?"

"I believe our resources are better applied to dealing with the charges at hand."

"What do you mean? These guys, especially Bonner, they'd do anything to get back at me."

"You don't seem to possess more than innuendo to pursue. That leaves—"

"No, that's not—"

Worth put his palm up. "Hold on, Mr. Lupinski. I understand there may have been strong disagreements with these men, but killing someone and making it look like someone else committed the murder is a complicated plot."

"But—"

"Before you rebut, I'd like you to explain how they planted your blood at the scene."

"I can't, but if we get someone to look into this, someone good, they'd find out what happened."

"Mr. Lupinski, it's my responsibility to provide the best defense for you, but I'm compelled to advise you that without concrete evidence of a scheme to implicate you in the murder of Mr. Stein, we should consider alternative options."

"What other option is there?"

"We must give a plea serious consideration."

"You mean saying I did it?"

"Yes, but to a lesser charge."

"That's crazy, man."

"I don't believe so."

"And why is that?"

"The charge against you is first-degree murder, a class A felony. The sentencing ranges from imprisonment for life with no chance of parole to a twenty-five-year term. If you're released, you'd be an old man, provided you survived the prison term to begin with."

"Twenty-five years?"

"Yes, at a minimum. But if we plead guilty to second degree, and I say second because I don't believe they'd accept manslaughter, which is unintentional, I believe we could strike a deal for a maximum sentence of fifteen years."

"Fifteen years?"

"Yes, but if we move quickly, before they invest any more resources into the case, we might be able to negotiate a parole hearing after eight or ten years."

"This is crazy, you don't believe me."

"Unfortunately, it's not a matter of belief, Mr. Lupinski. I deal in the law. It's early. However, between the witnesses placing you by Mr. Stein's home, and your blood at the crime scene, the state has the makings of a strong case."

"But I wasn't there."

"I understand your position, but I do believe it's in your best interests to consider a plea. I'll continue to develop lines of defense, but I'd like you to think this over."

The smell of a hot dog cart caused Cory's stomach to lurch as he stepped onto the sidewalk. He leaned against the building, trying to anchor his thoughts. He felt as if the people on the bustling sidewalk were a visual of what was going on inside his head.

Cars beeping their horns only added to the madness. He stepped back inside the lobby and closed his eyes. He couldn't go to prison. His family needed him. Tommy was just six. By the time he got released, his son might have a kid of his own. And Ava, he knew their relationship would never recover from this.

He couldn't let it happen. There had to be a way out of this, he thought as he went outside. In need of a drink as he walked in a sea of people to the subway station, an idea hit him. It wasn't optimal, but as a last resort he'd have to consider running away.

Living a life on the run was miles better than being in jail. It wouldn't be easy hiding, but the thought of being cooped up in a cell was worse. It'd be tough if not impossible to take his family with him. But maybe there was a way, he thought as he descended the subway stairs.

A poster advertising a trip to Italy raised his hopes. Hiding in Europe would be easier to take. He wondered how tough it would be to get fake passports for the family. Kids provided a measure of cover, but they brought complications.

Ava was too old to start over, and who knew what Linda would say. Leaving them behind would be painful. Cory pushed the thought of his family aside and boarded the RR train wondering if it was possible to slip over the Canadian border without detection.

7

As Cory peeled off his jacket, Tommy came running into the foyer.

"Daddy, see what I made at school."

Cory took the crayon drawing from his son. "Wow. This is super. You made this?"

"Uh-huh. Miss Judy said we had to make something we like to do."

"I can't believe what a good guitar you drew. It looks just like the ones we have."

"You like it?"

"I love it. We have to find a good place to hang it up."

"On the fridgerator?"

"Perfect. Where's Mom?"

"In the kitchen."

Cory pecked his wife's cheek. "My little man is super creative, isn't he?"

"Maybe you'll be an artist, Tommy."

"Yay, me and Daddy."

"Go change your clothes."

As soon as Tommy left the room, Linda said, "How'd it go?"

Cory exhaled. "A frigging disaster."

"Is that liquor on your breath?"

"I had one drink. That's all."

"Tell me what happened."

"Worth didn't want to hear about Bonner or Riley. Frigging guy wants me to make a deal."

"What kind of deal?"

Cory lowered his voice. "One that would have me going to jail. No way I'm doing that."

"I don't understand. Isn't there a way to defend the charges?"

"I certainly hope so, but I'm not sure Worth agrees. I don't know if he's looking for the easy way or not."

"A lot of lawyers like to make deals. Maybe he's just feeling you out."

"I can tell you, it didn't feel like that. Maybe he's not the right guy for this. It's like he sees the negative all the time. He doesn't believe that I didn't do it."

"I'm not saying you should make a deal, but what kind of a prison term are we talking about?"

"Twenty years."

"Oh my God."

As Linda's eyes teared, he said, "It's okay. Don't worry. That's not going to happen."

"What are we going to do?"

"I don't know, but worse comes to worst, I'll run."

"But what about us?"

"I just started thinking about it, you know, as a last resort, and I'm trying to figure it all out."

"Where would we go?"

"Canada? Or maybe Mexico."

"Mexico? No way, it's too violent there."

"I heard Costa Rica is nice, and there's a lot of Americans there."

"You'd get caught in a place like that in a heartbeat. You have to be low-key."

"I'm just throwing stuff out. I'm going to start checking around, see what I come up with."

"I'm scared, Cory. What about the kids? We can't just uproot them and go to some third world country."

"Maybe we won't have to. We could get new identities—"

"We'd be looking over our shoulders for the rest of our lives."

"Don't start jumping to conclusions. We're a long way from packing, okay?"

"And what about money? We'd lose everything we put up for bail."

"Take it easy, Linda. We're not going anywhere right now, if at all."

"Maybe you get another lawyer or at least talk to someone else. We can't be hanging our lives on one person."

"Trust me, I've been thinking about it."

"Tracy said she liked Worth better than the other woman. I think her name was McCarthy."

"Let me call her and set something up with her."

CORY DIDN'T THINK it was possible, but Donna McCarthy had less warmth than Worth. He thought it might be a technique to prevent defense attorneys from getting close to their clients.

Her office was a statement of contrasts: a rectangular

table was laden with law books and files, but her desk was clear. Only a fresh legal pad and a bright red pen spoiling it. McCarthy's chair was padded, but the visitor ones were wood.

"I understand you're looking for a second opinion, and I'm pleased at the opportunity to offer one. Please explain what happened and the current state of your defense."

Cory brought her up to date, finishing with, "I know it looks bad, but I didn't do it. I swear on my kids."

"The state will build upon your prior conflict with Mr. Stein. Unfortunately, it's a compelling narrative for a jury."

"I get the revenge stuff, but why would I wait so long?"

"There are ways to counter that, but based upon what you've told me, that's not the biggest issue."

"You mean the so-called witnesses?"

"No, eyewitnesses are notoriously unreliable. The elephant in the room is your blood at the scene of the crime. It's proof you were there, making a witness window dressing."

"I wasn't there."

"Are you suggesting that it was planted?"

"Yeah. It couldn't have gotten there any other way."

"Is there a person or persons you believe responsible for it?"

Cory told her about Bonner and Riley. McCarthy said, "You came here for an opinion, so I'll give you mine."

"Okay."

"If you're going to claim you've been framed, it's imperative that you be clear about it. Unless Bonner and Riley are working together, I suggest you determine who is doing the framing. Does that make sense?"

"Yeah, I understand, but I don't know who it is."

"The court and jury, if this goes to trial, are going to want evidence of collusion. You may not have to uncover the entire scheme, but more than hearsay is going to be required."

"Do you think a private investigator can figure it out?"

"It would depend on what actually occurred."

"Someone is framing me, and nobody believes me."

"The way to convert them is by providing proof. It's that simple."

"Do you use private eyes?"

"Many times, they're helpful."

"Would you use one if you represented me?"

"I'd need more detail on what the prosecution has, but it's a moot point as my current caseload prevents me from taking a case such as yours."

"What does that mean? That my case is too hard? That it's not winnable?"

"I was speaking to its complications."

"My lawyer said I should consider a plea bargain. What do you think?"

"It's an option in many cases."

"But you don't even know that I'd have to serve like, twenty years."

"After doing this for twenty-two years, I'm aware of what a negotiated plea would look like."

8

———————

Emerging from the Washington Heights subway station, Cory's phone pinged. He listened to the voice mail from Worth. His lawyer wanted him to call. After sitting on the train for almost two hours, talking to Worth was the last thing he wanted to do.

The angst over the long trip to Columbia Presbyterian Hospital faded when Cory stepped into a family waiting room. Five kids were hunched over, strumming their guitars. The sounds clashed, but to Cory it was sweet.

"Morning, guys."

"Hi."

"What a super cozy space. It's gonna work out good here. I can spend one-on-one time with each of you."

Cory's phone rang as he picked up his guitar. He swiped his wife's call away. "You know what would be a cool thing to do? How about we learn a simple chord progression? Then we'll add an easy melody and see how it sounds together."

Cory walked the children through a basic pop progression and taught them a melody using just four notes. It took half an hour for the kids to get close.

"You guys are the quickest learners I've ever seen. Let's put it together. We'll need three of you to play the chords and the other two the melody. Who wants to play chords?"

Cory assigned the roles. "All right, we ready?"

The kids nodded.

"Here we go. One, two. One, two, three, four."

It took three tries to get everyone through four bars. "This is sounding really nice. Let's try it again." As he counted the kids in, his phone vibrated. It was Linda, again.

After they played, Cory said, "That was amazing. Look, I gotta make a quick call. When I'm done, we'll do some one-on-one."

He stepped into the hall. "What's up?"

"Where are you?"

"Up at Columbia. I'll tell you, these kids are sponges. I can't believe they learn so fast."

"You have to call Worth. He's looking for you."

"What does he want?"

"He didn't say, but I don't think it's good."

"Don't worry, he's always negative."

"Call him and let me know what's going on."

"Okay, as soon as I'm done."

Feeling as good as he had since his arrest, Cory floated through the hospital's soaring lobby. A text sounded, reminding him to call Worth. He dialed his attorney as he walked down the circular driveway.

"Sorry, I was up at Columbia working with kids who have cancer. What's going on?"

"I received a call from the DA, and it isn't good."

Cory stiffened. "What did they say?"

"They claim that you left a threatening voice mail on Mr. Stein's phone."

"Uh-uh, it wasn't a threat. I was trying to get him to call me back."

"Why would you call him?"

"I needed some records that he had. The IRS is asking for some old documents, and he has most of the expense records."

"Why would you call him directly?"

"He didn't respond to my accountant. I was just trying to get my stuff. He had no right to screw with me."

Worth paused. "Did you reference the document request in your message?"

"I, I don't remember."

"That would go a long way toward explaining, but prior contact with the deceased will bolster the premeditated charge."

"What does this mean?"

"It's damaging. To what extent I won't know until I receive the transcript of the call."

"When will you get it?"

"Technically, they have thirty days, but we should have it in the next couple of days."

Cory held onto the strap as the subway rumbled south. He tried to recall what he'd said to Stein, but the only thing certain was it wasn't cordial.

He envisioned a slick prosecutor reading the transcript to the jury. The lawyers would twist everything to make him look guilty.

Cory couldn't let it happen. He had to have a plan if things didn't turn around. If he wasn't able to persuade the police he was framed, he'd have to run. The short time he'd spent behind bars convinced him there was no way he was going to jail—especially for twenty or more years.

Leaving his family would be painful, but maybe there'd be a way to see each other. He wondered whether the authorities would be able to trace video calls made through FaceTime. He could use a fake background, and as much as he would want to, wouldn't tell them where he was.

But wherever he went, there had to be a music scene. He'd have to play just to keep his sanity and to earn a living. He'd disguise himself, dye his hair, grow a beard, and wear fake glasses.

What name would he take? Something foreign but not too exotic. A flash of nerves hit him as he thought about language. He'd have to decide immediately where he was going and learn what they spoke if it wasn't English.

There were a lot of countries where English was required in schools, but you knew who was a native or not. He began thinking of a backstory that made relocation believable. He could say he was Canadian. A move to England would be easy, he thought, as the train rolled into his station.

"DADDY'S HOME. Hey, guy. What did you do today?"

"We played tag, and nobody could get me."

"That's because you're super fast."

"Where were you?"

"Teaching sick kids how to play the guitar."

"Did you show them what you showed me?"

"Only my Tommy gets the best secrets. Go get your ax out. I want to show you a new picking trick."

Tommy took off, and Linda kissed Cory's cheek. "What did Worth say?"

Cory shrugged. "There was a message on Stein's phone."

"From who? Don't tell me—you?"

"I called him about the IRS stuff. He wasn't calling Giordano back."

"Oh Cory, this is bad."

"What's bad, Mommy?"

9

—————

Tommy fell asleep as Cory read him a bedtime story. He put *Harold and The Purple Crayon* on the nightstand, turned on the night-light, and tiptoed out of the room.

Cory grabbed his laptop and resumed surfing for how to disappear. There was a surprising number of articles on how to become a fugitive. The first two he read didn't raise his spirits.

Neither of them addressed running as a family. One article pointed out that the odds of getting caught multiplied when someone knew where you were.

To be successful, he'd have to completely cut ties with his family. Cory leaned back, looking at a photograph of his kids and wife. What was worse? Seeing them once a month, through plexiglass, or never talking to them again?

Forcing the question out of his mind, he continued searching for advice. One guy, a bank robber, had been on the run for ten years. In addition to cutting ties, the fugitive said you had to ditch your devices, or technology would lead the authorities to you.

Cory closed the site and opened a private window. He

wasn't sure how much it would protect his browsing history, but it also raised a tool he could use. Why not leave a trail? Not to where he was going, but to throw the cops off.

Cory typed in Cabos, Mexico, in the browser and clicked on rentals when his wife and daughter came into the apartment.

"Hey, how was dance?"

"Okay. Mom, I'm taking a shower."

Cory asked his wife, "What's with the one-word answers?"

"She's upset at what's going on."

"And what do you think I am? I'm the one looking at going to jail."

"This affects the whole family."

"She hasn't said two words to me since the shit hit the fan. She probably thinks I'm guilty."

"She's worried and doesn't know how to express it."

"She's got to learn to talk about things."

Linda raised her eyebrows. "Really?" She smiled. "I remember a certain someone who kept his secrets and feelings locked up."

"That was different."

"It always is, isn't it?"

Cory took Linda's hand and pulled her onto the couch. "I've gotten better, right?"

"You're closing up again."

"Sorry, this is crazy."

"You can always talk to me."

"I know."

"What have you been thinking about?"

He lowered his voice. "I'm not supposed to say anything, but I've been thinking if it looks like I can't find who framed me, I can't go to prison. I just can't."

"I don't understand, you're not going to . . ." She put a hand to her mouth. "You're not thinking of taking your life, are you?"

"No, I'd never do that. I was thinking, you know, maybe, to run."

"Where?"

"I don't know. Mexico or something like that."

"What about us?"

"I don't know, I just started thinking about it."

"They always catch people who try to hide."

"I know, but there are a couple of guys I've been reading about who've been on the lam for ten years or more."

"What kind of life is that?"

"I don't know, but it's got to be better than a damn five-foot cell."

"Promise me you won't do anything rash. That you'll talk to me first."

Cory said he would, but he really didn't think he could afford to tell her. It was just too risky. He'd have to be as smart and alert as he could. Cory had to remain sober; there was no other way.

CORY SIPPED his coffee and read a story about Robert Vesco, an American financier who fled to Central America. He had enough money to change a law in Costa Rica that outlawed his extradition. It worked for a while, but American pressure rolled back the law, and Vesco ended up fleeing to Cuba.

He got up to make a second cup of java when his daughter said, "Great. Look who's on the news again." Ava got up. "I'm not going to school."

Cory turned to the TV. A picture of him on stage was over the anchor's shoulder:

"There's more trouble for fallen star Cory Lupinski. The musician, whose stage name is Cory Loop, was arrested on suspicion of murdering his former manager Lew Stein. The assistant district attorney handling the case made public a voice mail message on the deceased's phone. Here's a transcript of the message, purportedly left by Cory Lupinski."

The screen was filled with a typed message that the newscaster read: *Where the hell are you? I'm not going to let you get away with it, you bastard. I'm telling you, don't screw with me or you'll regret it. And I mean it.*

"We've reached out to counsel for Mr. Lupinski. We'll bring you their response to the damning evidence against someone who brought such joy in the past."

Linda shook her head. "You didn't remember threatening him?"

"It wasn't a threat. I just wanted the papers he had. He should've given them to me when we fired his ass."

"What is Worth going to do about this? You gotta say something."

"I'm calling him now."

"Mr. Worth, it's Cory. I just saw the news. Did you know about this?"

"I received a call from the DA's office just before they released it."

"What are we going to do?"

"We'll release a statement, with a plausible explanation, dismissing the message. You said it was related to records required for a tax audit, correct?"

"Yes."

"Bring whatever IRS documentation you received in regard to the audit."

"Well, I didn't get anything formally."

"I don't understand, Mr. Lupinski."

"You see, my new manager, Mr. Baffa, he said it was my responsibility to have the records in case the IRS wanted them."

"Are you stating there was no audit?"

"Not yet. But Mr. Baffa said because I was claiming losses against other years' income, that it would probably be audited."

"That presents a significant challenge. I'll have to consider this new information before deciding on a response."

10

———————

CORY HAD JUST FINISHED MIXING A CHILDREN'S SONG HE'D written. As he left the studio, his phone rang.

"Cory Loop?"

"Yeah, who's this?"

"Brandon from *Entertainment Tonight*. How are you?"

"Good. Why the call?"

"Every two years or so, we do a show focusing on entertainers who've had, uh, legal issues, you know, interaction with law enforcement. One of the cases the program manager selected was yours."

"Really?"

"You got to admit, it's an interesting case, being accused of murdering the manager who stole from you."

"I didn't have anything to do with Mr. Stein's death. You're wasting your time covering it."

"The segment is green-lighted; it's going to happen."

"You'll regret it."

"Why don't you come on and tell your side of the story?"

"There's nothing to tell. I didn't do it. It's one big mistake that we're going to correct. The police got the wrong man. I'd never do something like that. They shouldn't have arrested me in the first place."

"I'm not judging and don't know all the details, but from what our sources obtained from the prosecutor's office, there seems to be enough evidence to connect you to the crime."

"I don't know how many times I have to say it, I didn't do it!"

"Then come on the air and tell the world."

"I got half a mind to, but my lawyer doesn't want me doing any press."

"I'd hate to present a one-sided picture."

"Hold on! I'll call my attorney to see if he'll allow me to come on."

"That would even things out."

"Even things out? What, are looking to hang me or something?"

"No, it's not like that. It's just we have quite a bit of—"

"Forget it! Goodbye!"

Linda came in. "What's going on? Your nose is bleeding."

Cory swept his nose with a thumb. "It's nothing. It stopped already."

"Who were you arguing with?"

"I wasn't arguing. It was that damn TV show, *Entertainment Tonight*. They're doing a show on celebs with legal problems and want to do a hit job on me. Bastards want me to come on so they can rip me up."

"You said no, right?"

"Yeah, Worth don't want me saying anything to anyone."

"Good. Go wash your face."

Cory headed to the bathroom to clean up. Linda went to pick up Tommy's sipper cup and something caught her eye. She touched it with her fingertip. It was bright red and sticky. It was a drop of Cory's blood.

Fear ran up Linda's spine. Had Cory's nose bled at Stein's house? Is that how it got there? Linda replayed the day her husband's ex-manager was killed.

Cory woke up in a bad mood. He said he hadn't slept well. Cory had mentioned how much his manager had stolen from them at breakfast. At the time, she thought he might have been up worrying over money. She now considered whether he'd been unable to sleep because of obsessing over Stein.

She remembered Cory brooding as she left to take Tommy to school. He was gone when she came back, even though his studio session wasn't for several hours. When he came back later that afternoon, she remembered he was fidgety. She'd thought it was because he was craving a drink.

Linda also remembered that he'd stayed up late, claiming he wanted to work on a new song, but when she'd gotten up to use the bathroom, Cory was on the couch, staring at an infomercial.

Did he kill Stein? She had to know the truth. Cory had been violent in the past. It wasn't pretty, but she thought it was because of the drugs and drinking. Since he'd been trying to stay sober, he'd been moody at times but never violent.

Did Cory have a streak of violence in him that had emerged again? Linda's mind spun. What would happen to them if Cory went to prison? If he got off somehow, were they in danger? Would Cory's dark side strike again? Maybe hurting one of the kids?

Cory came back in. Linda said, "What are we going to do?"

"I don't know, but I got to call Worth and see if he can stop these idiots from running a hit piece on me."

"Not the show, Cory. Everything. What's going to happen to us if you go to prison?"

"I'm not going to jail. No way."

"How will you get out of this?"

"I'm not sure. Worth doesn't seem to want to hire an investigator, so, I'm thinking of getting one on our own."

"Did you do it?"

"What? Of course not."

"Don't lie to me, Cory."

"I'm not."

"Were you there?"

"No."

"Are you sure you didn't have a nosebleed at his house?"

"I wasn't there. Goddamn it! Why doesn't anyone believe me?"

Linda hugged him. "I believe you. I'm just scared, for the kids, for us."

"It's going to work out. Don't worry."

"We couldn't bear to see you in prison. It would scar the kids and follow them the rest of their lives."

"I swear, I'm not gonna spend the rest of my life behind bars. I'll run if I have to."

"Run? Where?"

"I don't know yet, but I'm checking into it."

"What about us? We couldn't go with you. It's terrible hiding like that."

"I know. It'd be tough on them and you but better than seeing their father in some shitty jail."

"Would we ever see each other again?"

"Unless I can find out who is framing me, probably not. The cops would be following you to see if you might lead them to me."

"We'd lose everything if you skip bail. What would we do for money?"

"I'm not going to leave you guys homeless. I'd never do

that. Maybe I can swing getting more of the royalties upfront. I'd say I need it to pay for my defense. We could put it aside somewhere safe, that the cops wouldn't know about it."

"But you'd need money to survive too."

"I know, but I can make a buck doing anything. I'd wash dishes until I figured something out. I don't want the kids or you to suffer."

11

———————

Cory's spirits lifted as he read another story on fugitives. Though many were caught, it was because they'd let their guard down. Those who were vigilant slipped through the cracks even though the law was looking for them. At the end of the day, the cops had too many people to track down and went after the easiest targets.

Besides avoiding contact with people in your former life, a couple of themes showed up in every success story: high-quality fake identity papers and altering your looks.

He'd undergone a transformation of sorts when the record label stylists took over. The look, which he still kept, was younger and edgy.

This time maybe he'd melt into the background by going to his original hair color, maybe even go gray or even shave it all off. The love patch would be replaced with a full beard.

Glasses would help, but to really change, he'd have to consider cosmetic surgery. He'd have to research it depending on where he ended up. Maybe a procedure in someplace like Mexico before moving on. Right now, the thing he wanted was an assurance he could get fake papers.

As a musician, Cory didn't have the kind of network to go undercover, but when he'd been blackmailed, a man was recommended to him to discover who was behind the extortion. Cory scrolled through his contacts and hit dial.

"Uh, Mr. Black?"

"Who's asking?"

"Cory Loop, Cory Lupinski. Remember, you helped me with the—"

"What's going on?"

"I don't want to talk over the phone. Can we meet?"

"One thirty. The end of Perry Street, by the water."

As the phone went dead, Cory reached for his jacket.

The wind was whipping off the Hudson River. Cory tucked his chin into his jacket as a runner headed north on the path along the water. He lowered his head as a gust of wind buffeted him.

Cory saw Mr. Black. He was leaning on the railing facing the Hudson River. Cory sidled up to him, wondering how he could stand the cold in a dungaree jacket.

"Thanks for meeting me."

Black nodded silently.

"You probably know, I'm being accused of killing my ex-manager. I didn't do it."

Black remained silent.

"I'm not saying I'm gonna do it, but if I can't be sure to beat this, I'm thinking of running."

"You?"

"Yeah, why?"

"You're not cut out for that kind of life."

"I have no choice. I can't go to prison."

Black nodded. "And?"

"I'm going to need a new identity. Can you get me a new passport and license?"

"Eight thousand."

"Okay."

"In cash."

"I'll get it. How long is it going to take?"

"Two weeks after you get me two photos."

"No problem, I'll get them fast."

"The Eagle statue in Battery Park, one week from right now."

"I'll be there."

Black nodded. Cory watched him walk away, stunned he could get what he needed so easily.

12

———————

Nerves jangled in Cory's stomach as *Entertainment* *Tonight*'s theme song faded. "Look at them, they're just waiting to tear somebody down."

Linda lowered the TV's volume. "It's what they do. Everybody knows it, so don't get riled up."

"They're gonna make me look bad, and that's not good for anybody on a jury."

"But Worth said he'd move the trial if he felt you couldn't get a fair one."

"I can't let it get to a courtroom. That would mean we never found out who was framing me. Look at the way this bastard is smiling."

The thirty-year-old host said, "Tonight's edition is a special segment focusing on the legal misfortunes of celebrities. I'm sure our viewers remember Cory Loop, whose real name is Cory Lupinski."

A picture of Cory holding an award filled the screen.

"Cory had a mercurial rise to the top of the pop charts, including three number-one hits. As with many, the fame and fortune created a stream of problems. Mr. Loop was the victim of an extortion scheme, which culminated in him shooting the blackmailer in the leg. Mr. Loop claimed it was in self-defense and served no time for the offense.

"His recent troubles revolve around Lew Stein, his dead ex-manager. The history between the two is long and complicated. At one point, Stein, who allegedly stole from Cory, was stabbed during an argument with the musician."

"Allegedly? What bullshit!"

"No charges were filed in the incident. Cory dropped out of the pop scene, moving to making children's music, focusing on finding a cure for childhood cancer, and improving organ transplant programs. We'll follow his story after a message from a sponsor."

"At least they're mentioning your charitable work."

"Trust me, nobody will remember."

"Let's get back to our coverage of Cory Loop. Unfortunately, the award-winning musician's current troubles are his most serious to date. He has been charged with the murder of his ex-manager, Lew Stein. Found in his home, Mr. Stein was suffocated to death.

"A witness put Mr. Lupinski near the victim's Brooklyn home, and he was arrested while giving guitar lessons at the children's wing in Columbia Presbyterian Hospital."

Video of a handcuffed Cory being led into a police station flooded the screen.

"Sources tell us that there are now two witnesses placing Cory Loop by Stein's home. Law enforcement officials also discovered an incriminating voice mail message left by Mr. Loop on his ex-manager's phone."

"Incriminating? Come on!"

"But the most significant piece of evidence is the drop of blood found next to Mr. Stein's body. DNA tests confirm it belongs to Cory Lupinski.

"*Entertainment Tonight* invited Mr. Lupinski on tonight's show, but he declined, refusing to make a statement."

"Bullshit! They never asked for a statement, I told them I didn't do it."

"With us tonight is John Steer, an expert in criminology and frequent contributor to this program.

"John, based upon what we know about this case, what's your opinion of the depth of trouble Mr. Lupinski is in?"

"Unfortunately, the history between him and the deceased, combined with the voice message, build a strong case for premeditation and thus, a first-degree murder charge."

"Explain what that is to our viewers."

"Essentially, that Mr. Lupinski planned the death of Mr. Stein. It wasn't an argument that spun out of control but a calculated event."

"What about the witnesses? How important are they?"

"Two is always better than one, but eyewitnesses are notoriously unreliable. They may help to sway a jury, but any inconsistencies will be exploited by the defense."

"It should be noted that Mr. Lupinski denies being there, begging the question of how his blood came to be next to the body."

"That single drop of blood may turn out to be the thing that convicts Mr. Lupinski."

"From what we know, on the day of his arrest there were no known cuts or scratches detected or photographed when he was booked. Where could the blood have come from?"

"Most likely a nosebleed. It would be a temporary event, and any evidence of one would be gone by now."

"Interesting."

"I'm not a splatter expert, but based upon my years of experience, after looking at photos of the crime scene, it appears as if the drop came from a height of five or so feet."

Linda said, "Oh my God."

"Shut this shit off!"

Linda clicked the remote. "Cory, you have to be honest with me. I'll stand by you no matter what you did. I don't care what happened, but we have kids. I have to know."

"Know what?"

"Did you . . . hurt that man?"

"How can you say that?"

"You get nosebleeds, and those people said you were at the scene."

"Nobody saw me in the house. They saw me outside, in the neighborhood. People know who I am, they just mixed up where they saw me. Worth and even the idiot on TV said witnesses can't be trusted."

"So, you didn't do it?"

"No. How many times do I have to say it?" Cory walked out saying, "Geez, nobody believes me, not even my wife."

13

Cory took the Amazon package into the bedroom and closed the door. He opened the box and took one of the items out and put it into his mouth. It didn't fit properly, but the instructions said how to mold it to your teeth.

He looked in the mirror and smiled. Instead of the porcelain veneers the record label had spent thirty thousand on, it looked like he'd never seen a dentist. He thought the slight buck look was even more effective than the crooked teeth.

Cory pulled out the glasses he'd bought and slipped them on. He liked the way the heavy black frames changed his look. He applied the fake mustache and bushy eyebrows. They were gray, making him appear older. Pushing back his hair, he held his palm on his forehead, envisioning himself bald.

He thought it could work and reached into the box for the last item. He fingered the latex as he read the instructions. Cory watched a quick YouTube video and applied the prop. He smiled into the mirror and went to show Linda.

His wife was at the sink. Cory cleared his throat. Linda turned and gasped. "Huh?"

"What do you think? Pretty good, right?"

"I thought someone was in the house. How did you do all that?"

"Bought it from Amazon."

"They can trace it."

"I had Donny buy it for me."

"You told him you were thinking of running?"

"No. It's almost Halloween. I told him I wanted to surprise you and the kids."

"I'm gonna get some pictures taken in case I need to get a new identity."

"Cory, promise me you'll tell me before you go."

"If I go. It's nowhere near a done deal. I have to be prepared."

CORY STOOD in front of the Eagle Monument gracing Battery Park. He kept a lookout for Mr. Black as well as a possible mugger. Out of the corner of his eye he saw a man emerge from behind a tree.

Dressed in the same thin jacket, Cory wondered if Mr. Black was someone who wore shorts all year.

"You got the money?"

Cory reached in his coat and handed him a brown bag of cash. Black stuffed it in his jacket.

"Here's the pictures."

Black took the photos. "Not bad, but you still can't let your guard down."

"I know. I'm going to—"

Black shook his head. "Less talking increases your odds."

"Okay, sorry."

"Pick a country that doesn't have an extradition treaty with us."

"That's a good idea. Where do you suggest?"

"Two weeks. Trinity Church, the Vesey Street side."

Cory watched Black walk out of the park. He wondered if he'd be able to adapt to life on the run.

He dug his phone out and opened an incognito tab. The list of countries that wouldn't heed an extradition request from the United States was long. It was also depressing. There wasn't a country you'd take a vacation in—a bunch of places in Africa and the Middle East.

Russia was on the list. It was where Edward Snowden went. And China, but Cory wouldn't consider either.

One place he recognized was Vietnam. He'd heard it was up-and-coming, and with the French having influenced it, there could be a Western music scene. The problem was getting there.

The easiest would be a place in Central America. He could cross the border and work his way down, but he didn't recognize any of the names as being in the region.

Cory tucked his phone in a jean pocket, wondering where some of the countries were. He hoped when he went to research them at home, that a couple of options would surface.

Walking down the stairs to the South Ferry subway station, Cory's phone rang.

"Mrs. Hirsh, how are you?"

"We're good."

"What's up?"

"I'm sorry, but Jimmy wants to stop taking lessons."

"What? He loves playing and he's making super progress. I don't understand."

"He changed his mind."

"I'd hate for him to stop. He's one of my top students. Can I talk to him?"

"I'm sorry, he's not here."

"I'll stop over, okay?"

"No. I don't want you coming here."

"All right. Tell him I'll miss him."

When she hung up without saying goodbye, Cory realized it was her, not Jimmy, who'd made the decision. He also knew it was about the murder case.

No one seemed to believe he wasn't guilty. When trouble came, people distanced themselves. It may have been natural, but it hurt.

He wondered what Linda truly believed. She said many of the right things, but something had changed. His kids were another matter. Tommy was six, and that meant dad was a superhero, but Ava had built a wall between them.

She was a teenager who didn't want the attention the case had brought. It was understandable to a degree, but if he couldn't convince his family, how would a jury react?

14

———————

Cory was cleaning his guitar. Linda was watching the news and said, "Zepher got off? That's impossible."

"What?"

"Joe Zepher, that actor that did the Batman movies and was in that stupid TV show on NBC."

"The one where he played the plumber who hit the lottery?"

"Yeah. That's him, bastard killed his wife and got away with it."

"Oh yeah, he was cheating on her, and the girlfriend changed her story about what he'd told her."

"The phony makes me sick. I knew he did it the first time I saw him on TV. Talk about fake tears."

"How'd he get off then?"

"His lawyer was that sleazebag Tower."

"Barney Tower? The guy who tried to screw me?"

"Yeah. He got the DA to drop the charges."

"I hate him, but he's a miracle worker. I don't know how he got me off when I shot Bonner. He's gotta have pictures of the judges having sex with animals or something."

"He's a creep."

"I wonder what he's gonna suck out of Zepher. He'll probably try the same shit he did to me. The bastard will bleed Zepher until he's broke."

"Who cares? He killed his wife. He should be in jail."

Cory polished his Gibson Sunburst acoustic. "You're right."

"You want this on? I have to get dinner started."

"No. I'm going to compose."

Cory retreated to his studio and hung up his guitar. He sat behind an electric keyboard and plugged in his headphones. His hands roamed the keys, his left playing chords and his right searching for melodies.

At the lower end, he hit the same dark chord twice. It sounded like a funeral dirge. It made him think of his own death. Life would end as he knew it if he went to prison. He'd probably die behind bars.

With the evidence against him and a lawyer who believed he couldn't win a trial, it was grim. He wanted a drink. He put his guitar down and got up.

Cory would run if he had to, but being cut off from his family and the life he knew would be painful. Realizing the only way out was to uncover who was framing him, he sat back down. He'd have to stay sober to have a chance at doing it.

CORY OPENED THE DOOR. "Hey, Donny, come on in."

"How are you, man?"

"I'm all right."

"You sure?"

"I'm not gonna kid you, it's rough. I don't know what I'm going to do."

"You'll beat this, man."

"I don't know, my lawyer isn't too optimistic. He's talking about some kind of a plea."

"Really?"

"Yeah, but I'd get like twenty years."

"What? That's crazy, man."

"I don't know what to do."

"I know he screwed you, but that Tower cat seems to get everybody off. Why don't you see what he says?"

"We didn't leave on the best of terms."

"It's life and death, man. The dude might be able to get you off. You have to patch things up with him."

"I don't know . . ."

"You just said things don't look good. It's worth a shot."

"I hear you. But I gotta think it through a little."

"Don't waste time, bro."

"I won't." Cory waved him to the studio. "Come on, I want you to hear two tunes I just penned."

Cory handed Donny two sheets of manuscript paper. "These are them."

As Cory picked up his acoustic guitar, Donny said, "You want me to lay down a bass line?"

"Listen to what I got first."

Cory tapped his foot, setting the tempo, and played the song.

"Man, the kids are gonna like that. The turnaround is cool. I can see them latching onto it."

"Really?"

"Yeah, man. I think you got a winner here. You have a name for it?"

"I was thinking 'Break in the Clouds.'"

"Maybe just 'Cloud Break.'"

"That's better. I like it, it's snappier. Let me play the other one."

Cory stutter-strummed his guitar and sang the composition. Repeating the last phrase, he faded out his voice.

Donny smiled. "You got a gift for this kids' stuff. You know it may sound crazy, but it has like a rap cadence in the bridge."

"Yeah, that's on purpose. I don't know if you remember that guy, Billy See, who was big when we were kids. I heard him say something on a podcast; he called it machine-gun phrasing."

"Billy See? Man, haven't heard that name in ages."

"You know his stuff seemed simple, but I studied it, and it's more intricate than it sounds."

"Most great music is. Makes me think of Jobim, simple, memorable melodies, but those bossas are a bitch to improv on."

"Amen."

"You want me to play a bass line on these?"

"I'm thinking to keep them acoustic, really stripped down."

"They did sound good. You send them to your agent?"

"Not yet, had to see what my buddy had to say."

"Send them, they're gonna love them."

***

AFTER PUTTING TOMMY TO BED, Cory sat next to Linda. He turned up the volume of the TV a notch and said, "I'm thinking of reaching out to Tower."

"The lawyer?"

"Yeah."

"Are you nuts?"

"Take it easy. The guy's a frigging genius or something."

"Genius? He's a crook is what he is."

"At this point, I don't care what he is. My life is on the line. I gotta do whatever needs to be done to get off."

"Cory, you gotta be careful with him. He can make things worse."

"Worse than going to jail for the rest of my life?"

"I don't know, he might twist things and try to screw you like he did with Bonner."

"Trust me, I hate the bastard, but remember the first time with Stein? He got me off and the same thing with Bonner, just like that."

"He doesn't have a magic wand."

"I know, but he's got contacts and gets things done."

"How does he do it?"

"I don't care. Maybe people owe him favors."

"Or he blackmails them, like he did to you."

"I don't care, I just want this over."

"You got to be extra careful."

"I know. I've been playing out stuff in my head to try to see what could be up his sleeve."

15

———

Watching the James Bond movie *You Only Live Twice* gave Cory an idea. Could he fake his own death and buy time to figure out who was framing him?

It was an option instead of running and hiding. The toughest part was no body to prove someone died. It would have to be an accident, maybe on the water.

He rarely went fishing, but maybe he could rent a boat, taking Tommy for a ride. Having his kid on a boat without adults would be dangerous but convincing.

Another idea that kept popping into his head was jumping off a bridge. After two decades of neglect, the George Washington Bridge was being repaired to keep it from collapsing. There were safety nets to catch jumpers and pieces of the structure as it deteriorated.

Could he leap off the bridge, landing safely in a net, and scramble into hiding? Without a body, faking his death would require cutting off contact with the life he knew. It was the same as running and hiding.

Cory opened a private browser and rooted around. One article caught his attention. It covered how someone had faked their death in an automobile accident in the Philippines. The piece mentioned that an underground ring kept dead bodies on ice to sell to those who wanted to disappear.

An accident or fire would be staged, and the dead body placed at the scene. The ring had contacts that would declare it was you who died and issue a death certificate that was accepted worldwide.

It was an interesting solution but would require getting to the Philippines. Cory wondered whether such an enterprise existed in America. He did a quick Google but came up empty.

He wondered whether searching what was called the dark web would help. It was an area of the internet where criminals and pedophiles operated. He'd heard of arms being dealt there as well as human trafficking.

It seemed to be the place to search.

16

Using a public browser, Cory searched for apartments in Mexico City. Then he hunted around Cabo San Lucas and Cancun. He also researched Lake Chapala, Mexico. It had Mexico's largest lake and was home to the largest expat community of Americans in the world.

Cory also rooted around Costa Rica and Chile. He wanted to leave behind a realistic trail for law enforcement to discover. He would buy a one-way train ticket to Tempe, Arizona. It was farther west and less known, lending credibility to a plan to escape over the border.

Adding to the head fake, Cory downloaded both Duolingo and an English-to-Spanish dictionary. Besides the news, he had no way to monitor how much law enforcement would believe his ruse.

The cash he'd withdrawn would bolster the belief he fled —though in reality, most of it went into a lockbox that Linda had opened. The bail would be forfeited, but Cory was hopeful he'd get the money back once he uncovered the framing plot.

Leaving his family would be tough, and he didn't want to

compound it by leaving them destitute. He had to get them as big a stash as possible.

———

Cory was trying to come up with lyrics for a new song when his agent called.

"Cory? It's Sandy."

"Hey, Sandy. What did you think?"

"I love both of them, especially 'Cloud Break.'"

"You do?"

"Yeah, I think they're both gonna move a lot of units. You have any more to make an album?"

"I have a dozen others but nothing I'm really digging yet."

"You never know, send them over. Either way, with these two to anchor an album, we'd be fine. We'd want to release them as singles anyway."

"So, the label is on board?"

"Not exactly."

"What does that mean?"

"Here's the thing; with all the publicity around your, uh, problem, they feel parents aren't going want to buy your recordings."

"That's bullshit. This is supposed to be America, you're innocent until proven guilty."

"I know, but that's not the way it works."

"Oh, come on—"

"Hold on. I talked it over with a couple of the legal guys, and we think we can put it out under a stage name."

"What do you mean?"

"We keep your name away from it. You'd still get the

composition and performance royalties, but the public wouldn't know the connection."

"I don't know."

"Or we could license the tunes to Raffi or Zanes."

"Let me think about this."

After hanging up, Cory went into the kitchen. "I got good news and bad news."

Linda said, "About the case?"

"No, my new songs."

"Oh, you had me worried. What's up?"

"Well, the good part is they really dig the tunes."

"That's great. I told you that if Tommy likes them, they're going to be hits. What's the bad news?"

"They think I'm a turn-off for parents and want to issue them under a stage name."

"There's nothing wrong with that. You still get the same royalties, right?"

"Yeah, I'm just thinking about a way to make sure you get money if something happens to me."

"Nothing's going to happen to you."

Cory shrugged.

"Call Baffa up, he'll know how to make sure of it."

"Good idea."

Cory pulled his cell out and dialed his business manager.

"Mr. Baffa, it's Cory Lupinski."

"How are you?"

"I guess as good as can be expected. I got a situation I need your advice on."

Cory explained releasing the new material under a stage name and asked, "If I agreed to something like that and I had to go to jail or something, would my family get the royalties?"

"There's a good chance a substantial fine would be

imposed. It'd be part of a sentence to give the state an opportunity to recoup the costs associated with a trial."

"How much would that be?"

"I have no experience in that area and would have to research it. However, that's maybe the least of the financial side of your problem."

"I don't understand."

"Given your public profile, it's likely the family of the victim would file a civil suit against you. If you're convicted criminally, chances are they'd be awarded a significant sum as monetary compensation for their loss."

"So, using a stage name wouldn't protect the money?"

"No, as you ultimately benefit."

"What if I listed my friend as the composer?"

"If he just passes the income to you, there's a likelihood it will be found out."

"What about my wife?"

"That would appear to be an obvious circumvention."

"But Linda and I have written together in the past. I mean not much, but we have."

"Has she ever been given composition credit on a published work?"

"Yeah, it's been a few years, but yeah, definitely."

"And it was a co-credit, with split royalties?"

"I gave her the composition end and took the performance. It wasn't a ton of money, but it happened."

"Did she work on these songs?"

"Yeah, she helped."

"You have to be certain, as it may be challenged in a court of law."

"She helped me with the lyrics, you know, what words to use."

"In that case, the wiser thing to do would be to consider co-crediting."

"But that would leave half of the money, and we're not talking a lot of money here, that I could lose."

"I understand, but at this point, that's my advice."

"But then my half could go out the window."

"True, but you want to avoid a challenge. If you only claim half the royalties, it should satisfy the state and settle any civil action."

"I get your point, and I'm no legal person, but don't you think these guys would take what they can get easy and then push to take my wife's?"

"It's likely they'd pursue the entire stream, claiming it was a tactic to shield the money, but they'd have to convince the court."

"I doubt these songs are going bring in a ton of money, so my family is going to need whatever royalties they generate."

"I understand your position, and it's your decision, but I still believe you shouldn't get too aggressive."

17

———————

Cory's mind raced. What would Tower say when he saw him? Would he refuse to see him or scream at him? Tower had a host of nefarious contacts. Would he sic one of his thugs on him?

Tower had tried to intimidate him after Cory recorded their conversation to stop Tower from continuing to blackmail him. Nothing had come from it. Tower had tried to scare Cory. It worked, and Cory was relieved when the harassment ended.

Cory pushed the idea of stopping for a drink out of his head and tried to calm down. He pulled his phone out and set the Spotify app to a classical music stream.

He tried to concentrate on the Vivaldi sonata, but it wasn't working. He stepped into the elevator and closed his eyes. On the ride up, he took deep breaths.

Sitting in the waiting room, his leg shook like a jackhammer. The receptionist led him to Tower's office.

Cory wiped his sweaty palms on his pants as the woman opened her boss's door. Barney Tower, in a crisp white shirt and blue tie, was leaning back in a burgundy leather chair.

He said, "Cory Lupinski."

"How ya doing, Mr. Tower?"

Tower smiled. "Absolutely fantastic."

"I'm sure you are, after that win you had with Zepher. It was super."

"As you're intimately aware, it's what I do."

"You sure do."

"As for you, you're not doing particularly well, are you?"

Cory spread his hands. "Look, I know we had our differences in the past, but I'm considering changing attorneys."

Tower smiled. "And you'd like to know if I'd be interested in representing you?"

"I didn't do what they're saying."

"Whether you did it or not is of no concern. I prefer not knowing."

"All right, but somebody is trying to frame me for killing Stein."

"So I hear."

"Let me ask you, what do you think of my case? If I hired you, what would you do?"

"I don't give away my strategies. If you want to know, engage my services and pay my firm's professional fees. Then, and only then, I'll share my approach."

"But how do I know you'd be better than who I have now?"

"You wouldn't be here if you didn't think I could help. Besides, you've benefited from my expertise and connections in the past."

"How much is this going to cost?"

"You can't put a price on saving a man's life."

"I know, but I gotta know. I don't want to go through what happened last time."

"That wasn't pleasant, was it?"

"I mean, I hope there's no hard feelings, but I had to do what I did. You understand, right?"

"I'm a transactional person."

"What do you mean by that?"

"I don't have time to get into it today. Let my office know if you wish to retain our services."

"But how much will I need to pay?"

"Five hundred an hour plus costs. We'll need a hundred thousand dollars up front as a retainer."

"I don't have too much money right now because of the bail thing."

Tower put up a palm. "That's your problem. I've got work to do."

"But—"

Tower stood. "Goodbye, Mr. Lupinski."

Cory walked down Madison Avenue. He didn't like Tower, but he was his only option. Worth was a nice guy, but Cory's life was on the line. He wasn't sure what Tower did to get the results he did, but he was sure he played dirty.

Tower was nasty, but Cory didn't have a choice. He had to have Tower's help if he wasn't going to spend the rest of his life behind bars.

He'd have one more talk with Worth about his chances. If the attorney still believed the best option was to plead guilty in exchange for a twenty-year sentence, Cory would hire Tower while continuing to prepare to run and hide.

LINDA WAS IN BED, tapping her iPad. Cory said, "We got to talk."

She put her tablet down. "You made your mind up?"

"Much as I hate the bastard, unless I find out who's behind all this, Tower's my best shot at getting off."

"I can't believe nobody else can help us."

"Tower's got the connections. Look at what he did for Zepher and me with Bonner."

"How do you think he does it?"

"Probably bribes people."

"He's so sleazy. I can't believe so many people are that corrupt."

"Right now, I don't care about anything but getting this over with."

"You have to be careful with him."

"Trust me, I'm on alert. As soon as Baffa sends over the publishing papers, you'll sign them and get them to the label. Once that's all in order, I'll pull the trigger with Tower."

"You sure about giving me all the credit?"

"Yeah, it'll be cool. Raffi wants to do the tunes; he needs material for a new album."

"You think we'll get sued?"

"Maybe, but if we stick to our story that you wrote the lyrics and used the chords from 'Around the Farm,' we're gonna be fine."

"I don't know, what happens if I have to go on the stand? I can't lie."

"Don't worry about it now. Let's see what happens. We can always change it up if things get too hot."

"I don't like this. Why does everything have to be so complicated?"

"I'm sorry. I just want to be sure you and the kids are going to be okay if I got to run or something."

"How do you expect us to be okay? Huh? You'll be a fugitive. The kids will never understand it. They'll be haunted by their famous father who's disappeared."

"What do you want me to do? Go to jail? Would that make you happy?"

"Don't be so stupid. We want you here, where you belong."

"Me too, but if I can't, prison isn't an option for me."

"Being on the run isn't good. We gotta find a way out of this."

"I'm trying. Maybe Tower can work some of his magic."

18

———

Between the upfront payment Baffa arranged for the tunes in exchange for a smaller royalty and twenty thousand from Linda's mother, Cory scraped together Tower's retainer.

Crossing the street, Cory pushed feeling terrible about borrowing money from his sick mother-in-law from his thoughts. Walking down Lexington Avenue, he hoped the effort would pay off.

Waiting for an elevator, two women pointed at Cory and whispered to each other. Cory turned his back and waited for the next ride up.

Tower's assistant, Brenda, led him down a hallway that smelled of cigar smoke. She knocked on his door and opened it. Tower, finger curled around a fat cigar, was reading a document.

"Sit down. I'll be a minute."

Cory eyed the bottle of Pappy Van Winkle on the desk. It had been his favorite bourbon, and it was no coincidence Tower had made it available.

"Feel free to pour yourself a drink, Mr. Lupinski."

"No, thanks."

"You sure? I hear nothing beats a shot of Pappy."

"I'm not drinking anymore."

Tower raised an eyebrow and turned a page. He set the papers aside. "Sorry about that."

"No problem."

Tower dragged a file to him and centered it. "We received the first set of documents from our discovery request." He flipped open the folder. "The prosecution has accumulated substantial evidence against you."

"But we can fight back, can't we?"

"Yes, what they have may be formidable, but it's not insurmountable."

"That's good."

"I never concern myself with an eyewitness, but they'll make the case that your phone location data corroborates you were there."

"I teach a student just a couple of blocks away."

"The DA is aware there's enough to elicit reasonable doubt. Being in the vicinity of the crime scene is an issue but explainable."

"Super. My old lawyer, he was so negative—"

"What is troubling is your blood being discovered near the body."

"I wasn't there, I swear."

"We must be careful in addressing it. A denial, no matter how vigorous, is not enough."

"What do you suggest?"

"We could have our forensic experts test and age the stain."

"You can tell how long it was there?"

"Exactly."

"How reliable are the tests?"

"They're highly accurate, but the prosecution will parade

experts providing an opposing conclusion no matter what the results are."

"But that will make more reasonable doubts. Won't it?"

"On its own, I'd tend to agree, but in concert with the witnesses and the incriminating message you left on the victim's phone, questions will begin to pile up."

"That message was old—"

"You don't have to convince me, it's the jury I'm concerned about."

"What are we gonna do?"

"I have a couple of ideas. There's a handful of people I'm going to reach out to. We'll see from there."

"That sounds good. You said you were going to look into the bail thing. What's up with that?"

"Good news."

"Really?"

"I had several conversations with the DA's office and a private discussion with the judge. They're agreeable to reassessing the amount posted."

"Oh, man, that's super. By how much?"

"It's not a done deal, but we're going to have a hearing this week on my motion to reduce by a million dollars."

"I can't believe it."

"If we're successful, and I believe we will be, there's going to be costs and people who need, let's say, taking care of."

"No problem. Do what you have to do."

"Are you sure? It's expensive."

"Absolutely. How much?"

"Three hundred thousand."

"Three hundred? That's steep."

"Not really. Getting a bail reduction of this magnitude is

highly unusual. If you want to halt the proceedings, let me know now."

Cory hesitated. "No, it's okay. Go for it."

"Excellent. I've got to get going, there's a charity dinner I must attend."

"Okay, but I think we should hire an investigator to look into who is setting me up."

"Right now, I want to focus on the bail hearing, but we can talk about that next time. Is there anything else?"

"You think I should take a polygraph test? You know, to prove I'm not lying."

"I'll have to think about it, as they're not admissible as evidence."

"HEY GUYS, I'M HOME!"

"Daddy!" Tommy ran to his father, and Cory picked him up and turned him upside down.

"Swing me, Daddy."

Cory held his son by the ankles and swayed him.

Linda came in holding a dish towel. "Be careful. How did it go?"

"It went super! Who wants to go out to dinner and celebrate?"

"Yay! I do."

"I have a chicken in the oven already."

"So what?"

"I've got to shower, and Ava has a paper that's due tomorrow."

"Can we go, Mommy?"

"Not tonight, honey."

"Don't worry, little man. After dinner, I'll take you for an ice cream."

"Yay!"

"You're in a great mood. It went well with Tower?"

"It was all good. Get Ava, I want her to hear the good news."

Dragging her feet, Ava followed her mother into the family room.

"Hey, Ava. I know this all has been tough on you, so I wanted to share some good news."

Cory sat Tommy on his lap and said, "Today, Daddy went to his new lawyer, and this man is very good. He's optimistic about the case, and he has a ton of contacts."

Linda asked, "What did he say?"

"He's in touch with the DA, and even the judge, and he's working on a plan to get this behind me."

"Did he tell you what he was going to do?"

"It was a lot of legal mumbo jumbo, but guess what?"

"What, Daddy?"

"My bail is going to be reduced, by a lot."

Ava said, "So? That don't mean anything."

"Yes, it does. It means they're starting to realize I didn't do it."

"No, it doesn't."

"Of course, it does. Why else would they lower it?"

"Bail has nothing to do with innocence or guilt."

"Who told you that?"

"We learned that in civics class. Bail amounts are based on what the court thinks the risks are of the accused going on the run."

Cory thought, how did a sixteen-year-old know this? "Yes, that's part of it, but the bottom line is they wouldn't give us back the money if they believed I did it."

Ava rolled her eyes and got up.

Linda said, "Where are you going?"

"I have to finish my paper."

"It's okay, let her go finish her schoolwork. Tommy, go get Trouble, I feel like playing a game."

"Okay, Daddy."

Tommy ran out and Cory said, "Even when I win, I lose. You'd think she'd be happy that something went our way."

"I don't understand what Tower said."

Their son came running in with the game. Cory said, "I'll tell you later."

19

Cory put Tommy to bed and went to the kitchen. "He loves Curious George. I remember reading that as a kid. Talk about a royalty stream."

"What happened with Tower?"

"It was good. He didn't seem to be holding a grudge or anything."

"What did he say about how he'd handle the case?"

"Not much. He said he's researching it and all."

"That's it?"

"No, he mentioned the witness and blood and how to deal with it."

"What exactly did he say about the evidence against you?"

"He's working on it. You know, he's reaching out, talking to the DA and stuff."

"I'm not trying to be negative, but it doesn't sound like any progress was made."

"That's not true. He's going to get the bail lowered. There's a hearing next week."

"I wonder how he did that?"

"He said he spoke with the DA and the judge. I don't know how he does it, but I'm telling you he has amazing contacts."

"That's good."

"Good? It's what we need. We'll have some breathing room financially." He lowered his voice. "We'll have to turn a lot of it to cash and hide it in the lockbox."

"I hate to say it, but Ava is right."

"About what?"

"As far as the case is concerned, a lower bail doesn't mean anything. I know it's a positive, but I had hoped to hear how Tower thinks he can get you off."

"I get it, but Tower is a crafty bastard."

"I need something we can hang onto."

"He doesn't say much. He works his magic behind closed doors."

"I hope so."

"Don't forget, last time around, he didn't say anything and got it done."

"I know, but this is different, Cory. A man is dead, and they say you did it."

"You think I don't know the difference?"

"That's not what I meant. The last time it was bad, but we knew Bonner was going to be okay. I know Tower is good, but this is a whole other level."

Cory nodded. "Why is someone doing this to me?"

"Is Tower going to hire investigators?"

"We're gonna talk it over next time. I'm sure he's putting feelers out. That's how he operates."

"You really think this guy walks on water."

"When he got me off, it said a lot."

"That was one case. I'm grateful, but it doesn't mean he can do it again."

Tower had not only saved Cory when he shot Bonner. He'd also scared off Linda's divorce attorney and had killed her attempt to take the kids away from him when they had marital problems. He couldn't tell her that. "Don't forget Zepher and when he got the governor off."

"I forgot about the governor."

"And Zepher's was a murder case."

Linda frowned.

"I'm telling you don't worry. Tower's the man."

"I can't wait for this to be over."

"Hang in there, hon. We'll get there."

CORY COULDN'T SLEEP. He replayed his meeting with Tower. Was Linda right? Had he overestimated what was said? The bail part was super, but he hadn't said much more. Cory took solace in recalling Tower had always been stingy with details.

Tower operated on the edges. It made sense he was secretive, Cory reasoned. To be as effective as he was, the lawyer had to play dirty. It was the one thing Cory was sure of.

His heart fluttered when he thought Tower might be playing him again. Could the lawyer really get Cory off the hook, or was his effort all about the money he'd earn?

Tower gravitated to high-profile cases. He hated to lose. Cory had seen that when he'd outfoxed him. Tower had gotten so angry, he thought he might stroke out. He'd also sent his goons to scare Cory by following him and his family.

Cory had to hope Tower took his case because he thought he could win, not as some twisted revenge scheme.

20

———

TOWER WAS ON THE PHONE WHEN CORY WAS SHOWN INTO HIS office. He was thankful the lawyer wasn't smoking a cigar. His assistant pointed to a chair. Cory sat and surveyed the room. It looked like there were a couple of new pictures of Tower and another of his horses in the winner's circle.

The light reflected off Tower's slicked-back hair as he disagreed with who he was speaking to. His gray silk suit jacket was thrown over the chair next to Cory. Hand-tailored, Cory figured it cost several thousand dollars.

As the lawyer finished his call, Cory wondered where Tower lived. Was it a Fifth Avenue penthouse or a mansion in Westchester?

He put the receiver down. "That ran a little longer than I expected. Time don't mean anything to a prosecutor."

"You were talking to a prosecutor?"

Tower nodded. "It takes them a paragraph to say hello. When some of them come to my side of the table, it's a huge adjustment for them."

Cory didn't know much about the interaction between

defense lawyers and the state, but he was surprised at how Tower had spoken to this one. "Tough case?"

Tower waved him off. "I just signed off on the bail documentation. The bonding company will process it and release the funds tomorrow."

"Super, I appreciate it."

"I'll cut you a check, less expenses."

"Oh. I thought—"

"I've given this case considerable thought. I'm not going to sugarcoat this; you're in a difficult situation. The prosecution has incriminating evidence against you, and they're not finished building their case. It's an uphill battle at this point, and I expect it will get steeper as the investigation moves forward."

"But you said the witnesses could be disputed and—"

"Yes, individually, we can attack, but combined they present a formidable challenge. You have to make it as easy as possible for a jury to come your way, and I have serious concerns we can."

"But—"

He pointed a finger at Cory. "You don't want to go to trial unless you know the results before walking in the courtroom."

"We have to look for who's framing me. Why aren't we hiring a private investigator?"

"I've reviewed the complete file the DA has. I'm not saying it doesn't exist, but there's no evidence of a conspiracy."

"That's because no one is looking for it. I'm telling you, they're framing me."

"Can we put that aside for a moment?"

"Okay."

"We have to decide on how to proceed with addressing

the charges. We don't have unlimited time, in fact, the case is already on the calendar for mid-February."

"The trial?"

"Yes."

"But that's, like, three months away."

"One hundred and fourteen days, to be exact."

"Is that enough time to find who's behind this?"

"Without concrete information on where to look, I wouldn't know where to direct an investigator."

"Start with Bonner. He had plenty of reasons to get revenge."

"I'll get someone to look into Bonner and any possible role he may have."

"That's super. I think it really could be him."

"And if it's not, I need you to start thinking of plan B."

"What's plan B?"

"Your best option is to change your plea from not guilty to one of self-defense."

"Self-defense?"

"Yes."

"But I wasn't even there."

"The evidence contradicts that claim."

"If I said it was self-defense, that would mean I did it, right?"

"Yes, but under the law it would be a justified killing."

Cory shook his head. "No, no. I can't . . ."

"I realize it may be shocking, but it's your best chance to avoid a long prison term."

"You want me to say I killed Stein in self-defense to get out of going to jail?"

"Exactly."

"But people would look at me differently. I told everybody, my wife and kids, that I didn't do it."

"People make pleas every day, admitting to crimes they haven't committed to avoid or reduce sentencing penalties."

"I know, but I don't know if I could do that."

"Think about it. I understand the concept may be shocking, but it's results that matter."

"I don't know what to think anymore."

"That's why you have me. Let me do the legal thinking for you."

"Thanks."

"Go home, talk it over with your wife, and we'll get together next week. Let's make it Thursday at noon."

"Okay, thanks again."

Cory headed to the door and turned around. "You're still going to check into Bonner, right?"

"I'll look into him, and you give serious thought to my suggestion."

CORY WAS SITTING on the couch. Linda came in with two bags of groceries. She looked at Cory. "What's the matter? It didn't go well with Tower?"

Cory shrugged and got up. He took the bags into the kitchen. Linda followed. "Tell me what went on."

As he put the milk in the fridge, he said, "He's going to get an investigator to look into Bonner."

"That's good. It's what you wanted. Why are you down?"

Palming a jar of peanut butter, he said, "He wants me to think about pleading self-defense."

"Self-defense? I don't get it."

"He said he's a little worried about the evidence. He thinks it can be defended, but he doesn't want to take a chance with a jury. He said you never go to trial unless you know how it's going to turn out."

"But that would mean you'd admit to killing Stein."

"I know, I didn't and wouldn't be happy about saying that."

"I don't like it."

"Me either, but he said if I did, I could walk away, no jail or nothing."

"He did? Hmm, maybe it's the way to go."

"What would we tell the kids?"

"Tommy is too young. Ava, well, we'll explain that people make deals all the time."

"She's going to be tough on me. I don't think she'll buy it, but over time she'll understand."

"She's at that idealistic age. They think they know how the world works, but they have no clue."

"I know. I hope Tower's guy can find something on Bonner. That would solve everything."

"How much time do we have?"

"Not much. The trial date is mid-February."

21

———

CORY PUT HIS GUITAR DOWN. HE COULDN'T COMPOSE WITH his mind fixated on the charges against him. Five days had crawled by since his last meeting with Tower. He had called the lawyer yesterday but never received a call back. He pulled his phone out and willed Tower to call. How was it that time could go so slowly, yet the trial date was quickly approaching?

Cory grabbed his jacket and headed outside. A blast of cold air hit him. He zipped his jacket, wondering who Tower had hired to check into Bonner and whether they found anything. It had to be the piano tuner. The bastard had black-mailed him, and Cory shot him. Who wouldn't want revenge? He couldn't think of anyone else except Riley. But though something was off, he knew the rhythm guitarist couldn't be the framer.

Walking toward Prospect Park, Cory rewound the last decade of his life. Was there someone he'd screwed, embarrassed, or treated badly enough to come after him? As a session musician in demand, he'd played with everyone and was reliable, always giving his best.

When he had his breakthrough, there wasn't a soul he could remember not happy for him. Embarrassed by how he'd reacted under the dual pressure of stardom and addiction, Cory examined his interactions. He looked at his shoes as he walked through the leaves. He'd been an ass. But a big enough jerk to motivate someone to make him spend the rest of his life behind bars?

Cory had cheated on his wife, but other than Joanne, none were long relationships. He thought about two that were married. He'd been aggressive pursuing them when clubbing, but why were they out if happily married? One of the women, redheaded Suzanne, had been cautious the times they'd been together. She refused to go to his apartment and always made sure their dinner dates were in private rooms outside the city.

She made references that her husband was some kind of gangster, and their secretive rendezvous made sense at the time. But looking back, did she know her husband would come after Cory if he found out? The timing didn't make sense. Their affair happened years ago. If her husband discovered her infidelity, he'd be understandably upset. But why wait so long for retribution?

Had he just become aware? It wasn't like a hood to shelve their anger until no one would suspect him. Cory remembered reading about a Russian mob boss who would wait until an enemy would least expect it. He felt waiting, sometimes as long as a decade, made revenge sweeter.

Could it be Suzanne's husband and his gang? It seemed remote, but the whole case was bizarre. Bemoaning his dalliance, Cory decided to try and track her down. Maybe she'd know something. But first, he'd call Tower again. Bonner was the likely suspect, and Cory had to know where he stood.

CORY WAS ABOUT to go to the bathroom when Tower's assistant waved him over. "He'll see you now, but he's extremely busy."

"Thanks."

She knocked on Tower's door, and the attorney growled to enter.

The lawyer tossed his reading glasses onto the desk. "Mr. Lupinski, you're certainly persistent."

"I'm sorry to bother you, but you know, I can't sleep thinking about this."

A smile appeared then vanished from Tower's face. "I understand you're anxious, but you have to trust the system."

"The system? They're accusing me of murder."

"And we're going to address the charges. Try to remain calm."

"Did you check into Bonner? Is he the one who framed me?"

"Yes, we did. However, Mr. Bonner has an alibi for the time in question."

"He could be lying."

"This is not my first rodeo, Mr. Lupinski. We vetted his story. He was out of town, visiting his sister in the Catskills."

"That's like, two hours away, he could have driven back. That bastard is as cunning as they get."

"That's doubtful."

"No, you don't understand, Bonner has it in for me. He's smart, look at the way he blackmailed me."

"My man is confident Bonner is not involved in any way."

"Who did you use? Was it Mr. Black?"

"I don't know who you're referring to."

"Are you sure? He knows you."

"I'm quite sure."

"Well, you should. Mr. Black is the best. I can set you up with him, if you want."

"My long-standing relationships have served me well."

"You're sure whoever checked Bonner is good?"

"It's not Bonner, and unless you have something tangible on someone else—"

"I do! You see, when I was riding high and partying too much, I played around on my wife. Anyway, I met this woman, Suzanne, her husband was a mobster."

"What's the point, Mr. Lupinski?"

"I think it could be him."

"And why do you believe that?"

"Well, I've been racking my brain trying to think who would do something like this, and it hit me yesterday. She said he was really jealous and super dangerous."

"Is that all you have?"

"Like I said, I just remembered this guy. I'm waiting on her to call me back. I'll let you know as soon as I hear from her."

"You do that. Now, I'm afraid I'll have to bring this conversation to a close. Today's schedule is a tight one."

"Okay."

"Have you given thought to my plea suggestion?"

"Yes, but I need more time."

"I understand. Just remember that the more time and resources the DA puts into a case, the less likely they are to negotiate."

"I get it."

Tower stood. "Your second invoice is waiting for you at reception. I'd like to remind you that it's due immediately."

22

———————

Cory hit redial, shaking his head when it went to voice mail.

"Suzanne, it's Cory Loop calling again. Hey, I know it's been a super long time, but I need to talk. Can you call me back?"

He flopped onto the couch. Linda came in. "Who you trying to reach?"

"It's a long shot, but some woman who was flirting with me, her husband is a gangster or something."

"What? Who are these people?"

"I, uh, met them backstage. They were friends with Dave. The husband freaked out at an after-party because she wouldn't leave me alone. He was super jealous."

"How long ago was that?"

"About six years ago."

"And you think he's involved?"

"I don't know, Linda. Tower said it wasn't Bonner, and I don't know where else to look."

Linda sat next to him. "You don't think it's Riley, right?"

"Nah. I don't like the little prick, but I know it ain't him."

"Maybe it's an unstable fan."

"You think so?"

"Why not? Some of them lose touch with reality. Look at all the stalkers."

"Yeah, but some lunatic waited until I faded out of the limelight to screw with me?"

"Maybe they're mad that you're doing kids' music."

"That's crazy."

"The point is, *they're crazy*. Don't you remember some of the fan mail that came in?"

"Do I. Remember that guy from Upstate New York? He had the words to 'Dead Silent' tattooed on his back."

"You can't make something like that up. Did you get any threats?"

"Most of it was just kooky. There was only one time, this guy, he'd send emails every day, and he showed up one night outside the arena in Orlando. He tried to get on the bus and went berserk. I felt bad for him, he was out of his mind."

"You never told me about that. What happened?"

"Security got him to the ground. But I told them to let him go after we pulled away."

"Scary stuff. You should call Helen, the president of the fan club back then, see what she says. Maybe she has an idea."

"HELEN, HOW ARE YOU DOING?"

"Cory?"

"Yeah, it's me."

"Oh my God. How are you, uh, doing?"

"The best we can, given everything."

"It's hard to believe."

"You and me both. I didn't do it. Somebody is framing me."

"Really?"

"Yeah, that's why I'm calling. We've got an investigator checking into some people, but I was wondering about the fan club you ran for me. Was there anyone you think was crazy enough to do this to me?"

"Hmm. You know, two guys come to mind. One was called Diesel. I don't know if that was his real name or not, but he was on the sick side. I was on the verge of calling the police one time when he scared me with his stalking. He always knew what we were wearing, and what hotel the band was in."

"Diesel? I never heard of him. Did he ever threaten me or the band?"

"Not directly, but it was borderline."

"Could be him. What about the other guy?"

"I think he was called Juan. He used to email that he wanted the set list in a certain order, and if it wasn't, he'd blow the place up. He was a nutjob for sure."

"Geez. People are crazy. Do you have their last names?"

"I'll have to check the records and get back to you."

"Thanks, Helen. I hate to push you, but my back is against the wall."

"The files are in the office. I'll get back to you, Cory, don't worry."

Cory hung up, muttering, "Yeah, don't worry."

He wondered what he was going to do with the information. Tower seemed uninterested in pursuing possible suspects. He wanted Cory to plead self-defense. Was that the best option, or was it the easiest one for the lawyer?

Towel wrapped around her head, Linda came into the family room. "Did Helen come up with anything?"

Cory told her about the two men. She said, "No shortage of nuts. Remember that guy who got up to our floor in the old building? He scared me so bad, I almost dropped Tommy."

"Thank God he was harmless."

"Maybe it is a fan."

He shrugged. "How are we going to track all this down?"

"Tower should be doing that."

"I don't think he believes it. He wants me to go the self-defense route. Maybe he's right, maybe I should."

"You changed your mind?"

"No, I don't want to, or at least not until I have to, but this is going to cost a ton of money. Money we don't have."

"We'll find it."

"How?"

"I don't know, it'll work out. You'll sell some more songs, and I can get a job."

"No way. Not until Tommy is older."

"We'll cut back on expenses."

"Don't make it too obvious. I don't want Ava resenting me any more than she already does."

"She doesn't resent you. She's having a tough time dealing with this. I'm sure the kids at school are being jerks about it."

Cory hung his head. "I feel terrible."

"It's not your fault."

"Oh yeah? If I didn't lose it the first time with Stein, I wouldn't be screwed. Man, how long do I gotta pay for a mistake?"

"Beating yourself up isn't helping. Maybe you should go see Dr. Bruno and talk it out with her."

"And spend another two hundred?"

"You can't put a price on your health. Why don't you go play some music? It'll help clear your mind."

Cory said, "Yeah, I need centering."

Cory picked up his Gibson L-00. The prized acoustic guitar was his favorite. He scanned the nine others hanging on the wall. His stomach dropped when he thought he'd have to sell any to fund his defense.

It wouldn't happen. He'd been broke before and rebounded. All he had to do was write a couple of songs. They didn't have to be hits; he paid the bills composing midlist tunes.

Cory noodled around, trying to find a catchy phrase he could anchor a melody on. Nothing seemed interesting enough. He closed his eyes and fingerpicked low notes. It was mysterious. He played the six-note phrase over and over. It was dark and depressing.

He swung the guitar off and hung it up. He couldn't write a kids' song in his current state of mind.

23

———————

Cory was at the keyboard trying to reharmonize a lesser-known Louie Prima tune. It was catchy and he thought simplifying the chords might give him something to lay a melody over.

The old-time performer had a knack for creating songs people sang along to. That was a winning formula for the children's market.

While notating a dominant chord, his phone vibrated. The number looked vaguely familiar. "Hello?"

"Cory?"

"Yeah."

"It's Suzanne."

"Oh wow. How are you?"

"Pretty good. And you?"

Cory looked at the phone; she didn't know about his troubles? "So-so. I'm embarrassed to ask, but what was your last name?"

"O'Rourke."

"That's it. That's your married name?"

"Yes. Why are you asking?"

"What was your husband's name?"

"Why are you asking these questions?"

"I was just thinking about the old days, and I remembered when he lost it backstage that time."

"Billy has a temper."

"How's he doing?"

"Fine."

"What did he do again?"

"He's a businessman."

"What kind?"

"I have to go. Nice talking to you."

Cory minimized the composing software and opened a new tab. He typed in Billy O'Rourke in the search bar. A long list populated. Cory scrolled down and went back to the search bar, adding crime to the name.

Cory leaned in. The top result was for an Irish crime boss named William Dublin O'Rourke. He clicked onto the link, and an image of the man nicknamed The Monk appeared. Cory zoomed in.

Was it the same man? The picture was of a much younger man. Was O'Rourke the kind of guy who had his goons rip a camera out of a person's hands if they took a picture of their boss? Cory went back to the article.

The *New York Post* write-up was short. O'Rourke was suspected of ordering the beating of a man who stole a crucifix from St. John's Church. Cory read it twice. The theft took place in 2015. Cory scrolled to the top. The article was written on November 10, 2017.

O'Rourke had waited over two years. Cory leapt up. Was it him? It had to be. He ran into the kitchen.

"Linda, I think it's him."

"Who?"

"This guy, his name is O'Rourke. He's an Irish mobster."

"What's the connection?"

"He's the guy who got twisted over his wife flirting with me at an after-party."

"How long ago was this?"

"I don't know. One of the tours we did when I was hot."

"I don't get it. You're saying this woman was flirting with you and he freaked out?"

"Yeah."

"Come on, Cory. You were screwing her, right?"

"No, I swear. That's not it."

"And you want me to believe he waited years to frame you?"

"Come here, read this. You'll see this guy is whacked out."

He showed her the web article. "Now do you believe me?"

"This doesn't make sense."

"It's crazy, right?"

"You better be straight with me. Don't tell me you didn't do more than flirt with that woman."

"It was a long time ago. I—"

Linda stormed out. "Shut up before you dig a deeper hole."

Cory watched his wife walk away, thinking, of all the guys it could be, did it have to be the husband of someone he'd slept with? He needed a break and it looked like he had one.

He Googled the mobster, but there wasn't much out there. He searched using the nickname The Monk. He scanned the results, smiling when he saw a definition of Monk as someone with patience.

He called Tower's office. The lawyer wouldn't get on the

phone. Cory passed over the information on O'Rourke and hoped Tower would take it seriously.

Cory hung up. He was too wired to go back to composing. He went into the kitchen.

"I called Tower, but he wouldn't get on the phone."

"Okay."

"I told his assistant. You remember Brenda, right?"

Linda nodded and opened a drawer.

"Anyway, I gave the information on O'Rourke. It's the first time I'm feeling hopeful."

Linda silently put a tea bag in a mug.

Reaching out, Cory rubbed her back and Linda stiffened. "I'm going to try to finish that song I was working on."

Cory exhaled. She was right to be pissed, but did he have to keep paying for every mistake he made?

Seated behind his Yamaha keyboard, Cory repeated the nickname Monk in his head. It made him think of the jazz pianist, Thelonious Monk. He fingered a couple of dissonant chords the old player was famous for. The clashing sounds wouldn't work for kids, he thought. Or would it?

Cory played with variations of harsh chords when Linda came in. "Cory! Mom's being rushed to the hospital."

"What's wrong?"

"Mary went there, and she was out of it. Her legs were swollen, and she couldn't catch her breath. She called 911. They're taking her to Mount Sinai."

"Let's get moving."

"She needs kidneys. She's not going to make it."

"They'll move her up the list."

"I got a bad feeling. Mom's not going to get them in time."

Cory wiped a tear from her cheek. "She'll be all right."

The couple burst out of the elevator onto the nephrology

floor. Hustling down the hallway, Cory wondered why it was so quiet. Rounding a corner, they almost ran into the doctor taking care of Linda's mother.

"Dr. Faulkner, how is Mom?"

In green scrubs and somber, the physician said, "I'm afraid she's experiencing acute renal failure."

Cory put his arm around Linda's waist, asking, "She needs a transplant. Is she going to get one?"

"I hope so."

Linda said, "We got to get her kidneys. She won't make it if—"

"I'm aware of that, Mrs. Lupinski, but all I can do is keep the transplant unit informed of her condition."

"This is crazy. My mother is dying! Why isn't she getting a kidney?"

"Take it easy, Linda. Let's go see her, and then we'll talk to the people in transplant."

Cory held his wife's hand as they entered her mother's room. Seeing the gaggle of hoses and lines attached to her, he swallowed hard. His mother-in-law was unconscious. Linda's legs buckled, and Cory eased her into a chair.

Tears streaming down her face, Linda took her mother's hand and kissed it. "We're here, Mom. You'll be okay."

Cory stood beside his wife, staring at his mother-in-law. Her leathery face had a yellowish tint. Seeing how terrible she looked made him wonder if there was anyone he could reach to help her leapfrog the transplant list.

24

Holding a fire truck, Tommy came into the studio. "Daddy, why is Mommy crying?"

"She's upset that Grandma doesn't feel good."

"But she's getting better, right?"

"A little bit. Go give Mommy a kiss."

As Tommy ran off, Cory tapped a number in his phone.

"Hi, it's Cory Lupinski."

"Hello Mr. Lupinski."

"No one from the transplant board called me back."

"We advised them you called. You have to give them time to respond."

"But it's been over a day."

"I'm sure they'll return your call."

"Look, isn't there something you can do? My mother-in-law really needs the transplant. She's very sick."

"I'm sorry, Mr. Lupinski. I know you've done marvelous work with our child patients, but Mount Sinai's transplant board is completely independent. I'm sure you understand; for it to operate properly it cannot be influenced by contacts—"

"This isn't influence. She's dying."

"I'll let them know you called, again."

"I'm not going away!"

"Goodbye, Mr. Lupinski."

Cory flung his phone onto the couch. "Goddamn it!"

Linda came in holding Tommy's hand. "Who was that?"

"Mount Sinai. Nobody's calling me back."

Her shoulders sank. "She's going to die."

"Grandma's gonna die?"

"No. A friend of Daddy's is sick." She got on her knees. "But Grandma is very sick. Mommy and Daddy are trying to help her."

"I can help too."

Linda hugged him. "You certainly can."

Cory lowered himself to the floor. Tousling his son's hair, his phone rang. "I got to get this. It's Helen."

Walking out of the room, he said, "Hey, Helen."

"Hi Cory. I pulled out the records and found some info on the guys we talked about."

Cory sat at his workstation and grabbed a pencil. "What do you have?"

"Diesel's last name is shown as Jameston. There was no return address on the envelopes he used, but the postmark was Jersey City, New Jersey."

"How many threatening letters did he send in?"

"We saved fourteen."

Cory opened his laptop, saying, "Wow. He's obsessed. Can you scan the letters over? My lawyer will want them."

"No problem. There was a note that we had alerted Tracy on five separate occasions."

"I remember getting some security warnings."

"I've been doing this a long time, and though you have to be careful, most of them are just over-zealous fans."

Cory typed in Diesel Jameston in the search bar. "Maybe not this time."

"Maybe. Now, the other man is Juan Foster. We found six letters that we marked as unusual. We also reported them."

"Where does this guy live?"

"Starrett City. In Brooklyn."

"If you can send those over, with his address, we'd appreciate it. I hope my lawyer can track these guys down."

"I'll send them now."

Cory's eyes scanned the search result. "Thanks. I'll talk to you later."

There were ten results, making Cory wonder who named their kid Diesel. None of the names were connected with New Jersey, and Cory had no idea what the man looked like. Most of the men pictured were thirty to forty years old.

Cory studied one face. The man had an earring and a scar crossing his chin. Could this be him? The fact the guy was an illustrator didn't fit. He'd have to leave it to Tower to identify who Diesel was.

But what about this Juan Foster? He did a search, and the third line had a reference to Brooklyn. Cory clicked the link, and a Facebook page opened. Foster was a thirty-year-old with thinning hair. His profile background was a montage of rock album covers.

Foster was into music and had gone to Brooklyn's New Utrecht High School. The occupation section read self-employed. Cory took that to mean he wasn't working. He wasn't a 'friend' and couldn't view his posts.

Cory thought about sending a request but was worried he'd tip off Foster. He called Tower's office. The lawyer was in court. Cory made an appointment for the next morning and went to tend to his family.

Tommy was brushing Linda's hair. "See how nice Mommy's hair is?"

"It's super beautiful."

"How are you doing, hon?"

"I'm okay." She pulled her son onto her lap. "Tommy made me feel better."

"What time you want to go to the hospital?"

"I was waiting on you."

"I'm ready, but we should wait for Ava to get home. The kids should come."

Linda nodded. "She'll be home in an hour. I told her no dance today."

<hr>

CORY TURNED the lights on and opened the shade. Linda said, "You're going to wake her up."

He threw a chin toward their children at the foot of the bed. "It's depressing in here."

Linda bent over and kissed her mother. She stroked her cheek as Cory put his arms around his kids. "Talk to your grandmother."

"But she's sleeping, Daddy."

"She can hear you. It's good for her."

Ava sniffled and stood beside Linda.

Cory said, "I want to see if I can talk to a doctor."

"See if they moved her up the list."

"They better have."

At the nurse's station he asked for an update. A pregnant nurse came around the counter. "Hi, I'm Erin. Mrs. Moran is in my section."

"How's she doing?"

She took a breath. "She's holding her own."

"What does that mean?"

"She's fighting but needs a transplant."

"I know. But as of this morning she was like number twenty on the list."

Erin shook her head. "We don't have enough donors. It's really unfortunate."

"And that's it? It's unfortunate? My mother-in-law is going to die, and we're supposed to watch her go? What's wrong with this place?"

"I'm sorry, sir. I realize it's frustrating, but the problem is not limited to Mount Sinai. Until we get the public on board with donating their organs, we're not going to be able to meet the demand."

"This is screwed up, man." Cory turned his back and headed back to the room. He tried to think of what to tell Linda and the kids.

25

―――――――

Cory yawned as he was shown into his lawyer's office.
Tower got up, moving from the round table to his desk.

"Didn't sleep last night?"

Cory shrugged. "At the hospital until two in the morning."

Tower suppressed a smile. "Case getting to you?"

"My mother-in-law is in ICU. She needs a transplant really bad. I was going to ask you about it."

"We do law here, not medicine."

"But you know everybody. Don't you have a contact to get her a kidney or two?"

Tower hesitated. "The transplant world is a universe unto itself—"

"You have someone?"

"It's an expensive endeavor."

"To jump to the top of the list, you have to pay somebody off?"

"No. Transactions like these are done outside of the system."

"Not through the hospital?"

He shook his head. "No. The system frowns upon offering incentives to donors."

"So, it's a private transaction."

"Exactly."

"I saw something on TV, I think it was *60 Minutes*. I'm pretty sure it was in India. They had people getting paid to donate a kidney, and people from the US and Europe would get them."

"Something along those lines."

"Can you put me in touch with someone?"

"I'm afraid your mother-in-law's case is too advanced."

"Why do you say that?"

"She's in ICU. It requires travel, and it takes time to make the arrangements. Time your mother-in-law doesn't have."

"What kind of travel?"

"There are several surgery centers outside the New York metropolitan area that are supportive of matching donors and receivers."

"She could probably handle something like that. How much time would be needed?"

"Six to eight weeks."

"Okay. I'm going to check, I'll let you know."

"Have you given consideration to the self-defense plea?"

"What happened with Billy O'Rourke?"

"There's nothing to indicate his involvement—"

"What are you talking about? The guy's a mobster."

"That may be, but we're not finding evidence of it."

"I don't understand."

"Our investigative team is top-notch."

"All right, but I got the information on two men who could be involved. They're fans who are off their rockers."

Tower leaned back but said nothing.

Cory pulled out a handful of documents and put them on

the desk. "Here's their names and last addresses. These guys made a ton of threats against me. This Diesel guy said he was going to blow up one of my shows."

Tower didn't pick up the papers. "Mr. Lupinski, I think it's time for a reality check."

"What are you talking about?"

"I realize how difficult these circumstances are to accept, but you can't keep digging up anyone who cursed at you over the last twenty years as suspects."

"These people threatened me. Repeatedly." He picked up the documents and waved them. "They put it in writing. It's all right here."

"We'll look into them, but I believe it's time you consider the plea. Time is not on our side. The trial date is rapidly approaching."

"I know, I know. Just check into these guys. I'm telling you, they're nasty. If they don't check out, I'll really think over the self-defense thing."

"I'm afraid it's your only option."

Cory kept replaying Tower's warning. It meant the lawyer either didn't believe the names he gave him would pan out, or was it that he wouldn't even waste resources on them? If that was the case, Cory would have to hire someone on his own.

Siren wailing, an ambulance caught Cory's attention as it sped down Lexington Avenue. Jarred, he thought about his mother-in-law. She was just sixty-four years old. He wondered how long she'd live.

You didn't have to know anything about medicine to understand she was at death's door. She needed a miracle to get the transplant. Why didn't people want to donate their organs? It's not like they had a use for them.

Going down the subway stairs, Cory knew he was as guilty as the next person. Only after being exposed to suffering children waiting for a transplant did he decide to become a donor.

This was a fixable problem. Why didn't the media spread the word instead of focusing on celebrities and the weather? And where was the government?

Tower mentioned an option outside the system. Was it illegal? As Cory thought it over, he realized it didn't matter if your life was on the line. If Tower knew about something like that, it had to be safe. The question was whether his mother-in-law could survive the wait and move from the hospital to a clinic. Stepping into a subway car, Cory felt if she could, it was worth a shot.

"I'm home!"

As Cory squirmed out of his jacket, Linda came in. "How'd it go?"

"The usual. He said he'll check into the fans, but he pushed the self-defense thing again."

"What about that gangster guy?"

"He said there's nothing there."

"You don't believe him?"

"I don't know what to believe, but hey, I asked Tower for help getting Mom a transplant."

"You did?"

"Yeah, he said he couldn't do anything about the list but said the other way to get an organ was outside the system."

"What do you mean?"

"He didn't get specific about it, but it's a private way of getting an organ."

"You have to pay someone for it?"

"Yeah. Not the person directly, but remember that *60 Minutes* piece we saw?"

"That was horrible. Making poor people give up their organs for money."

"I know, but maybe this isn't like that. Maybe they have a supply of donors, say on life support or something."

"You think so?"

"I can find out, but she'd have to be moved out of the hospital, and it would take six to eight weeks to get one—"

"Unless she improves, she doesn't have that kind of time."

"We got to try, no?"

"Only if it's from someone who's brain-dead."

"I agree. We can't take advantage of someone who's poor. Call her doctor, see if you can get them to commit to how much time she has. I'll get more details from Tower on who the actual donor would be."

26

———

"I'M SORRY, MR. LUPINSKI, MR. TOWER IS VERY BUSY. HE said there is nothing to report on the names you provided."

"Tell him I wasn't calling about that."

"What's the nature of the call?"

"Mention transplant to him."

"Transplant?"

"Yes. Tell him I want to ask him a quick question on it."

"Hold on."

Cory cringed at the smooth jazz playing while he was on hold. It was tinny and annoying. He held the phone inches away until hearing Tower's voice.

"Mr. Lupinski. What can I do for you?"

"I wanted to ask about the transplant arrangement you mentioned."

"Yes?"

"How much would it cost for a kidney?"

"Two hundred thousand."

"Wow. That's expensive."

"Everything is relative."

"Where do the organs come from? A living person?"

"Of course. All donors must be alive."

"No, I meant, is it, say, someone who needs the money or somebody who is brain-dead?"

"I don't understand the relevance of the question."

"We don't want to take advantage of someone who needs money."

"What does it matter if the person is poor or brain-dead? The fact that someone needs an organ and can get it is all you should be concerned about."

"We don't feel comfortable buying a kidney from a healthy person."

"But you're comfortable allowing your mother-in-law to die?"

"No, of course not. It just feels immoral paying for it."

"We'll see how being virtuous works out for you."

"What does that mean?"

"Goodbye, Mr. Lupinski, I don't have time for these kinds of discussions."

Cory looked at his phone. "What a hard-ass."

He trudged into the kitchen. "I talked to Tower. It's two hundred grand for a kidney."

"Oh my God. Where would we get that money from?"

"We can use the money we got back from the lower bail instead of saving it for when I run."

"Run? You're not—"

"It just came out that way."

"What did he say about where they get the organs from?"

"He won't say."

"That's not good."

"I know. It felt like they're paying people who need the money."

"That's horrible."

"I know. We're really going to have to think about this."

Linda exhaled. "Why can't Mount Sinai just get the kidneys for her?"

CORY INSERTED his ear pods and played a Bill Evans album. Music from the jazz pianist always helped him to think. Pushing through the front door, he wrapped a scarf around his neck and walked along the sidewalk.

Accused of murder and with Linda's mother fighting for her life, he wondered if life could get any more complicated. He felt bad for his mother-in-law. Since his mother's passing, she'd been a ceaseless supporter. She even threaded the needle when their marriage went through a rough patch.

Cory thought of his mother. She used to say God gave you what you could handle. He bought the line sometimes but not now.

Crossing Flatbush Avenue, the pianist tapped the same quarter note over and over. It reminded Cory of a ticking clock. He had two of them: the trial was looming, and his mother-in-law had even less time.

As hard as it was, he had to accept the reality his mother-in-law wouldn't get the transplant. There just wasn't enough time. She was weak, hanging on by a thread. Losing her would hurt like hell, and the kids would be devastated. But over time, they'd recover from most of the pain.

Everyone lost people they loved, especially grandparents. It was a cold fact better off accepted than fought.

But if Cory went to prison, the damage would never be undone, particularly if it was a long sentence. He didn't kill Stein and felt the truth would come out. He hadn't found the person framing him, but he would. The world would find out he was innocent.

Considering a trial, Cory's confidence waned. Though it was rare, people were behind bars, convicted of crimes they never committed. Could that happen to him?

Tower was arrogant, but he sounded right when he said not to go to trial if you didn't know what the outcome was going to be.

27

Cory was about to join Linda in bed when she said, "Get the heavy blanket out of the closet."

"Yeah, it's cold. You think the kids are all right?"

"I put their comforters on earlier."

Cory put the throw on and slipped under. Reaching to shut the lamp, Linda said, "We got to help Mom. I want to try the transplant thing with Tower."

"Really?"

"She deserves a chance. I know it's a lot of money, but I couldn't live with myself if we didn't try."

"If it were reversed, she'd do it for us."

"In a heartbeat. Plus, we got to show the kids we don't give up."

"I'm not saying we shouldn't do it, but it's a slippery slope. How do people decide when to try something and when to say no? Nobody wants to be a science experiment by doctors who don't know when to stop treating a patient."

Linda sat up. "You think that's what we're doing? That she's a helpless cause and we're unrealistic?"

"No, no. Not us. I'm just talking in general."

"But you think we should do it?"

"Absolutely, we got to give her a shot. I'll call Tower in the morning; tell him we're going ahead with it."

"Okay. Should we go to the bank?"

"Yeah, we'll get the money, and I'll take it to Tower."

"You should make an appointment with him to make sure he has time. I don't want to have all that money in the house."

"If there's cash to be had, Tower will make the time."

<hr>

CORY WORE his backpack in front. He wanted to keep his eyes on the money. The Uber stopped in front of Tower's office and Cory scooted inside.

He was whisked into the lawyer's office. Tower smiled. "Good to see you, Mr. Lupinski. You have the funds?"

"Yeah."

"Put it here." Tower pointed to the center of his desk.

Cory swung the backpack off and placed it in the cleared spot

Tower unzipped the bag and took out a bundle of cash. He brushed the stack, checking that they were hundreds. He reached in and began placing them in stacks of five.

"There's a hundred there."

"That's right. A hundred now and a hundred when she's accepted at the facility. She'll get in, there's no doubt about it."

"If so, you'll get the rest, there's no doubt about it."

Tower's faced darkened. He tossed the backpack to Cory. The lawyer opened up the credenza behind his desk. He punched the keypad on a safe and swung the door open. Tower put the money in and closed it.

"I'll let you know when the arrangements have been made. Is that it for today?"

"Did the investigators get anywhere on who's framing me?"

"Mr. Lupinski, don't you believe I would have called you?"

"Just checking."

"There's nothing to suggest a conspiracy. As recommended, your best option is a self-defense plea."

"I've been giving it a lot of thought. Tell me how this would work."

"I reach out to the DA and court, informing them we're changing our plea from not guilty to not guilty due to self-defense."

"I thought I'd have to plead guilty."

"In essence you'd be admitting to the murder, but it was a justified killing."

"You think it will work?"

"I have a high degree of confidence it will."

"How high?"

"It's difficult to put percentages on things like this. But it should work."

"Should? That doesn't sound good."

"It was a poor choice of words, but let's not get distracted. Your options are limited. You either take a chance with a trial, hoping you'll be exonerated, or you plead self-defense."

"I'm not sure I understand what makes something self-defense."

"There are five elements that justify the use of deadly force: innocence, imminence, proportionality, avoidance, and reasonableness."

"Imminence?"

"That Stein, in this case, posed an imminent threat to you.

But the overriding one here, and frankly in most cases, is reasonableness."

"So, it comes down to me acting reasonably when he died?"

"Exactly. Now, we'll have to go over your testimony. Make sure it's airtight and that you stick to it."

"You mean, create a story about what happened?"

Tower nodded.

"Stein was suffocated. So, he was attacking me, and I had no choice. I tried to stop him, and it just got too far. I didn't know he was dead. When I left, I figured he was just unconscious."

"You'll need to explain why you were there and how an argument broke out and why you felt threatened."

"I can do that."

"I look forward to hearing the details. Once you have your, uh, version of things, we'll bulletproof it."

"For the DA?"

"Yes, and in case they are unwilling to drop the charges."

"They won't drop the charges?"

"It's uncertain and unlikely they would drop—"

"What? That means there'd be a trial?"

"I don't understand your apprehension. You're going to go on trial whether you plead not guilty or use the self-defense angle."

"I guess so, but I thought with self-defense it would just go away somehow."

"No, it wouldn't disappear with a change in plea. What would change is the strategy in a trial."

"How so?"

"The prosecution has the evidence to prove just about every element of the crime. You have a violent history with the victim, you left a threatening message on his phone, you've been placed at the scene of the crime, and your blood was found near the body."

Cory sank into his chair as Tower kept talking.

"As discussed, creating doubt on each of these will be difficult and risky."

"Okay, okay. I get it."

"Shall I advise the court of your decision?"

"I got to speak to my wife first."

28

Cory waved to Linda, who was peering out the window.
She met him at the door. "How'd it go?"

"Good."

"Everything is set?"

"Yeah, he'll let us know when and where we have to bring her."

"I hope he hurries. I just got off the phone with the nurse's station. The treatment isn't working. She's not showing any improvement."

"Damn, we're so close."

"I know. What did Tower say about the case?"

"I hate to say it, but he made good points about a self-defense plea."

"Like what?"

"A bunch of legal crap, but the bottom line is that it's too risky to plead not guilty. So, it's either I go the self-defense route or run."

Linda's lip quivered. "Running scares me. I know you don't want to admit to anything, but maybe it's the best way. What do you have to do?"

"I'd have to make up a story about what happened. You know, I went to see Stein about the tax papers, and he went off at me. I felt threatened and tried to stop him. I thought he was unconscious and took off."

"You'd have to have all the details down."

"I know. I'd say I was in the neighborhood teaching and figured I'd stop over, blah, blah, blah, but keep it short and sweet."

"You'd have to say why you didn't call 911."

"Think it's better to say I didn't know he was dead, or that I panicked?"

"Oh, I don't know. I guess most people would be scared and try to hide it. But I don't know how many would believe you didn't know he was dead."

"I got to get that part right."

"Maybe Tower can help. He should know what juries believe."

"I should've asked him if he was going to get one of those jury experts."

"They're important. You need to get the right people."

"Tower's good. He probably has that lined up."

"What about the blood? How you going to explain that?"

"I think the nosebleed is the best. Stein swung at me and hit my nose."

"That makes sense."

"What about when you left Stein's house? Where'd you go? What did you do?"

"I came home?"

"You got to remember you'd be upset, nervous. You just had a fight and had to subdue Stein."

"I'd want to get away from there as fast as possible."

"Or maybe try to make it look like you weren't in a hurry. Did you stop anywhere?"

"I don't think so. It was so long ago, I can't remember."

"Do you usually stop somewhere when you teach out there?"

"Yeah, I can say I stopped and bought a pretzel from that old guy with the cart by Cadman Plaza Park."

"Don't make something like that up. You'll get in trouble that way. Who knows, that guy might have been sick that day."

"With my luck, he would. You know, you're giving me better advice than Tower."

"He'll probably get into it after you decide."

"Either way, I have to figure out what I'm going to say."

"Stick to the truth as much as you can."

"The truth is, I didn't do it. Now I gotta make this bullshit up."

"Take your time. I'll help."

"I'm going to start writing down some ideas."

"Don't write it down until you have exactly what you're going to say. Besides, you should know what happened off the top of your head, plus, who knows, if they seize your computer, they could use it against you."

Cory exhaled. "I'm going in the studio to think this over."

Cory sat at his workstation. Coming up with a story was scary, but he was going to keep it simple. All he had to do was say he walked from his last lesson to Stein's house. Having been inside before, he pictured the foyer. He remembered the striped wallpaper along the wall with the stairs.

What if Stein had redecorated? If he was on the stand getting hammered by a prosecutor, how would it look if he couldn't remember something like that? It could ruin his believability.

Tower had to know about things like that. But why hadn't the lawyer given him guidance on crafting what happened?

Cory reasoned that Tower was worried about tainting himself if it came out he instructed his client to lie.

Cory would put together his version of what happened and tell Tower. He was sure the lawyer would have suggestions to strengthen the self-defense claim.

Tower mentioned reasonableness as the key to a successful plea. What was considered reasonable when killing someone? The words seemed at odds with each other. Wrong or right, the internet had information on everything.

Cory opened a private browser, typing "self-defense plea" in the search bar. He looked over a page of results, clicking on the third one.

It led to a defense attorney's website and was written to attract potential clients. Cory read a long blurb touting the use of a self-defense claim. This lawyer also keyed in on reasonable responses to a threat, but what leapt out was his references to imminent threats.

The lawyer posited that the use of deadly force was almost always justified in the face of an impending threat. If you were sure that an aggressor was going to do you bodily harm, your reaction wouldn't be held against you.

Cory hit the back button and clicked on another site. It was yet another attorney fishing for clients. The information was similar; you could kill someone if you believed you were in real danger.

It was comforting, but Cory realized he'd have to find a way to concoct an appropriate threat. He went back to Google and scrolled down. There was a link to a New York lawyer who touted he'd worked for the DA before switching sides.

Cory clicked on the site. It didn't seem to have the 'salesy' feel the other lawyers' sites had. The sidebar had links to specific sections of the judicial code. He double-clicked on self-defense.

As he read, bile began splashing against the back of his throat.

29

THIS ATTORNEY WASN'T A FAN OF USING SELF-DEFENSE. HE said it was rare that a defendant could surmount the burden of proof an affirmative defense demanded. He stated that if a defendant met the elements of a self-defense claim, that they wouldn't face prosecution in the first place.

It was a powerful concept that had Cory reeling. He recalled an incident where a man with a machete was threatening a woman in Central Park. The woman, a Brinks guard, was on her way to work when the encounter occurred. The woman shot and killed her menace but was never charged.

Cory went back to reading. He didn't understand the part that said even if prosecuted, the defendant wouldn't need the instructions of an affirmative defense to be read to the jury because the jury would simply refuse to convict, either on a lack of intent or under its mercy-dispensing authority.

He didn't know what the instructions part meant, but he got the overall meaning: self-defense would have to be obvious to work. He cycled ideas, but they depended on whether a weapon of any kind was found at the scene.

Cory wondered whether if there were successful cases

where a weapon wasn't used. Maybe he could say Stein was choking him and he responded.

Then an idea hit him. Cory could say he wrestled a knife away from Stein, and he took it with him when he left. Cory liked that idea. If Tower approved, he'd go with it, saying he threw it in a trash can on the way home.

Cory closed the laptop and went into the kitchen. After telling Linda the idea that Stein had a weapon, she said, "It sounds okay, but you better check with Tower."

"I will. I think the district attorney has to tell Tower if they found a weapon or whatever at the scene."

"I'm pretty sure that's right."

"I'm going to scout out a place to say where I dumped the knife."

"Start thinking what kind of knife it was."

"Maybe keep it simple, a kitchen knife."

"They'll count his silverware—"

"Maybe a Swiss Army knife. A lot of guys his age have them."

"Only if you can somehow find out if he owned one."

"Ugh! I'll think about it. I got to get going. I have three lessons. What time you going to the hospital?"

"Around four."

"I'll meet you there."

"I think we better tell Ava about the self-defense plea before you tell Tower you'll do it."

"I know. I'm afraid how she'll react."

"We'll just have to explain that it's the safest way. Kind of like what Tower says."

"I wish she'd believe me about the framing."

"She'll come around."

"I hope so."

THE SUBWAY CAR WAS EMPTY. It was earlier than when he would have ridden it on the way back from killing Stein, but neither times were rush hours. He wondered whether anyone would remember seeing him. He wasn't in the spotlight any longer, but a lot of people still recognized him.

Would someone say he acted nervous? He went back over his story. It would come down to what he did in the house, where the knife came from, and what he did with it afterward.

In his mind's eye, he saw a red handle connected to a shiny blade. He tried to understand why the vision came to him as he carried his guitar up the stairs to the street. Was it the Swiss Army knife on his mind, he wondered, as he made his way to his student's apartment?

"Hey, Mr. Loop, let me show you this riff I made up."

Cory resisted the urge to cover his ears as the twelve-year-old played a distorted run of notes.

"Pretty good, Jimmy, but play it slowly. Get the notes to sing. It'll sound better if it's cleaner."

"Like this?"

"Better keep it in time. Here, let me set the metronome at sixty."

"Sixty? That's way too slow."

"Trust me, Jimmy. If you can play it slow, you can play it fast, but not the other way around. You hear me?"

"But—"

"No buts! Play it. Slowly!"

Jimmy picked the notes.

"No. No! You're way ahead of the beat. Listen to the metronome."

The kid started playing again.

"Don't you hear it?"

The kid's mother came in. "Everything all right?"

"Yeah, he's just not listening."

Jimmy said, "I'm trying, Mom. He's always yelling at me."

"I'm not yelling, just trying to get you to slow down."

The mother said, "Uh, Mr. Loop, can I talk to you a second?"

Cory followed the woman out of the room. She lowered her voice. "Is everything okay?"

"Yeah, why?"

"You've been teaching Jimmy for five years now, and you've never raised your voice."

"I wasn't yelling, he couldn't hear me."

"You sure you're all right?"

"I guess I'm not feeling too good. I got a lot going on, and maybe I'm feeling the pressure a little."

30

Linda said, "I'm exhausted."

"That's okay. Go to bed."

"It's only eight."

"That doesn't matter, you're tired."

"I don't know why. I didn't do anything but go to the hospital."

"You were there all day. It's stressful sitting there all that time."

"How can you get tired doing nothing?"

"Look, between your mother and what's going on with me, you can't have any more stress."

Linda collapsed on the couch. "When is this going to end?"

"Soon, hon. Hopefully, Tower calls about the transplant, and I'm close to telling him to go for the self-defense plea."

"If we survive this, nothing can touch us."

"I hope so, but I couldn't have predicted anything that's happened, good or bad, the last ten years."

Linda burrowed into Cory. "I worry about the kids."

"Don't. They're tougher than you think."

"I don't know. They need a safe, predictable environment."

"Look, it's tough on them to see what Mom is going through, but sooner or later they'll realize everybody dies."

"You don't think she's going to make it?"

"We have to be prepared. She's weak, and a transplant is not exactly routine."

"I know. I just don't want her to suffer."

"Nobody does, that's the worst. We have to be realistic, that's all."

"What do you mean?"

"Let's see how it goes. If it goes against her, we may have to let her go."

Linda nodded.

"Go to sleep."

"I don't want to go by myself."

"Can you give me a little time? I need to record a solo for something Donny's working on."

"Okay. Go ahead, I'll watch something."

Cory kissed her cheek. "Super. I'll see you in a bit."

He closed the studio door and played the tune his friend had sent over. It leaned toward rock. He listened to it again, singing ideas he might use in a solo.

Cory played the recording one more time. Closing his eyes, he tried concentrating on Donny's bass line. He couldn't make out the upper extensions his friend was playing on some chords.

Cory took his Les Paul Gibson off its stand. The Starburst was his favorite electric guitar. He plugged it into the console, put headphones on, and warmed up. He ran scales but couldn't identify the tension he heard in those chords.

He stopped trying and began playing blues licks over the recording. Noodling around over the solo spot, Cory exhaled.

He'd been holding his breath. It was something he never did. He reminded himself you couldn't make music if you were tensed up, and restarted the tune.

Waiting for the solo space to come around, Cory hit the record button. Two beats before it came, he launched into it, playing an opening line he liked. He tried to build on the idea, but instead of letting the feeling flow, he was thinking about each note a nano-second before playing them.

He listened to what he'd created; it sounded mechanical and forced. Cory tried two more times before giving up. He hung his guitar up and left the studio.

The TV was on. Eyes closed, Linda was on the couch. Cory bent over her, whispering, "Linda. Come on, let's go to bed."

"Uh, I dozed off."

Cory clicked off the TV. "That's okay."

"You're done?"

"I'm gonna lay it down tomorrow, nothing good was coming out. I got too much on my mind."

The couple got into bed. Five minutes later, the cadence of Linda's breathing told him she had fallen asleep.

Cory thought about his mother-in-law lying almost comatose in a hospital bed. She'd caught a bad break with failing kidneys and had suffered the last two years as the disease progressed. She was just sixty-four, too young to die, but she'd seen her daughter get married, giving her two grandchildren.

He imagined his own exit at sixty-four. Would he have walked Ava down the aisle? Would either of his kids have children? It was probable, but if he was behind bars or on the run, he wouldn't see them.

Admitting to something he didn't do gave him stomachaches, but he hoped a self-defense plea could be the answer.

Cory went over the story he'd made up. Being in the area giving lessons was a double-edged sword; it put him near the crime scene but also gave him a valid reason to be there. The knife was still the thing that could trip him up.

How the knife entered the argument and where it had been dumped were details he had to get right. He was going to say he put the knife in a dumpster behind Panda Express, a Chinese restaurant in the area.

The attorney would know if it was believable. He thought about Tower. If he hadn't changed lawyers, where would he be?

Cory knew the answer; he'd be on run. But why hadn't Worth recommended a self-defense plea?

Worth was a button-down type of guy. He probably wouldn't have mentioned it because Cory had said he didn't do it. Tower was a rule bender. He'd do anything to get his client off the hook.

Tower didn't seem to care whether who he was defending was guilty or not. He only gave a damn about winning. It was an ugly approach, but you couldn't argue with the results. Cory still couldn't believe Tower had gotten him off after he shot Bonner.

Somehow, he'd saved Cory's ass then. Did Tower have another ace up his sleeve? Was the self-defense plea just a way to work around a scheme Tower had arranged?

Though Tower had proven the value of his connections, the stakes were too high now. If he admitted to a justified killing of Stein and something went wrong with Tower's deal, Cory would spend the rest of his life behind bars.

Cory had done some research. Conceptually, self-defense

was simple; you either killed or risked being killed. Everything balanced on whether the risk was real and imminent.

The ex-prosecutor's site he'd visited also made a simple argument as to why a self-defense plea wasn't necessary. What he said made sense; if it was self-preservation, the authorities wouldn't bring charges.

Cory slipped out of bed. The floor was cold. Instead of putting on socks, he headed directly to look something up.

31

Cory opened a private browser, navigating his way to the site skeptical of self-defense pleas. He read the opinion again. Cory didn't know much about the law, but the reasoning was as logical as it got.

Who was this lawyer named Michael Mashetta? He went to the bio area of the website. The attorney had a list of credentials, including awards as a prosecutor and working for the defense.

Cory threw his head back. Who was right? Was it Tower or this ex-prosecutor? He wasn't equipped to know, and there was another unknown. The jury. If he'd been able to find the framer, he wouldn't have to deal with this.

He cycled through the people he believed might be responsible. He had been certain Billy O'Rourke was involved. But Tower had said no. He even said O'Rourke wasn't a gangster. How could Tower say that? The guy had been in the papers. Why would Tower deny it?"

Was he involved with Tower somehow? Cory's mind was whirling. He had to focus on what he could control, and that was the story.

He'd tighten up what he claimed happened and see what Tower thought about it. Cory closed his laptop, wondering why Tower hadn't counseled him on what he knew was the most important part of his defense.

Heading back to bed, he felt it had to be a protective thing. Then he stopped in his tracks. Was Tower trying to submarine him? He blew it off. Tower was a lot of things, but he wasn't a loser.

Cory wasn't the high-profile star he'd been, but the case still attracted a lot of attention. Tower wouldn't want to lose with the cameras on.

Linda was snoring. Cory covered her shoulder and slipped under the blanket. He couldn't get Tower off his mind. He remembered his first encounter with the lawyer. Cory was in a panic. He called Mr. Black for help, and the unorthodox operative told him to call Tower.

Tower took control immediately, hiding Cory in a hotel room as the cunning lawyer worked his case. Cory remembered being shepherded by Tower when he surrendered to the police. The attorney wasn't warm, but there was no doubt he'd been protective.

How Tower had extracted Cory from the nightmare was a mystery. One that Cory was afraid to look at too closely out of fear it would disappear. The attorney was not only incredibly effective but quick to resolve anything presented to him.

It got too easy to bring a problem to Tower, and Cory was guilty of depending on him. He wondered if his dependency had driven the lawyer to get greedy. Either way, it was wrong and ended their relationship.

Had the attorney changed since their blowup? There were little signs, but he was human, not a machine. Tower agreed to represent him quickly, surprising Cory. But on reflection, it made sense. Tower said he was transactional, and Cory likened him to a poker player. He'd lost the last hand but was ready to play again.

Cory didn't play cards but knew playing poker against Tower was a losing proposition. Wondering if Tower bluffed when he played, Linda's cell phone rang. He popped out of bed and rushed to her nightstand as Linda woke.

He grabbed the phone. Mt. Sinai Hospital was calling.

Groggily, Linda said, "Who is it?"

Cory answered, raising a hand as he went into the bathroom. Linda followed him. "What's going on? Is it Mom? Is she okay?"

Cory hung up. "Mom's, uh, not doing well."

"Oh my God. What's the matter?"

Cory reached into his closet for his pants. "Get dressed. I'll get the kids up. We got to get down there."

Ava and Linda held hands walking down the hallway. Tommy felt heavier than usual as Cory carried his sleeping son into the intensive care unit. Nurses were hurrying between rooms. Though there was a lot of activity, it was conducted quietly.

They checked in and were led to his mother-in-law. Linda said, "How is she doing?"

"I'm sorry. Your mother is extremely weak."

Linda gasped when she saw her and reached tentatively for her hand. Cory looked at his mother-in-law's chest. Her breathing was shallow and intermittent.

Cory lowered his son to the ground. "Say hello to Grandma, Tommy."

"Is Grammy sleeping?"

"Yes, but she can hear you."

Ava buried her face in Linda's chest. They were both

crying. Cory wrapped his arms around them. "It's going to be okay. She's peaceful, and she's going to a better place."

"Mom, look at this one." Ava held a picture of her grandmother holding her as a newborn.

"She was so happy when you were born. They say having a grandchild is better than having your own kid."

Ava ran her finger over the photo. "I think we should put it on the board."

"Sure. We need to find one with her holding Tommy."

Cory said, "She was a special lady. From day one she treated me like a son."

"Mom loved you. She used to protect you when you did something stupid. It used to annoy me she didn't stick up for me."

Ava said, "I guess Daddy was the son she never had."

"He got away with everything. Remember when you wrecked her car?"

"You crashed Grandma's car?"

"It was an accident. I was reaching in the glove box for a CD and I took my eyes off the road and hit a parked car."

"More like sideswiped the whole block."

"Oh my God, Dad. Did you get hurt?"

"No. But it was super embarrassing. I was more afraid to tell your mother than Grandma."

"What did Grandma say?"

"She was cool. Said she knew I didn't do it on purpose, and as long as I wasn't hurt, that was all that mattered."

Tommy said, "Daddy, why didn't they give Grammy the kidneys?"

"It's very complicated, but Grammy got sick really fast and there wasn't enough time."

"But why not?"

"Look through these and find a good picture of you and her. Daddy has to make a call."

Linda looked at Cory. He said, "I'm going to call Tower. You know, about the arrangements and get our money back."

32

THE FUNERAL ARRANGEMENTS DISTRACTED CORY. AS THE last person to leave the wake mentioned the transplant, Cory realized Tower hadn't called him back.

His family was getting into the limo to go to the cemetery. Cory stuck his head in. "I got to use the bathroom. I'll be right back."

Stepping into an empty viewing room, Cory called Tower. Expecting to be told he wasn't available, Cory was surprised to hear the lawyer's voice. "Mr. Lupinski."

"Hi, I wanted to let you know my mother-in-law passed away."

"Yes, I'm aware. Please give my condolences to your wife."

"You knew she died?"

"Of course."

"How did you find out?"

"We monitor all of our clients."

Cory felt it was odd he referred to her as a customer but let it pass. "Well, I'm calling about the money. When will we get our deposit back?"

"That wasn't a deposit but a payment to make the necessary arrangements."

"Okay, but when are you going to refund the money?"

"A refund will not be forthcoming."

"But she's dead. We don't need the kidneys."

"That's unfortunate, but we're well into the process and have already expended funds to secure the resources."

"But we just told you to get started, like, a week ago."

"You know we move quickly."

"We really need that money. Can't we get some of it back?"

"I'm sorry, Mr. Lupinski, but we simply can't do that."

"I don't understand. You can take whatever you spent already out of the hundred grand."

"A contract is binding."

"I didn't sign no contract."

"It was an oral contract. You hired us to make arrangements, and we did. It's unfortunate that your mother-in-law died, but it doesn't change what we already did."

Cory heard Ava call for him and he said to Tower. "I have to go, but I gotta tell you, what you're doing is unconscionable."

CORY CAME into the family room. "Tommy fell asleep before I finished reading a page."

"Everybody's wiped out."

"It's been a tough couple of days. You know, my nose is still stuffed up from the daylilies."

"I don't like them either. Anytime I smell one, I think of a funeral parlor."

"Ava seems to be handling it okay."

"She's a smart kid, and we told her all along how dangerous Mom's condition was."

"How are you doing?"

"I'm all right. I mean, I miss her like crazy, but since she went into the hospital, I . . . I knew."

"She was some lady. We'll miss her, but at least she's not suffering."

"I know. I really didn't think she'd survive the transplant."

"It's crazy, but it could have gotten worse for her."

"I know. It's going to be hard to clean out her apartment."

"I'll help you, and there's no rush."

"It's okay. I want to get it over with. Oh, you have to call Tower and get our money back."

Cory took a deep breath. "I did, but he's not giving any back."

"What? Why not?"

"He said he spent money, made the arrangements, blah, blah, blah."

"It was a hundred thousand dollars. No way he spent it all."

"I know, but he wouldn't budge."

"That's so unfair. I'm going to call him."

"Maybe that's not a good idea."

"Why not? She was my mother, and it's our money."

"I know, but he's handling my case, and I don't want to piss him off or anything."

"So, he's allowed to push us around? I won't stand for it."

"Take it easy, hon."

"One thing has nothing to do with the other."

"I'm going to see him. I'll bring it up again. I'm sure he'll bend some."

"He better."

"We'll see what happens, but right now, let's try and relax. Everything is so damn negative these days." As soon as it came out of his mouth, Cory regretted saying it. "No, it's not. We have each other and the kids."

Linda raised her eyebrows. "Really? You forget you're accused of murder?"

"You know what I meant."

Linda shrugged.

"We need to lighten things up. Let's watch something funny. You up for some Sebastian Maniscalco?"

An hour later, the couple went to bed. The comedy hadn't been the magic Cory hoped for. Linda put her head on his chest, and Cory felt the wetness of her tears. "I don't know what I'm going to do without her."

"It's tough, but it'll get better after a while."

"She was always there for me."

"And she's still watching out for you. She's your guardian angel now."

"I know you lost your mom way earlier, but I don't know, I feel cheated."

"That's natural. She was taken too early."

"I feel bad for the kids. They won't have a grandma around. And Tommy will forget her."

"No, he won't. Both kids have great memories of her, and we'll make sure they remember their grandma."

"I hope so. Maybe it's because she's the last to go, but when Dad died I felt bad, but nothing like this."

Cory hugged his wife. "It sounds terrible, but it's because you're an orphan now. We both are."

"Oh Cory, I can't lose you too."

"Don't worry. I'm not going anywhere."

"I hope not."

"I'm going to tell Tower to get the self-defense plea going. We got to end this."

"I can't wait."

"Start planning a vacation."

"A vacation? Where? We don't have the money to go somewhere fancy."

"I don't care where, as long as it's warm. Donny was telling me it was cheap in the panhandle of Florida."

Linda yawned. "I'll check online tomorrow."

As she moved to her side of the bed, the questions he had about the biggest decision of his life amplified in his head. The primary one was whether he'd have to stand trial. If the DA didn't buy his self-defense story, he'd have to sell it to a jury.

Tower seemed confident and had delivered every time Cory was in a jam. However, what the other attorney had written crept back into his head.

But what were his options? If he didn't go along with Tower's suggestion, it was either pleading innocent despite the evidence against him or running away. None of the options were good. There was no room for error.

33

CORY SMELLED COFFEE. HE FELT LIKE CRAP. HE PULLED THE blanket over his head and tried to fall asleep. Tussling with what to do, he'd come to an uneasy agreement with himself that self-defense offered the best way out.

There were still questions that needed answering, but he resigned himself that he would tell Tower to move ahead. Cory got out of bed and padded into the kitchen. "Morning. How'd you sleep?"

Linda said, "Terrible. I had a bad dream about Mom."

"Sorry." He kissed her cheek and grabbed a cup of coffee. "You sleep okay?"

Cory shrugged. "Not really. Was thinking over this self-defense thing. I think it's the only way to go."

Linda reached for his hand. "It'll work out."

"I gotta tell the kids."

"Now?"

"Yeah, I don't want Ava hearing about it from a friend or the news."

"I can't wait until it's behind us."

"There's no guarantees this is going to work."

"It will. You have to trust Tower. He knows what he's doing."

"That's the problem. I don't know if I can trust him."

"Why? Nobody thought of using self-defense."

"I know he wants to win and all, but maybe he doesn't care that much. If he loses, it's my ass in jail. He still gets paid, and the bastard's got the money from the transplant."

"We got to get some of that money back, but don't let that interfere with your case. He told you about that way before Mom . . ."

Linda started crying. Cory said, "It's okay." He gave her a napkin.

Ava came in. "What's the matter, Mom?"

"She's upset about Grandma."

"I'm okay."

"You sure, Mom?"

"Yes. I like that blouse with those jeans."

"Grandma got me this for my birthday." She held up her arm. "And this was the bracelet from Christmas."

"It goes perfect together. Eat something before you go to school."

"I'm not hungry. I'll take a bar with me. I gotta go. See you later."

Cory said, "Hang on a second. Sit down, I have to tell you something."

"What? What's wrong?"

"Nothing, honey, Daddy just wants to let you know in advance something about his case."

"What?"

"Under the advice of my attorney, I'm going to change my plea to self-defense."

"What do you mean?"

"That it was a justified killing."

"You killed him?"

"No, I didn't, but the lawyer said it was the best way to be sure I don't go to jail."

"I don't get it. Why would you admit to something you didn't do?"

"Daddy's only saying that because Mr. Tower said it's the way to go."

"So, now you're lying also?"

"Hold on, Ava. I know it's shocking to hear, but I didn't kill Mr. Stein. I wasn't even there. This is nothing but a legal strategy to make sure I don't go to prison."

"I don't believe this. This is crazy."

"People do this every day."

"Yeah? But once you say you did it, you can't take it back. You'd be known as a murderer."

"The people who know me, the ones I care about, would know the truth."

"What truth? The one where you didn't do it, or the one where you did?"

"I'm only saying it was self-defense to be sure. Otherwise, I have to take a chance with a trial, and Mr. Tower said that would be dangerous. It's all about trying to manage a bad situation."

Ava shook her head. "I don't know how you can say you did it. It'll be all over the news and everything. You can't just take it back; it'll be there forever."

"It's hard to understand, but you got to trust me. It's the best option we have."

Ava stood. "I'm going."

"Have a good day, honey."

The door slammed.

"Geez, that went well."

"I'll talk to her later."

"She's right, though. Her whole life we taught her to be honest, to watch what she said, and now we're telling her it's okay to lie."

"You don't have a choice, Cory."

"I don't know, but it feels selfish. A good father would fight the charges, be an example of integrity."

"You're a wonderful father."

"It doesn't feel like it."

"You are, and let me tell you, doing what you're doing makes sure you'll be around for the kids. What good are you going to be for the kids if you're in prison?"

TOMMY HAD A NIGHTMARE, and Linda had stayed with him until he fell asleep. She tiptoed into the family room. Cory was watching TV. "He's out?"

"Snoring like an old man. What are you watching?"

"A documentary about people faking their own deaths."

"Oh, come on, not again."

"No, I'm not thinking about it anymore, but it's crazy. There were two guys, both in Florida. One guy was a pilot, and he went up and put the plane on autopilot. Then he parachuted out over Mississippi, where he had a stash waiting for him."

"The plane crashed?"

"Yeah. He thought it would make it to the Gulf of Mexico, but it petered out before it got there."

"They caught him?"

"Yep. And this other guy, he took his boat out and made it look like he drowned in the Florida Keys. He had some sort of makeshift submarine he hooked up with. They were looking for him for days until he was spotted in Orlando."

"That was stupid of him."

"I know. The Coast Guard billed him like four hundred thousand for the searches."

"Put the news on. I want to see the weather. Tomorrow Ava's doing a walk for Alzheimer's. I hope it's not going to be too cold."

Cory changed channels. "I think it might be flurrying."

"It better not be windy."

"Wait a minute, that's the O'Rourke guy. The guy I asked Tower to check into."

"The one with the supposedly flirting wife?"

"I told you it was nothing. The guy is a gangster. They're saying he's involved in a gambling ring."

"Didn't Tower say he cleared him?"

Cory jumped off of the couch. "Yeah, and that he wasn't a mobster. What the hell is going on?"

34

"Tower lied to you then. He probably didn't believe you about the framing and didn't check O'Rourke out."

"Could be, or maybe O'Rourke is involved, and Tower's trying to protect him."

"Why would he do that?"

"How the hell would I know?"

"Don't get mad at me."

"Sorry, I'm just trying to figure out what's going on."

"Maybe nothing. All you know now is he seems to be involved in organized crime, and Tower told you he wasn't."

"Yeah, but why?"

"Like I said, Tower may never have checked him out."

"Oh, Tower would definitely do it. He's all over everything and everyone."

"He's not God, Cory."

"You don't know this guy. Tower doesn't miss a beat. Something is going on with him and O'Rourke."

"You're getting paranoid."

"Yeah, but it's my ass on the line."

"That's totally unfair. Whatever happens to you, happens

to this family."

"You're right, sorry."

"Let's step back and talk about this rationally. Okay?"

Cory nodded and Linda said, "You told Tower to look into O'Rourke, but it wasn't the first time you said someone could be framing you."

"Right, he was the third or fourth."

"And nothing came up on the others."

"Yeah, but who knows if Tower even checked into them?"

"There has to be a file on them. You can ask to see what he came up with. For now, let's assume he investigated them and found nothing. Tower doesn't want to waste time. His strategy is to have you plead self-defense. Does that sound logical?"

"I guess. But maybe O'Rourke killed Stein, and Tower is causing a diversion."

"By framing you?"

"I know it sounds crazy. Forget it. I'm all screwed up."

"It's okay. The O'Rourke thing is just a coincidence. Concentrate on what you're going to say happened."

"You're right. It's key to the self-defense plea. I got just about everything down about it and want to run it by Tower."

"Good. I'm sure he'll have a suggestion or two."

Cory took his phone out. "I'm going in the studio to call him."

"Ask him about getting our money back."

Tapping his phone, Cory said, "I will."

"I'm leaving to pick up Tommy. He's got tae kwon do, and Ava's got dance. I'll grab pizza from Gino's."

"That's cool with me."

After a five-minute hold, Tower came on. "Mr. Lupinski, how are you?"

"Okay. Say, I wanted to go over what I'm going to say

happened. You have time tomorrow?"

"Of course. Let me check my schedule."

Cory heard Tower tapping. "How would eleven fifteen tomorrow morning work?"

"Good."

"Fine, I'll see you then."

"Uh, hold on a second. My wife is really upset about the money we gave you for the transplant. We both feel we should get some kind of refund."

"We've had this discussion. The matter is closed. Now, if you have no further questions . . ."

"I was wondering about seeing the files you have on Bonner and O'Rourke."

"Files?"

"Yeah, what your investigators dug up on them. I'd like to see it."

"I'm afraid that's not possible."

"Why not?"

"The information is subject to a nondisclosure agreement."

"But I'm the customer. Ain't I paying for them?"

"Technically, but it's our firm who engages their services. I wish I could accommodate your request, but I'm simply unable to."

"That's ridiculous."

"I'm sorry you feel that way, but it's a necessary arrangement to ensure we get the information we require. As you can imagine, some of it involves unconventional methods. I'll see you tomorrow."

Tower hung up. Cory thought, there was that word again —unconventional. He took it as an admission Tower straddled the legal and illegal worlds. It made him uncomfortable, but he wanted to benefit from the lawyer's devious methods.

<hr>

CORY WAS CRUSHING pizza boxes when Linda said, "I'm going to get Tommy ready for bed."

"Let me read to him."

"You sure? You said you had to work on that jingle for the radio commercial."

"I don't want to miss any chance to spend time with him."

"Be my guest."

"Did you say something to Ava?"

"No. Why?"

"She was quiet eating and went straight to her room."

Linda said, "You're too sensitive. She does that almost every night."

Cory shrugged.

"Oh, I forgot to tell you. Ava wants to try playing lacrosse."

"Lacrosse? Why?"

"Said it would be a good sport to try and get a college scholarship with. She's going to need equipment. It would be a good way to spend time with her."

"Nice idea. I'll talk to her. Let me go read to Tommy."

Cory came into the family room smiling. "He really likes that new book I got him."

"He said he wants to be a fireman."

"No way. It's too dangerous."

"You never told me what Tower said."

Cory told his wife that it didn't look like they were going to get any money back and that Tower wouldn't let him see the investigator's reports. He finished with, "I'm telling you, I bet he didn't check anybody out."

"You think so? Why wouldn't he?"

"I don't know. Maybe he doesn't believe I didn't do it."

"I'm sure he saw everything they have on you. It's a lot."

"Don't remind me."

"He may have figured the best path was self-defense."

"For him maybe, not me. I don't like admitting to something I didn't do."

"I know, but at this point, the trial is coming up fast."

"Don't I know it."

"I hate to say it, but you've got to do the self-defense thing."

"This sucks."

"Sorry."

"Look, I got to go write. Take my mind off this crap."

Cory picked up his Gibson. He strummed the acoustic guitar, trying to force his mind to think about the jingle he had to write. This was the second one they had him doing. He liked doing them, and the money was decent. But Cory wondered whether the radio station would give him another gig, or anyone for that matter, after he pled guilty.

How would he provide for his family once people heard his admission? What would his family and friends think, especially Ava? She was confused and embarrassed by the jam he was in.

Linda mentioned her interest in lacrosse. She was right; it would provide an opportunity to repair some of the damage he'd done.

Cory visualized the weird equipment lacrosse players used to catch and throw the ball. He'd only seen the game on TV once. The memory made Cory put his guitar down. He opened his laptop and typed into the search bar.

Looking at the results caused him to think of the larger picture. Cory knew he faced the most difficult decision to make. Nothing would ever be the same again. There was no going back.

35

Cory leaned back in his chair and stared at the screen. Ava was only sixteen, but she was right; there were consequences He zeroed in on the young men in their lacrosse uniforms. Their lives had been changed forever.

Even though the Duke University players had been exonerated, the reputations of three men had been permanently tarnished by the false accusation of rape. People judged you immediately, and even if the information changed, their opinions rarely did.

Cory knew his situation wasn't the same; it was worse. Ava correctly assessed the repercussions; if you said you were guilty, you couldn't take it back.

Whether Cory did it or not, his reputation would be smeared forever. He could see the tabloids dragging him through the mud. As a former number-one recording artist, the whispering and conjecture would be off the charts.

He wondered about Tommy. His son wouldn't question him today. But as he grew older, Cory knew doubts would arise in Tommy's mind. Everything going forward would be tainted by his guilty plea.

He had to find who was behind the plot or he'd be tainted. Cory thought about pleading it was an unintentional death caused by defending himself from Stein's attack. Tower thought it would work, and if he stayed out of prison, he could mount an effort to uncover the framing conspiracy.

He didn't believe Tower had taken a serious look at Bonner or the others. Cory thought Bonner had the biggest motive. He played it in his mind again: the piano tuner had blackmailed him, and Cory had lost it, shooting him in the leg.

Who wouldn't want revenge against someone who not only took your gravy train away but shot you? And then there was O'Rourke. Linda had been right; there was no proof he was involved, but O'Rourke was a gangster and Tower had either lied about it or never looked into him.

Cory had to dig into the people he suspected, especially Bonner, but couldn't do it himself. The only person he knew was Mr. Black. Cory was pissed he hadn't called him earlier instead of relying on lawyers.

He told his kids it was never too late to do something, but he knew it was. Any investigation would take weeks, and if there was something, they'd have to dig further and get the court involved.

Maybe Tower could get the trial date pushed back. If he could get it postponed two or three months, it might be enough time. Cory didn't want to think about the alternatives. He'd just about given up on sticking with the claim he was innocent, so that left him with pleading self-defense or running.

Cory took his phone out. There was no time to waste. He called Mr. Black and left a message. He would see Tower in the morning. The meeting would set the course of his life.

36

———————

Walking behind Tower's assistant, Cory took a series of deep breaths. No matter how many times he'd met him and despite the fact he was paying him, Tower made him uncomfortable.

The lawyer was on the phone and didn't look up when they entered. The way he was talking made Cory think he was speaking in some kind of code. Nothing was specific. It was a string of nondescript words: "that thing," "him" and "place."

One of the few things he remembered from his father was his continual lament that it 'came down to who you knew.' As he started out pursuing music as a career, Cory didn't believe the arts were like that. But he found out getting gigs at bars and restaurants required a connection.

Tower hung up without saying goodbye and motioned to a chair. "Sit down."

"Thanks."

Tower raised his hand over his head and smacked it on the desk. "Got you!" He scraped something off his palm into a wastebasket.

"What was that?"

"An ant."

Cory thought it was an unusual way to kill an ant. He usually pressed a finger on one. "Oh."

"I'm glad you came to discuss your version of events. The trial date is coming up, and you must be prepared."

Cory didn't like he said you instead of we. "Well, one of the things I wanted to talk about was getting a postponement."

"A trial date deferral?"

"Yes."

"It's unlikely the court would grant one."

"Why not?"

"A variety of reasons, but there's no need for one."

"I'd feel more comfortable with more time."

"You need to get this behind you. What are you planning to say regarding the events that led to the death of Mr. Stein?"

"Well, I was in the downtown Brooklyn area, you know, I give guitar lessons to a couple of students who live there. Anyway, I finished teaching Juan, and on the way home I remembered needing documents Lew Stein had. He was my manager for a while, and my new manager, Mr. Baffa, said we needed tax papers he had. Do you think I should mention that Stein stole from me?"

"The prosecution will bring it up on cross-examination."

"Leave it out?"

"It doesn't matter."

"Okay. I'll say something like, I fired him because he was stealing money from me."

"Continue."

"So, I went to his house. He was surprised to see me but said to come in. I asked him why he never called me back, and he started getting in my face."

"What did you do?"

"I told him to calm down, that the documents he had were mine and that I needed them. He told me to fuck off. Can I curse on the stand?"

"I would use eff off instead. What happened next?"

"I asked for the papers again, but he started ranting that I'd ruined his career and that he wanted to kill me. I figured that would be good to say, right?"

"It could be. Please continue."

"So, he's threatening me, and I'm telling him to cool out. And that if he gives me the papers, I'd be on my way. He gets super close to me and tells me to get the eff out of his house. I can see his face, it's all red and I'm thinking maybe I should take off; then he turns around and walks away. I'm figuring he was going to get my papers, and the next thing I know, he's coming at me with a knife.

"It's a big one with a red handle and I start backing away. He lunges at me, and I skirt away from him. The blade just missed my face. I got amped up, and when he came toward me again, I kicked his arm and hit him in the wrist, making him drop the knife.

"It was like, unreal; we both stood there looking at the knife, and I thought I better get him before he picks it up again. So, I jumped on him, and we kind of staggered toward the couch. I was on his back and just pressed his face into the couch. He was trying to get me off, and I just stayed on him until he stopped moving.

I didn't think he was dead, just unconscious. I wanted to get out of there. I went straight for the door and saw the knife. I didn't want him to come after me again, so I picked it up and left the house."

"What did you do with the weapon?"

"I had it in my jacket and was really nervous. I was

looking for a place to dump it and saw this Chinese restaurant, Panda Express; they had one of those big green trash bins. I threw it in there and went home. What do you think?"

"You have to be prepared to answer questions about every minute and action you took."

"I was going to keep it simple, just stick to what I said."

"They're going to ask about everything. Who you saw on the way there and back, for example."

"I wasn't paying attention. That's the truth. I go there every week, and I couldn't tell you who I passed on the sidewalk, unless something happened, like one time this guy on the subway was hassling people for money."

"I understand. You'll need to have a time line for everything."

"That's easy, because I finished my last lesson, like, three o'clock. I could say I was at Stein's, like, fifteen minutes later. The whole thing at the house took no more than ten minutes. I was home around four fifteen p.m."

"You can't waver, no matter how hard the prosecution presses."

"I won't. What can I do to make it better?"

Tower smiled. "It seems fine the way you have it."

"Really? Isn't there anything I can do to make it more believable?"

"Nothing comes to mind. Why don't we let it sit where it is and think it over?"

Cory left his lawyer's office with mixed feelings. The relief he felt revealing his version of events faded as the elevator dropped. Tower hadn't given him much feedback. The only person Cory knew who was stingier than Tower with information was Mr. Black.

The meeting didn't make him feel any better. It was up to

him, Cory realized. He had to do what he felt was necessary. After all, it was his life on the line. Stepping onto the side-walk, Cory palmed his phone to call Mr. Black again.

37

———

WALKING TOWARD THE FLATIRON DISTRICT, CORY FELT BAD about coloring what he'd said to Linda. He was careful not to lie but gave her the impression it went well and that both he and Tower felt good about what he'd say happened.

He wasn't trying to mislead her. Cory just needed the space to think about it. Cory crossed Twenty-Third Street and headed into Madison Square Park, eyes on the lookout for Mr. Black.

A dusting of snow covered the grass surrounding a large sculpture. Cory jammed his hands into his pockets and looked at the piece. It was a modern interpretation of an elephant. He wondered what Tommy would say about it.

Considering why the artist had left out ears, he saw Mr. Black approach. His jacket was unzipped, and it looked like he was wearing a tee shirt under it. Cory lifted his chin out of his coat and said, "Thanks for meeting me."

"What's up?"

"I got a job for you. I need you to look into a couple of people. One of them is probably the guy that's framing me. It should be pretty easy. One of them is Bonner."

"Easy? Why don't you do it?"

"No, I meant easy for you. It was a compliment, man."

"Bonner and who?"

"I got a couple of others, but one guy is Billy O'Rourke. You know him?"

Cory wasn't sure if Black had nodded, and said, "Plus there's a guy that used to be in my band and—"

"I don't fish. From what I hear, they got witnesses placing you there."

"Yeah, two of them."

"Give me their names."

"The witnesses?"

"If you're being framed, somebody put them up to it."

"Thomas Rizer and Robert Ford." Black repeated the names and walked away.

Cory watched him leave the park. He thought about the witnesses. It made sense. The witnesses had to be in on it. Maybe they were being paid, or possibly the person running the conspiracy had something over the witnesses, forcing them to lie.

It was something Cory never considered, and it scared him that the plan was bigger than he'd imagined. But pressing the witnesses seemed an easier way to find out who was trying to put Cory behind bars.

A gust of wind plowed into Cory. He tucked his chin into his coat. He was freezing, but a surge of hope coursed through his body. Cory stomped his feet, took a picture of the sculpture for Tommy, and left.

CORY HUNG UP. "Tower is pressing me to sign the plea agreement."

"So? What's the problem?"

"I want to give Mr. Black time to check the witnesses out."

"How long is that going to take?"

"He wouldn't say. But with Bonner he was pretty quick."

"That should be okay."

"That's what I told Tower."

"You told him you hired Mr. Black?"

"No, no. I just told him there were a couple of personal things I had to tend to. He had the balls to ask me what they were."

"Why would he do that?"

"He's a frigging control freak."

"But you said he didn't tell you what to say."

"I think it must have something to do with his liability or legal stuff, 'cause lawyers are like officers of the court or something."

"Probably. You know I still can't believe he won't give us any money back. It's not right. Can we suc him?"

"Maybe, but not until this is over."

"It shouldn't be more than a month, right?"

"Probably longer."

"Why? The trial is three weeks away. It can't take that long."

"You never know with these things. It may not go like we're hoping."

"Don't tell me Tower said you might get a sentence."

"It's not that."

"Then what is it? Tell me what's going on?"

"I really don't know. If Mr. Black gets something, I may have to go underground for a while."

"Underground? What does that mean?"

"I'm not sure."

"Cory, if you're planning something, you better be straight with me."

"Take it easy, Linda. I'm just trying to say we got to be ready for anything."

"You'd tell me if you're going to run, right?"

"Don't worry."

"You just said you might have to go into hiding. That's nothing to worry about? What would I tell the kids?"

"If it comes down to that, I'll handle it. Did you cash that royalty check?"

"Yesterday."

"You put the money in the safe deposit?"

"Yes. You're scaring me. Something is going on."

"Everything is good. I just want to be sure you guys will have as much as possible if this blows up."

"Blows up? What the hell does that mean?"

"Nothing. It was the wrong word. I was just saying that if something comes up, we got to be flexible, that's all."

"You better not be hiding something from me."

Cory put his arms around his wife. "You're worrying too much. It might take some time, but I didn't kill Stein, and I'm going to make sure I clear my name."

"Just get this over with. I know you don't want to admit to something you didn't do, but going back to clear your name just prolongs everything. Can't we just get it behind us?"

"Let's see what surfaces."

Cory's phone pinged with a text. He dug it out. It was from Mr. Black.

38

———

Cory dodged traffic crossing the Avenue of the Americas and headed into Bryant Park. He recalled taking Ava to the library that anchored the east end of the park. He smiled, remembering how mad Linda got when he perched Ava on one of the lion statues that guard its entrance.

A handful of accomplished skaters were taking advantage of the midmorning lull at the popular ice rink. Cory watched an older man who might have been a hockey player decades ago. The old man was graceful. He was carving a tight turn when Cory felt the presence of someone.

It was Mr. Black. Cory said, "This old-timer must have been something years ago."

Black nodded. He was wearing leather gloves and his jacket was open. "He still has it."

"No doubt. Did you find out anything?"

"Whoever's behind this is good. Neither of them cracked, no matter how hard I pressed."

"What do you mean?"

"They're either too scared to talk, or a ton of dough is gluing their mouths shut."

"But can't you do something?"

"What else you got? You have another lead?"

"I don't know. I mean, there was the blood. They said it's mine, but it's not. I wasn't there."

Black squinted. "That won't help. You'd have to know who placed it there."

"What else can we do?"

"You want me to look at Bonner and O'Rourke?"

"Yeah, definitely."

"You got the money for this last one?"

Cory dug into his coat and handed an envelope over.

Black stuffed it inside his jeans and dug into his breast pocket. He pulled out an envelope. "These are yours."

"What is it?"

"Proof I did the job."

"Hey man, I trust you."

"Take 'em. They're surveillance photos of the witnesses. I got no use for 'em."

"Okay."

"I'll be in touch."

Cory watched Black exit the park. He opened the envelope Black had given him. There were three photos of each man. Both the men looked ordinary. Cory thumbed through the images. Black had photographed them coming out of their apartments and on the city's streets.

He stared at them. They appeared harmless. The saying that appearances and reality are polar opposites couldn't be truer, he thought, and put the pictures away.

He was running out of time and options. If Black couldn't get overwhelming evidence, and the self-defense didn't work out, he'd be convicted. Wiping his runny nose with a sleeve, Cory wondered whether he could handle being behind bars while waging a campaign to exonerate himself.

It'd be tougher working from jail. On the bright side, the public liked getting behind a story to free someone wrongly imprisoned.

How long would it take Black to develop evidence he'd been framed? He tried recalling the documentaries he'd watched that followed these types of cases. He was sure it was ten to twenty years. He'd be an old man by then and a stranger to his kids.

"WHAT TIME IS your meeting with Tower?"

"Two. I screwed up the times. I have a session at Silvertone Studios. The downbeat is three, and it's all the way downtown."

"What are you going to do?"

"We need the money, so, I can't be late. Especially since Red's producing, and he's not my biggest fan."

"But you've worked with him on a bunch of projects."

"Yeah, but he was close with Stein."

"See, it's not your playing. You're just worried what he might think about the case."

"I guess."

"Can't you get in to see Tower earlier?"

"I tried moving it, but they said he's preparing for some deposition and that was the only slot he had."

"Go earlier anyway."

"That's what I was going to do. I'll tell them some BS that I got to take Tommy to the doctor or something."

"Don't get used to lying."

"What am I supposed to do?"

"Just be careful."

"I will. I'm going to get going. The session will be a couple of hours, so don't wait on dinner for me."

Pulling on his wool cap, Cory tried to figure out why Linda was upset at the lie he was going to tell Tower. It's just a little fib, especially compared to the stuff Tower is going to have me say on the stand.

The rocking of the subway car made Cory sleepy. He closed his eyes and nodded out. He bolted upright. Cory erased the vision of Tower's hand smacking him down and stood the rest of the way.

Cory emerged from the subway station. He adjusted his scarf, wondering how it could be below twenty if the planet was warming. He checked the time. It was a quarter to one. Nice and early.

The elevator dinged, and Cory stepped into Tower's office. Out of the corner of his eye, he saw a familiar face get on the next elevator. He did a double take but couldn't place the face as the doors closed.

The receptionist was frosty, and Cory took a seat. It was one o'clock. Cory picked up *National Geographic* magazine thinking Tommy would love the penguins on the cover. He found the article on Antarctica, but before he read a word it hit him.

He sat back. Could it be? His heart raced. Cory put the magazine down. He stood up. "Hey, I'm sorry. tell Mr. Tower I had to go."

Pushing the elevator button, the receptionist said, "His secretary said he could see you now."

"No, I'm sorry, family emergency."

Blood pounding in his ears, Cory stepped into the elevator and jabbed the lobby button. Cory pushed through the doors and stepped onto the sidewalk.

He looked around and pulled his phone out. He called Mr. Black. It went to voice mail. "Call me. It's super important. Please hurry."

39

Cory took the steps two at a time. He burst into his apartment and went straight to his study.

"Cory? Is that you?"

Cory pulled the envelope Mr. Black had given him out of a drawer. "Yeah."

"What are you doing here?"

Cory stared at a photo.

"Cory! What's going on?"

"This guy was just at Tower's office."

"What guy?"

He stabbed the picture. "Him. One of the witnesses putting me at the scene."

Linda grabbed the picture. "Oh my God. What was he doing at your lawyer's office?"

"Tower is the one framing me."

"Are you sure? The guy could have been up there for a reason. Maybe a deposition or something."

Cory jumped out of his seat. "Bullshit! It's him. He's getting revenge on me."

"Take it easy, Cory. You can't say something like that

without proof."

"Oh, I got more than I need."

"You have nothing. All you did is maybe see one of the witnesses at Tower's office. You don't even know if it was him for sure, and if it was, he could have a valid reason for being there. It could be Tower who asked him to come up."

"Yeah, he probably did, to pay him."

"Why don't you just ask Mr. Tower why he was there?"

"He'll give me some bullshit answer."

"I know Tower is not your ordinary lawyer, but we got to be sure. You can't be making accusations until you're certain. If it turns out to be nothing, he'll get mad, and it might affect your case."

"You don't know him."

"And you don't know how attorneys and the law work. It could just be a normal thing."

"I don't know . . ."

"Why don't you just ask Tower what he was doing there?"

"No way. He'd know I was onto him."

"What are you going to do?"

"First off, I'm calling Mr. Black, and I'm thinking maybe I can ask my old lawyer Worth why this guy would go see Tower."

Cory left a message for Mr. Black and punched in his ex-lawyer. It was the second time he'd had to call him, but Cory didn't care what anyone thought anymore. His life was on the line.

He stared at the image of Tom Rizer as he waited for Worth to get on the line. Cory typed the witness's name in the search bar. The ten results on the first page were all social media accounts. From Facebook to Pinterest, there were several links.

Cory exhaled. The name was a common one. He clicked the first Facebook link and a guy in a tuxedo kissing his bride came up. This Tom Rizer lived in Connecticut.

"Hello, Mr. Lupinski."

"Hi, Mr. Worth."

"What can I do for you, sir?"

"I know we're not working together anymore, but I need to know something, and you can send me a bill, it's okay."

"I'll do my best to answer your questions."

"And anything I tell you, it's protected by the attorney-client thing, right?"

"If this concerns the case we were engaged on, you have nothing to be concerned about."

"You remember the police said they had two witnesses who said they saw me by Stein's house?"

"Yes."

"Well, one of them, Tom Rizer, I saw him at my new lawyer's office today."

"Are you certain it was him?"

"Yeah, it definitely was him."

"That is unusual."

"My wife said he could have been there giving a deposition or something."

"That's highly unlikely."

"Are you sure?"

"Depositions are rare in criminal cases, Mr. Lupinski. They are used only if the witness is out of state for a prolonged period or is incapacitated."

"Why would he be there?"

"It's impossible for me to speculate."

"I think Tower is the one framing me."

"That's a serious charge, Mr. Lupinski."

"You're not kidding. Thanks, I really appreciate your help.

Linda!"

His wife ran in. "What's going on?"

"Worth said it would be super unusual to do a deposition on a witness."

"Could there be another reason?"

"I asked, and Worth said he had no idea."

"Oh my God. I can't believe Tower is behind this."

"There's just no other answer."

"What are you going to do?"

"I don't know, my head's spinning. I want to go to this bastard's house and ask him why he's trying to ruin my life."

"Don't you dare, Cory. Maybe we should rehire Mr. Worth. He might have a way to deal with all this."

"I don't know. He's a good guy, maybe too good to go up against Tower. I want to see what Black has to say."

"You got to talk to Tower. This could be one big mistake."

"I don't think it is. Confronting Tower could be a huge mistake. He'd know we were onto him. I don't know how he'd react, but it won't be good."

"Promise me you won't do something stupid, Cory."

"What do you think I'm going to do, huh? I couldn't kill that bastard Tower if I wanted to; it wouldn't change a damn thing."

"I know, just stay away from him and the witnesses."

"That means the other guy is lying too." Cory reached for the pictures Mr. Black gave him.

"How can these people live with themselves? And what would make them do something like this?"

"Money, or Tower has something on them."

Cory's phone pinged. It was a text from Mr. Black. He told Cory to meet him in Washington Square Park at 6 p.m.

40

THE PARK WAS SHROUDED IN DARKNESS. CORY CROSSED Waverly Place and looked around before entering. He was glad Black set the meeting spot at the Washington Square Arch. The marble structure was bathed in white light.

Just off to the left, standing next to a leafless tree, was Mr. Black. He caught Cory's eye and pointed with a finger. Black took a step into the park. Cory hustled over. Cory's eyes adjusted to the dark.

"Thanks, man."

"What's going on?"

"You're not going to believe it, but Tower is the one framing me."

"What told you that?"

"I saw a witness, Tom Rizer, leaving Tower's office. There's no reason for him to be there."

"Interesting, if true."

"It is. I checked the photos you gave me. It's him."

"How did I miss that connection?"

"That's okay, man. Forget it. I want to know what to do."

Black shifted his weight. "I still have more checking, but I found out Tower represented Billy O'Rourke on an assault and weapons charge about two years ago."

"You think O'Rourke killed Stein?"

"It's early, but he could have or maybe one of his goons. Then he goes to Tower for help, and Tower decides to pin it on you."

"I still can't believe it."

"It's a clever ploy and vintage Tower."

"What do you think we should do?"

"We? Going up against Tower is something I don't do."

"Aw, come on, man. The guy is screwing me. I got kids, a wife—"

"It's bad for business."

"Nobody would know. Besides, somebody has to hold Tower accountable, otherwise he'll keep doing shit like this. He'll come after you one day."

"I don't like it. Tower finds out before we out him, and we're done."

"Oh, please, man. I got no one to go to. Can't you help me?"

"This is extremely delicate. You'd have to keep your mouth shut and do everything I say."

"No problem. Whatever you say, man."

"And I mean everything. There's not much time. Your trial is around the corner."

"Tower's trying to trap me with the self-defense plea. He knows it's not going to work, and I'll go to jail."

"I'm not a lawyer, but overturning a conviction, even with solid proof, would take years."

"I can't do that kind of time behind bars. I'll go on the run."

"I told you, running isn't easy."

"What choice do I have?"

Black pursed his lips. "I need to think this through."

"But you're going to help me, right?"

Black smiled. "Yeah, I'm in. Taking down Tower is dangerous, but it's got to be done."

"Thanks, man."

"Meet me by the Lightship Ambrose on Pier Sixteen. Tomorrow, two p.m."

CORY KEPT his coat on as he headed into the kitchen. "Man, it's freezing out there."

Mug of coffee in hand, Linda was sitting at the table. She put her iPad down. "What did Mr. Black say?"

"He didn't want to get involved. But I convinced him."

"Why wouldn't he help?"

"Because it's Tower. He knows how dangerous he is."

"What's he's going to do?"

"He already discovered that Tower represented O'Rourke in the past on a weapons and assault charge. He's going to look deeper into that connection for sure."

"Makes sense. Anything else?"

"He wants to meet tomorrow."

"How long will it take him to unwrap all this?"

"Who knows? But Black is worried we're not going to have enough time before the trial date."

"What can we do?"

"I'm going to ask Tower to try for a postponement again."

"He's not going to do that."

"I know."

"Then what?"

"Let me talk it over with Black. He's got a couple of ideas he wants to think over."

"I can't take the pressure anymore."

Cory hugged his wife. "I'm sorry, but it'll be over soon."

"It doesn't sound like it will be."

"Maybe, maybe not, but we got something to work with now."

"I hope it works."

"It will."

Linda broke out of his arms. "I have to run to pick up Tommy, he's at Marissa's."

"No, I'll get him."

"Are you sure? Don't you have to work on the music for that commercial?"

"It can wait. I want to see Tommy."

"Where's Mommy?"

"Home. I figured it would be fun to surprise you."

"Okay."

"Hey, who wants to go to Toy Space?"

"Me! Me! Me!"

"All right, let's get going."

"Can we get a video game?"

"We'll see. Let's look at something we can do together. Maybe there's a cool-looking model we can build. Or an erector set."

"What's that?"

"I used to have one when I was your age. It's a bunch of metal pieces that you put together and you can make a building or a bridge."

"A bridge? That's cool."

"Yeah, and we can put it in your room forever. Maybe we can get a model car. They may have a Tesla one like we used to have."

"We had a Tesla?"

"Yeah, when you were little. If they have one, we'll get it and build it. I wish I had kept some of the things I made with my father. It'd be super to see them now."

"DADDY, hurry up, so we can make the car."

"I am. Finish your vegetables."

"Do I have to? I don't like broccoli."

"Me too, but I eat it because it keeps me healthy."

"You know, Tommy, when I met Daddy, he never ate vegetables. He used to live on pizza and junk food."

"I wasn't that bad."

"I like pizza. Can we have it tomorrow?"

"No. We had it last week."

"How about we make a deal, tiger? You eat all your veggies, and we'll get some pizza tomorrow?"

"Okay. Then can we make the car?"

"Absolutely."

Tommy gobbled his broccoli, and Cory told him he had to wash his hands before they built the model. As his son headed to the bathroom, Cory said, "What time does Ava need to be picked up?"

"Eight fifteen."

"I'll get her."

"You looking to earn a father of the year award?"

"No. Just feel like doing it."

"What's going on, Cory?"

"Nothing, it's just that because of me, the kids have been through a lot."

"We'll get through this as a family."

Cory exhaled "I hope so."

41

Though the wind was whipping off the East River, crowds of tourists, half of them snapping selfies, flooded the Seaport District. Cory flipped up his collar and headed for the lightship.

He eyed the restored vessel that used to leave the harbor to act as a lighthouse for the shipping channel into New York. He thought about how technology had changed things. Today, you could pinpoint a location within a couple of feet.

Cory wondered whether there was a technological answer to the jam Tower had put him in. He spied Black. He was leaning on the railing with his face to the wind.

As Cory approached, Black turned around. Cory said, "Don't you get cold?"

"You've got to train yourself."

"I don't know. My blood's too thin."

"The bottom line is you have to ignore it. Focus your mind on something else."

"Maybe I'll give it a try sometime."

"It takes discipline."

Cory searched for a response, but Black said, "The key to

getting Tower is figuring out what makes him tick. Is it money? Power? Or something else? Everybody has a secret. What's Tower's, and is it big enough to bring him down?"

"Maybe we can uncover a case he fixed and use it against him."

"Don't you go poking around. You'll tip Tower off."

"What'll we do if he finds out?"

"We'll deal with it, if and when that happens."

"But—"

"I don't waste time on hypotheticals. I deal in reality. Now, you're going to have to play along with Tower, make it look like you're going with the self-defense plea. He never lets his guard down, but I want him as relaxed as possible."

"He knows I want a postponement."

"That's good. Tell him it's family stuff, you have kids; he'll buy it."

"What else do you want me to do?"

"If I need something, you'll know about it. Otherwise, stay out of the way."

"What about getting ready to run? Maybe to Mexico or—"

"As far as disappearing goes, I got an idea. It's outside the box, but I've used it before."

"Whatever you say."

Mr. Black explained his plan.

"I like it."

"If you're going to do this, you can't tell anyone."

"I know. Don't worry."

"Not a soul, not your wife, mother, kids, nobody."

"I got to say something to Linda."

"Not if you want this to work."

"But—"

"No buts. The only way you can keep a secret between two people is when one of them is dead."

Cory knew Mr. Black was right. How many times had someone confided in him, saying not to tell anyone? Not only had Cory broken the vow, but he'd learned others knew the secret before he did.

"Okay, okay. I get it."

"You leave the slightest trail, they'll track you down in a month."

"I'll keep it between us."

"There's no second chances with this. You do it, there's no turning back."

"I got to do it. There's no other way."

"I'll set it up."

"How will I know?"

"You'll hear from me, and when you do, be prepared to go immediately. No excuses, no delays."

Mr. Black's warning not to tell anyone, even his wife, ricocheted in his head. He trusted Linda implicitly. She was his soul mate and partner. They'd ridden the roller coaster of life together, and though he'd screwed up, she'd stuck by him.

But this was different. She'd be under enormous pressure from the authorities, Tower, and who knew who else. Was Black right? Cory forced his mind off his wife. The visualization of her pain when she would learn he had gone was too difficult to bear.

The faces of his kids swam through his head. How would they react when they learned Daddy wasn't coming home? They'd wonder how he could leave without saying goodbye.

Linda might be able to explain it to Tommy, but Ava would use the disappointment to cement her antagonism toward him.

It was a no-win position to be in. Cory had to do it, but doing so would crush those he loved. If it turned out that proving Tower had framed him was impossible, he'd never be able to return. He would disappear, without explanation.

He had to use whatever time remained to shower his family with love. But it would only go so far; Tommy was too young to have lasting memories, and Ava would be angry.

He'd have to write something they could look at a year or five from now. Something to assure them he loved them and had no other choice. He wouldn't be able to mail it, unless he did it on the way out the door. Would it be enough, or would Ava rip it to shreds?

He fished out a notepad and sat at his workstation. Cory wrote several opening sentences, crossing out each of them. The right tone was hard to strike. He crumpled the pages and got up.

Cory sat behind his electric piano. He took manuscript paper out. Plugging his headphones into the keyboard, he played with bits of melody. He wasn't used to putting his feelings in a letter. It wasn't much different than writing lyrics, but composing a tune came easier.

He'd need three separate songs. They'd express his love, but each of them would have to be different. Since he'd been writing children's tunes, he started with one for Tommy. Jotting down a couple of guiding words—hopeful, persistence, dreams—

Linda knocked on the door. "I'm going to bed."

"Okay, I'll be in later."

Two hours passed. Cory had finished the one for Tommy, naming it "Chasing Rainbows." He was altering the rhythms in Ava's song when Linda knocked again. "What are you doing? It's two in the morning."

"I'm almost done."

"Finish it tomorrow."

"I can't. I'm going to see Tower, and Donny needs me to cut two tracks with him."

"You're going to burn yourself out."

"I'm okay. I'm feeling creative."

Linda exhaled, "All right, but you need your rest."

"Go to bed, I'll see you later."

He finished the first draft of all three tunes. They needed tweaking, but Cory had something. He read the lyrics to each one last time. It was five fifteen. He tiptoed out of the studio and opened the door to Tommy's room.

Cory pulled the covers over Tommy and slipped in beside his son.

42

––––––––––––

Cory kept telling himself to relax. It was important Tower be convinced he was moving ahead with the self-defense plea. As the elevator doors opened, he assured himself it was natural to be nervous, his lawyer would expect him to be.

Announcing himself, he saw Tower heading toward reception and did a double take. The lawyer was smiling as he pushed a woman in a wheelchair. As they neared, he heard the lady say, "But I can't afford to pay your fees, I'm on Social Security."

Tower replied, "Don't worry, Mrs. Parma. I'd be more than happy to provide our services on a pro bono basis."

"What is that?"

"Free. It will cost you nothing."

"Oh my, Mr. Tower, you're a good man."

He rolled her to the elevators, saying, "We do our part."

"Thank you."

He pressed the elevator button and said to the reception-ist, "I'll be back in a minute. I just want to make sure Mrs. Parma gets off okay."

Tower and the lady got on the elevator, and Cory said, "Who's that? A relative?"

"No. Just someone who needs a lawyer."

"Boy, I'd like to get represented for free."

The receptionist smiled but said nothing. Cory took a seat wondering if there was another side to his lawyer.

Tower bounded out of the elevator, and Cory followed him to his office. The attorney slid behind his desk.

"You ready to finalize the plea?"

"Did you speak to the DA to drop the charges?"

Tower sat back in his chair. "Yes. I've had several conversations. Unfortunately, they're unwilling to go that far."

"I'd much rather avoid trial."

"I would as well. But you're credible, and the jury will believe your version of events."

"Are you sure?"

"As sure as I can be."

"I'd really like to spend as much time with my family as possible. Isn't there a way to postpone the trail?"

"I'm afraid not."

"Not even a couple of weeks? If this doesn't work out, I'd like to have had enough time with my children. My youngest is only six. Doesn't the court care about that?"

"Family situations are rarely considered by the court, especially in criminal court and when there's another parent to care for the children."

"That's unfair."

"The system does a poor job in dealing with children. Both as victims of a crime or as family members of a perpetrator or victim."

"That's a shame."

"It is. Lasting damage is inflicted on many defenseless

children. So, are we ready to proceed with the affirmative defense?"

"Yes, but I want to hold off as long as possible. The press will start up as soon as it gets out. Last thing I need is them hounding me and my family."

"I understand. The DA will not look kindly on a last-minute change, and we don't want to antagonize them. Let's settle on two weeks before the trial date."

"If we have to, all right."

"I'd like you to give a sworn statement as to what happened with Mr. Stein. I'd like to schedule that for tomorrow."

"Uh, tomorrow doesn't work. I have a studio session that's going to last a couple of days. Let me see how it goes the first two days, and I'll let you know when I can break free."

CORY HEARD the sound of a bass playing on top of a drum machine before he reached the stairs to Donny's house. When the bass stopped playing, Cory rang the bell several times.

The door creaked open. Donny smiled. "Hey, man." He looked at the guitar Cory was holding. "You came to do a little jamming, like the old days?"

"Figured I'd pop over and see how my man was doing."

"Come on down."

Cory followed his friend down a flight of stairs. The room in the basement served as the bass player's makeshift studio.

"I liked that line you were playing."

"Which one?"

"Doom, da-da, doom, uh, dat doom, uh, dit doom."

"I was hearing something from Bobby Dee's session."

"When was that?"

"Yesterday. I don't know why he didn't have you on it. I don't like Chris's playing."

"Since they charged me, I'm getting shut out."

"That's bullshit."

"Tell me about it. Whatever happened to the innocent until proven guilty stuff?"

Donny shook his head. "Sorry, man. What's going on with the case? Last time, you said you were going to do the self-defense thing, even though you didn't do it."

"You got to keep that between us, Donny. If it gets out that I'm saying I did it, it'll work against me."

"I didn't say anything. You still going with it?"

"Uh, maybe. I'm not sure. You know what Ava said to me? She said if I said I did it, I couldn't take it back."

"She's a smart kid. But you got to do what ends this madness."

"It's not going to be over for a while."

"What do you mean?"

"I can't say, man. Just call it a feeling."

"What's going on, man?"

"Do me favor, will you?"

"Sure, man, anything."

"Whatever happens to me, I need you to promise me you'll look out for my family. Okay?"

"Sure, man, but I thought things were going to work out."

"I think they're going to, it's just not gonna be a straight line."

"I don't get it."

"Donny, we know each other since we're five, you gotta trust me on this. Can you?"

"Of course. Whatever you need, brother."

"They should have enough money, but if they need something, you know I'm good for it."

"Stop with that. I got your back, man."

Cory hugged his friend. "Thanks. It takes a load off my mind knowing you'll be there for them."

"No problem."

Cory pulled away from his friend and pointed to his guitar case. "Do me favor and hold onto my Gibby for me. Something happens to me, I want you to give it to Tommy when he turns sixteen."

43

A week later, Cory was walking along the High Line to a meeting place picked by Mr. Black. Though it was dark, the elevated park was full of people who didn't care what time it was: teenagers and tourists.

As he passed the Twenty-Eighth Street entrance, he saw Black sitting on a park bench. Black rose. "Let's walk."

"Haven't been up here in a long while."

"And you won't be for a while."

Cory stopped walking. "Is it time to go?"

"Yes. Everything is set. You leave in the morning, after rush hour, say ten o'clock. Okay?"

Cory nodded.

"You sure you're ready?"

"Yeah, it just feels surreal."

"Focus. You get sloppy or sentimental, it's over. You understand?"

"I get it."

"Act normally around your family. I don't want you tipping off anybody."

"No problem. I'm ready."

"This could be going on a lot longer than you think."

"I'm hoping sooner than later."

"All right, you need to memorize what I'm going to tell you. If you need to, write it on your body, somewhere nobody can see."

Black gave Cory details of his plan. He handed him an envelope and disappeared down the Thirtieth Street stairs. Cory looked at the black sky. He stared at the sliver of the moon, silently repeating what Black said.

Satisfied he'd remember what was necessary, he took a deep breath and started for home. It was seven fifteen. It would take him forty-five minutes to get home. He called Linda.

After telling her that the visit with Mr. Black was nothing more than a touch base, Cory asked her to let Tommy stay up late tonight. He said he wanted to read a book to him.

He expected Linda to give him a hard time, as she believed kids needed a regular schedule. But she didn't. She understood his need to connect. Cory knew his wife was one of a kind.

He understood what Mr. Black said about telling anyone, but Linda was different. He searched his mind for a time when she'd broken a vow and couldn't come up with any. Besides, Linda rarely, if ever, gossiped.

The subway jostled him, and Cory reached for a bar. He steadied himself and realized Linda had been the stabilizing force for him and the children. She deserved to be told. It wasn't right if he left without telling her.

Cory ran it through his head again, deciding to tell her. He considered saying something when he got home, but the kids might pick up on it, and it would leave too much time for

Linda's emotion to spring a leak in the secretive plan. He'd tell her in the morning, right before leaving.

Cory read the last page to Tommy. "You see, if you keep at something, you make progress."

"I know, Daddy."

"Don't ever forget to give it your best, okay?"

"Uh-huh."

"You want me to read another story to you?"

"You can?"

"Sure. How about *Harold and the Purple Crayon*?"

"I like that one."

Cory opened the book, and before he finished the first page, Tommy fell asleep. Cory woke him up. "Good night, son."

"'Night, Dad."

"Always remember, Daddy loves you. Okay?"

Tommy nodded and closed his eyes. Cory shut the lamp and watched his son for a minute. He slipped out of the room and knocked on Ava's door. She was sprawled on a bed covered in papers.

"Still studying?"

"Yeah, reviewing old tests."

"Can I help you with anything?"

"It's algebra, Dad. You hate math."

"Just because I don't like something doesn't mean I didn't work hard at it."

"Whatever."

"No. It's not whatever. I want you to know in life, a lot of times, you can't pick and choose what you want to do. Sometimes you have to do things you don't like. At your age, one of those things was math. I didn't like it, but I worked hard and got solid grades."

"I thought you failed out in geometry."

"Uh, yeah. But I worked my tail off and turned things around. What I'm trying to say is, you can do whatever you want to, as long as you commit to it and are willing to work at it."

"I know, Dad."

"Nothing good comes easy. If it did, you wouldn't appreciate it, you know?"

"Okay, Dad. You're preaching a little too much."

"Sorry, just want to make sure you know a little hard work is good for you."

"I got to get back to studying."

"Okay, good luck on the test."

"I think I'm going to do good. We get the results back Thursday."

"Good. Okay, good night, I love you."

He hung in the doorway. Ava raised her head. "Good night, Dad." It pained him that all he got was a good night, but he told himself she was sixteen as he headed to the family room.

Linda was on the couch. "I thought you fell asleep with Tommy."

"I was talking to Ava."

"She's got a big exam tomorrow. How was she?"

"Good, good. I wish I had a closer relationship with her. We used to be so close when she was small."

"It's normal, she's a teenager."

Cory sat next to her. "I feel bad for putting her in the middle of all this. I hope she'll forgive me one day."

Linda took his hand. "She understands more than she lets on. She's just giving you a hard time to protect herself."

"You really think so?"

"No doubt about it. It's normal to take it out on your parents. We're easy targets."

"I hope you're right."

"You're a wonderful father. We'll get over this."

Cory slipped his hand between her thighs. "Why don't we go to bed?"

44

———

Linda stirred. Cory kissed his wife's shoulder. "You sleep okay?"

"Yeah, first time in a week."

"You think it had something to do with my lovemaking skills?"

"Maybe." She pecked his cheek. "I got to get up."

As Linda got out of bed, Cory fished under the pillow, pulling out her negligee. "Here you go."

Cory admired his wife as she slipped the gown over her head. Watching her walk into the bathroom, Cory began thinking about how to tell her he was leaving today.

He'd wait until the kids were out of the house, but figuring out how to start it off was difficult. He had to be sure to stress it was only to buy time to unmask the plot against him.

Linda would want a fixed time line. It didn't exist, and though Cory knew it wasn't true, he was going to tell her three months.

What was harder was knowing the kids would ask questions. He was sure Ava would be angry and Tommy confused.

He felt bad Linda would have to deal with them but relieved he wouldn't have to explain it to them.

He'd ask Linda to say he didn't want to plead self-defense because it would require him to say he did it. He hoped that that would console Ava and would prove his innocence.

He began a mental checklist. He wasn't taking much, but every item was essential.

Cory heard Tommy talking to Ava as Linda headed to the kitchen. Cory dressed quickly and followed her. "Hey, who wants pancakes?"

"Me, Daddy, me."

"Chocolate chip or blueberry?"

Tommy looked at his mother, who said, "Whatever you want, today only."

"Chocolate chip!"

"You got it, tiger. How about you, Ava?"

"No, thanks."

"You sure?"

"I said no."

"Okay, no problem."

He pulled a pan out of a cabinet. "Tommy, get the milk."

Cory took his time walking back home after dropping off Tommy at school. As he walked up the stairs to their apartment, he decided he was going to march straight in and spill his guts.

He pushed open the door. Linda was on the phone and shook her head at him. Hanging up his jacket, he heard Linda say, "Okay, Donny, take care."

"Who was that?"

"Donny. He said you went there yesterday."

"Yeah, so?"

"He said you were acting strange and that you left your

guitar there, telling him to give it to Tommy when he was sixteen. What's going on?"

Cory knew Mr. Black was right; you couldn't trust anyone. He couldn't tell Linda; she'd tell Donny, and then the news would spread. "Nothing."

"You gave him your favorite guitar and it's nothing?"

"I just want to be sure that if we get sued in civil court, that I won't lose her. I want Tommy to have it at some point."

"You sure?"

"Yeah, that's why we set up the lockbox."

"If there's something I should know, you better tell me."

"I'm just doing everything I can, you know, to prepare and protect the family, that's all."

"Okay. I got to run. I have a yoga class."

"Have fun."

Cory wanted to kiss her, but she grabbed her mat and coat and said, "See you later."

The door closed behind her. Cory walked around the apartment surveying each room. Sadness washed over him. He sat on Tommy's bed and stared at the Tesla model they'd made together. He was going to miss him.

His phone rang. Cory jumped to his feet. He hoped it was Black calling it off. It was spam. Damn. Doubt crept into his head. He couldn't leave his family.

He thought of Mr. Black and what he said: "You got to focus." Cory nodded to himself and sprang into action.

45

GLAD IT WAS COLD ENOUGH TO JUSTIFY WEARING GLOVES, Cory put sunglasses on and stepped into the sunshine. He patted the false stomach he had on. It looked like he had a beer belly.

Cory made a beeline for the subway station and used his wife's Metro Card to take the train to Lower Manhattan. He wasn't taking chances there was some way they could track him using his card.

When the train pulled into his stop, he exited and sat on a bench, feigning to tie a shoelace. He slipped a smooth pebble into his shoe and got up. Limping as he made his way underground, Cory took the Path Train into Newark, New Jersey. He looked around before heading to the Amtrak platform—nothing but commuters hurrying to the office.

Cory instinctively reached for his phone. The panic he felt when he couldn't find it retreated when he realized he'd left it home. He pawed the ticket to Boston Mr. Black had given him last night.

Back against a stanchion, Cory tugged his baseball cap lower and ran his tongue over the false teeth he wore.

Cory felt the vibration running through the platform. The rumbling increased as the local train rolled in. The express was hours faster, but with fewer stops, easier to trace. The doors slid open and he waited, watching people pile on. The conductor signaled the operator, and Cory stepped on as the doors closed.

He slid into a row of seats. The woman by the window was watching her tablet and didn't look up. Cory took a paperback out. He opened it, turning a couple of pages before laying the Spanish novel, cover up, in his lap.

The five-hour-plus ride dragged, but Cory was relieved it was uneventful. Tucking his chin in his coat, Cory hailed a taxi. He paid for the short ride in cash and walked three blocks to his destination.

Cory raised his head, surveying the tall building he'd call home for who knew how long. Built over Boston's North Station, streams of people were walking in every direction. It was a newer building featuring a touchless entry, but new meant surveillance cameras. He curled his arm up, placing the back of his hand under his armpit.

Added to his altered gait, it'd be assumed he had suffered a stroke or had a muscular affliction. Cory ambled slowly to the entrance. He dug out the key card and waved it over a pad. The glass doors slid open and he entered. None of the front desk personnel lifted their heads and Cory headed to a bank of elevators.

His key card automatically programmed the elevator to the fifteenth floor. No one got on with him, but there was a camera hanging in the corner. He kept his face near the control panel, his spirits rising with the elevator.

Cory's heart raced as he approached his temporary home. The door clicked open. He closed it behind him and leaned against it. He had made it.

He looked around—a studio with a sleeping alcove. He pulled open the fridge. It was stocked. The cabinets were filled with canned goods. He clicked the remote, and the TV came to life. Stripping off the pregnancy belly and teeth, he went to the galley kitchen.

Cory opened a can of tuna and watched the evening news. It was too early for trouble, but the reassurance felt good. He picked up the tablet Black had arranged. A note with *private browser* written on it was taped to the border. As a test, Cory jumped on the internet.

He started typing his name into the search bar before realizing he should be using a private browser. Cory told himself to slow down. If there was one thing he had while on the run, it was time. Using the safer way to search, there was no current news on him.

Cory found what he was looking for in a box under the sink. He cut the tape and opened the carton. Inside were seven phones, each marked with a day of the week and chargers. Black had said to only call in an emergency and that he'd reach out when he had something to report.

Black wanted him to use the burner phone infrequently and never the same one within the same week. He cautioned Cory on using it to call anyone else but him. Cory picked up a phone, wondering, if they were untraceable, then why couldn't he use one?

If he did, who would know? Did Black have some way of knowing? He decided Black probably could track it and put the phone back. As he stuffed it under the sink, he saw something under the bed.

Cory got on his knees and smiled. It was a guitar case. He opened it. It was a blond, low-end Fender, but it felt like Christmas to Cory.

Picking it up, he strummed. Cory tuned the acoustic

instrument and quietly played "Tablet Blues." It felt good to softly sing the tune he'd ridden to the top of the charts years ago.

He laid the guitar on the bed. Black had known without asking that it would occupy Cory for hours a day, lessening the chance he'd do something stupid out of boredom.

Black had thought of everything, not only renting the apartment online from a corporate landlord, but stocking it as if an apocalyptic event was about to occur. His suggestion of essentially hiding in plain sight was miles better than melding into the dusty Mexican countryside.

It was up to Cory not to screw it up by getting sloppy.

46

THE COLD WOKE CORY UP. HE WAS ON THE COUCH, AND HIS shoulder was killing him. He got up and shut off the TV. Rubbing his collarbone, Cory went to the bathroom in the dark. The apartment was nice, but the sofa was no better than a table.

He looked out the window, and the wind was blowing snow horizontally. There were scores of buildings in his view. They housed thousands of people, but Cory didn't know a soul. He pictured his wife lying awake in bed wondering where he was.

Cory had to get a message to Linda. She deserved to know if he was alive or hurt. He'd ask Mr. Black to let her know. He propped himself up on the bed and stared into the darkness. The reality of his isolation sank in.

He reached for the remote and put the TV on. It was night number one, and he had to develop a routine. As *The Usual Suspects* played, he tried to come up with a plan to while away the days. He'd get up, have coffee and exercise. Some push-ups and sit-ups, maybe look on the web for things to do without weights.

He didn't have manuscript paper to compose music on. He figured he could plug chords into his phone. But then he remembered he didn't have a phone. There had to be a program, maybe Google Docs, that he could use to notate. Either way, he'd have to bury himself in writing new tunes. He always lost track of time when he wrote or played.

It would soak up time and he hoped to have a small library of songs he could sell. The one thing he'd miss would be playing with other musicians. The interplay and creativity that went on was a place he was used to getting lost in for hours.

Cory tucked the blanket under his chin. Though it was freezing out, he'd miss being outside. It spurred his imagination. He cycled through the channels, hoping he'd get *National Geographic*. Maybe he could get a dose of nature from the boob tube.

LINDA WAS POURING milk into her coffee and Tommy said, "Mommy, where's Daddy? Isn't he taking me to school?"

"I'll take you. He had to go to work early."

Ava said, "No, he didn't."

"He did, Ava."

"What musician works at seven in the morning?"

"I think they're shooting a music video."

"That early in the morning?"

"The streets are empty. It makes it easier."

"That's cool. He didn't say anything."

"You know your father; he doesn't make a big deal about things."

"I wish he'd go back to making pop music, instead of that kids' stuff."

"Maybe he will, but right now he's able to be around while you're still . . . uh, in the house."

Linda dropped Tommy off at school and made a call. "Donny? It's Linda."

"Hey, what's going on?"

"Cory never came home yesterday."

"What?"

"I left for yoga yesterday morning, and when I got back, he was gone. I didn't get worried until dinner. I tried calling him, but he left his phone home."

"He forgot his phone?"

"Yeah. Do you know where he is?"

"I wish I did."

"Are you sure you don't?"

"I swear, I have no idea."

"I don't know what to do. He could be hurt or—"

"Did he say he was going somewhere?"

"No. He was home and gone when I got back."

"If he left without his phone, maybe he was rushing—"

"For what? If it was some kind of emergency, I'd know about it."

"Let me make some calls. Maybe he was playing somewhere and just crashed."

"Something is wrong. I know it. He had an appointment tomorrow with his lawyer."

"Don't panic. Maybe you should call the police."

"I was thinking of that, but . . . I got to tell you something, but you can't repeat it, okay?"

"Sure, what?"

"Did he ever say anything about going on the run?"

"You mean, like a fugitive?"

"Yeah."

"No, he never said anything."

"He told me he was thinking about it. He was even playing around with disguises."

"Are you kidding me?"

"Not recently, but when things were looking bad, before he changed lawyers."

"He mentioned something about not being cool with saying he did it. You know, he felt it could work against him."

"What else did he say?"

"Just, you know, if something happened, for me to watch out for you and the kids."

"He took off."

"I didn't take it like that. I thought he meant if he had to go to jail or something."

"No, he's hiding somewhere. I just know it."

"Where would he go?"

"He said somewhere like Mexico."

"Mexico? Unless he flew, he's still in the States somewhere."

"He didn't fly. Cory gave up his passport as a condition of bail."

"I can't see him sneaking over the border."

"It's so dangerous. I'm scared, Donny."

"It doesn't sound good, but maybe there's an explanation. He could come walking through the door any minute."

"I know he's not."

"I'll make some calls, see if anybody knows anything. Why don't you call the police?"

"No, if Cory is on the run, he wouldn't have gotten far yet."

"Hmm. Why don't you call the hospitals in the area? I know it's a long shot, but he could've had a heart attack or something and . . . hold on, did he take his wallet with him?"

"I don't know. Hang on, let me check." Linda ran into the bedroom. She opened the drawer of Cory's nightstand. His wallet was sitting in it.

"It's here! He's on the run."

"Maybe not. He could have gotten some kind of an urgent call and just—"

"Stop it, Donny. Cory's hiding out somewhere."

After hanging up, Donny replayed what Linda said about Cory being on the run. When he recalled what she said about him trying on disguises, he remembered Cory asking him to buy stuff from Amazon.

Cory had said it was for Halloween, but he now knew that he'd played a role in his buddy's disappearance. Would he have done it if he knew?

47

Linda looked through Cory's phone. There were no obvious clues as far as she could see. Linda wondered why he'd left the phone behind. Why not toss it in the river if he didn't want to be traced?

She wondered if there was information he wanted the authorities to find, and went into his studio. Sitting on his workstation was his MacBook. She'd seen enough cop shows to know they could find out what sites Cory visited.

Linda wasn't sure what to do. Should she hide them? If she knew the police could get information off the devices, she was sure Cory knew. The question was whether he had forgotten to ditch them or had left them behind on purpose.

Questions flooded her head: Where had her husband gone? Why hadn't Cory let her know he was leaving? Was Mr. Black helping him?

She scrolled through the contacts on Cory's phone. There was no entry for Mr. Black. Had Cory used a code for him, or did he delete the information? She went through the list again. She found one for Tower but not Mr. Black.

Cory had a meeting scheduled with the lawyer today.

She debated whether to call him and give him an excuse or wait to see what happened. Or had Cory canceled it himself?

Linda flopped onto the couch. She couldn't figure out what to do, and she had to guess what Cory had done as well. She looked at the red fire truck sitting on the coffee table. What would she tell the kids?

She cursed her husband. At the least, he could have left a letter. The thought made her jump up. Linda had seen an envelope tucked under his MacBook. Maybe a message was in it.

She moved the laptop. The envelope was unsealed. She pulled out three sheets of manuscript paper. A blue Post-it was stuck on the top sheet. The note was in Cory's handwriting: *Sorry, I couldn't say anything. I have to clear my name. I love all of you and wrote these songs for you. Recordings are in the Family Music Folder.*

Linda navigated to the song he wrote for her. Eight bars into the song, she broke down crying. She composed herself and ran her hand over the manuscript paper he wrote on. It was the most beautiful song he'd ever written.

She played the song twice more before listening to the ones he composed for Ava and Tommy. They were perfect. Cory's love for his kids was apparent, and the lyrics were clear. She hoped it would help soften the reality when they learned what the situation was.

THREE HOURS LATER, Cory's phone rang. It was Tower's office. Hustling into the studio, Linda answered, "Hello."

"Is Mr. Lupinski available?"

"This is his wife, Linda. What can I do for you?"

"Mr. Lupinski had a meeting scheduled with Mr. Tower, but he never showed up."

"I'm so sorry. I forgot to call you. He isn't feeling well. I'm sorry."

"That's okay. Tell him we hope he gets better and to call when he's up to it. He needs to reschedule as quickly as possible."

"I'll make sure to call you, maybe tomorrow. Let me see how he feels when he wakes up."

She pocketed his phone. Linda sat next to Tommy, who was watching TV, and waited for Ava to come home.

Ava breezed into the house, peeling off her backpack. Linda said, "How was your day, honey?"

"All right. I'm starving. Is there anything to eat?"

"You didn't have lunch?"

"I wasn't hungry then."

Linda got up. "There's hummus, or I can make tuna fish."

Ava frowned. "That's it? There's never anything to eat in this house."

"If you want something specific, tell me and I'll buy it. How about some eggs?"

"Okay. Soft-boiled. I'm getting changed."

"Tommy, you want anything?"

"Can I have a cookie?"

"Sure, sweetie."

They sat down to eat, and Ava said, "Did he come home yet?"

"Don't call him 'he.' He's your father."

Ava rolled her eyes and broke the egg in half. "So, Dad didn't come home."

"Finish your egg, and I tell you all about it."

Ava set her spoon down. "What's going on?"

"Eat first."

"I don't want to. Tell me."

"Tommy, listen to what I'm going to tell you and Ava. Okay?"

Nibbling a gingersnap, her son nodded. Linda took the envelope Cory had left and took the sheets of paper out. "Your father wrote these songs. One for each of us."

Tommy reached out. "Cool. Lemme see."

Linda handed him a song titled "Chasing Rainbows." "Be careful with it. Ava, this one is for you."

Her daughter took the sheet music named "Be True to You."

"Mommy, what one did Daddy make for you?"

"It's a beautiful song, called 'Us.'"

"'Us'? That's all?"

"Yes. Wait till you hear it. It's the best one Daddy ever wrote."

"It's nice he wrote these for us, but where is he?"

"He's gone away for a while."

"But why did Daddy go?"

"Let me explain, Tommy. We all know that somebody is accusing your father of doing a very bad thing. Daddy said he had nothing to do with it, and I believe him."

"So, why'd he run? Why can't he get justice at a trial?"

"It's complicated, Ava. He said he didn't do it, but there is evidence suggesting that he did. His new lawyer recommended he plead self-defense. Your father didn't want to admit to something he didn't do. It offered a way to end this nightmare, and he was going to take it to make things easier on the family."

"So, why'd he change his mind?"

"One of the things you said to him, about not being able to take back what you said, really got to him. He was concerned that it would look like he did it, and he didn't want to give off that appearance."

"I don't understand. If he runs away, it makes him look guilty."

"That's true, but the trial date is coming up, and there's not enough time to get to the bottom of who is trying to hurt your father. We have a good idea but need more information. Once we have it, Daddy will come home, and it will all get straightened out."

"How long is Daddy going to be gone? We were going to go ice skating Sunday."

"I'm not sure, honey. But I'll take you Sunday. Daddy recorded the songs. Why don't we go listen to them?"

48

LINDA WAS IN THE STUDIO, LISTENING AS CORY SERENADED her. She missed him, but hearing his voice dulled the pain. She wondered how long the effect would last on her and the kids. She got up and ran her fingers over the strings on Cory's Les Paul.

Trying to calculate how long it would be before she would see him again, Cory's phone rang. It was Tower's office. "Hello."

"Mrs. Lupinski?"

"Yes."

"I'm calling for Mr. Tower. Is your husband there?"

"Uh, yeah. He's in the shower."

"He needs to meet with Mr. Tower. How soon can he come in?"

"Maybe next week I think would work."

"I'm sorry, but Mr. Tower must see him no later than tomorrow."

Tomorrow?"

"Yes. I've been advised it's critically important. I believe there are some documents to execute in regard to the change in plea."

"Okay. I'll tell him to be there at, uh, four."

Linda hung up with a bad feeling. She didn't know what to do but had to go food shopping before picking up Tommy.

Wheeling a cart filled with groceries down her block, Linda saw two men in suits near the entrance to her building. As she got closer, she realized they didn't look like businessmen.

"Mrs. Lupinski, we'd like to speak to your husband."

"Who are you?"

"We're from Mr. Tower's office."

"He's not home."

"Where is he?"

"I'm not sure, but he's going to see Mr. Tower tomorrow."

"Are you sure about that?"

"Yes."

"Why are you answering his phone? Who is he hiding from?"

"No one. I swear. Look, I have to get these inside and pick up my son."

"You tell Mr. Lupinski to make sure he makes his appointment. Mr. Tower is extremely busy."

THE MORNING after missing the meeting with Tower, the doorbell rang. Linda answered it.

"Mrs. Lupinski?"

"Yes. What do you want?"

"I'm Detective Lopez. Is your husband home?"

"No."

"Where is he?"

Linda's lip quivered.

"It's okay, ma'am. Tell me the truth, and we'll go from there."

"I don't know where he is. I swear. He never told me, he just disappeared."

"When's the last time you saw him?"

"Uh, couple ofdays ago. I went to my yoga class, and when I came back, he was gone."

"Where do you think he might have gone?"

"I don't know. Honestly, I've been trying to figure it out."

"Have you spoken with him since he left?"

"No."

"Any texts or email?"

"No. He left his phone behind and, uh, his laptop."

"We're going to have to confiscate them and search the apartment for any evidence to where he might be."

"Search? My children are coming home."

"I'm sorry, ma'am. Is there a neighbor they can stay with?"

TOWER WAS ADDRESSING a handful of reporters outside the Center Street Courthouse. "It's unfortunate that my client, Cory Lupinski, didn't possess enough faith in our ability to administer justice and chose to flee rather than face the charges against him.

"We must do more to instill confidence that our legal system works for the average citizen. It's imperative that trust be built between the accused and the system that is supposed to assume their innocence, to protect the powerless.

"This nation's sacred institution of justice is in danger of collapsing when citizens decide a life on the run is more palatable than a jury of their peers.

"Let this be a reminder to the powers that roam the halls of justice that fairness is a critical component of the system itself.

"I have time for a few questions."

"Did you know Cory Loop was going to run?"

"No. However, I knew he was concerned, not only in regard to how the system was going to treat him, but also about the manner in which the press was covering the allegations against him."

"What bothered him about the media coverage?"

"These are his words, not mine, but my client felt the press contributed to the belief he was being railroaded."

"How did he explain the evidence against him?"

"Let's just say that we were prepared to defend the baseless charges against Mr. Lupinski in the strongest of manners."

"How? His blood was found at the scene?"

"You'll just have to wait, but I can tell you, when the time comes, we'll present a vigorous defense."

"How do you respond to the rumors that Mr. Lupinski was going to use self-defense as a way to justify his actions?"

"I'm sorry, but I don't address rumors, it only lends credence to them."

"How is Cory Loop's family reacting to this development?"

"They're doing well, and I'd ask the media to respect their privacy. That's all the time I have today."

SHAKING HIS HEAD, Black shut the TV off. Tower was good, a chameleon without peer. He wasn't sure how to classify Barney Tower. Everyone knew he was a fighter who'd do what he could to win. Rumors had swirled for years concerning his tactics, but that's all they were, rumors.

Were other lawyers frustrated by Tower's legal prowess? Black had obtained a transcript of the lawyer's record while at Fordham Law School. Tower had compiled an impressive 3.9 GPA, graduating at the top of his class.

Tower was arrogant and had outhustled opposing counsel time after time. It made sense that some of the stuff in circulation was born out of jealously. But Black had started digging. It hadn't taken him long to question how Tower had amassed real estate holdings valued at fifty million dollars.

Black looked into Tower's family, wondering if he'd inherited wealth, but came up empty. There wasn't much on Tower before law school, but the fact he'd received a needs-based scholarship cemented Tower's underprivileged background.

He'd have to probe Tower's past, but the first place Black was going to probe was a case that defied logic. He just needed another piece of proof that Tower had gotten his client off through extortion and bribes.

49

CORY WRAPPED THE BLANKET AROUND HIS SHOULDERS AND got out of bed. He popped a pod in the coffee maker and went to the window as the machine heated up. It was another gray day. Cory had been in Boston two weeks, and the sun had come out once.

He hit the brew button and got the powdered milk. As the coffee streamed into a mug, Cory envisioned the chaotic scene at his apartment on weekdays. Linda would be making sure the kids ate something, and Cory would keep Tommy focused on getting ready for school.

It was tough getting the day started that way. Cory preferred to ease into it, having his coffee and reading the news, but he wished he was back in Brooklyn. He sipped his java and put his name in the tablet's search bar.

Three results from yesterday came up. Cory clicked on the *New York Post* article. In the piece there was a quote from the DA stating that they were aggressively pursuing Cory Lupinski. Cory wondered whether aggressive meant anything special or just a way for the prosecutor to sound serious.

The DA also said there was no evidence that Barney

Tower had played a role in his client's disappearance. He qualified the statement with a 'thus far,' but if Cory was apprehended, he'd do his best to drag Tower into his getaway scheme.

Cory moved to a post on the *New York Times* website, "The Chase for Cory Loop." The story was a seesaw for him. It referenced several high-profile fugitives, making clear that eventually the authorities got their man, but quoted a source from New York's Finest that they believed Cory had fled to Mexico.

He was about to click on the third result but decided on a second cup of coffee instead. Cory took a sip, sat down and watched the Tower video again. It was the fifth time he'd seen the person he believed was framing him talk as if he were protecting him like a parent.

Each time he saw Tower conning the media, it made his stomach pitch. He was putting himself up as some kind of guardian, despite the fact he was the one forcing Cory to run. Tower was the reason he was separated from his family, from his children. Cory tossed the tablet aside.

He put his mug in the sink and pulled the box with the cell phones out. He needed to hear Linda's voice. The kids were still home. Maybe he could talk to them.

He paced the small apartment. If Black found out, it wouldn't be good.

But how would Black find out? It was impossible. Cory turned the day's phone on. He watched it power up. Cory took a deep breath and typed in his wife's number. His finger hovered over the green button when the phone vibrated. A call was coming in. Cory deepened his voice.

"Hello?"

"It's me. You carrying the phone around?"

"Didn't want to miss your call."

"You need anything?"

"No, but it's not easy being cooped up in—"

"Don't cry. I told you it was gonna be tough."

"I know. But can you get a message to my wife?"

Black remained silent.

"I just want to let her know I'm okay."

"I'll think about it. I wanted to check in, let you know I'm onto something that might be big."

"What is it?"

"Can't say. Got to go."

"Oh, come on, man, I need something to hold me over."

"It's another crazy case with the same judge."

"What do you mean?"

"Can't say. I'll be in touch."

"Wait—"

Cory looked at the phone. What had Black uncovered? He thought it was a crooked judge. Maybe that was how Tower was able to get people off. Cory wondered if it was the same judge who oversaw his shooting incident.

It could only be one of the underhanded methods Tower used, because everybody would realize a particular judge was involved in too many unexpected verdicts. How Tower turned on him made Cory convinced the lawyer also used extortion to get the results he wanted.

Cory wondered what tactics Tower used. Did the lawyer set up his victims, plying them with drugs or sexual favors? Did he bribe people and use the bribery against them?

Tower's network had to be extensive. Cory knew Tower had legitimate cases that he'd won on merit, but it made him question how many people were cast into similar situations by the crafty lawyer.

Cory acted badly when he'd been unable to handle fame and the pressure of keeping secret that he'd stolen the songs that became hits. But taking drugs and cheating on his wife wasn't close to what Tower did regularly.

How could Tower knowingly ruin someone's life? How could he sleep at night knowing Cory would be behind bars, separated from his family? Cory was convinced Barney Tower was heartless.

Tower was pissed at Cory for outfoxing him and ending the extortion. Trying to get revenge was childish, but as twisted as it was, he saw why Tower wanted to hurt him. But his family? Cory had kids, a six-year-old and a teenage daughter, and a wife. Why make them suffer?

Cory wondered whether Black would get a message to his wife. No one would know about it. Nobody would be able to trace it, would they? Cory believed Black was worried Linda would say something and the police would find out. Or was it the authorities were monitoring Linda's calls?

The hope he felt that his family would find out he was safe evaporated. The DA said they were using every resource possible to track him down. It made complete sense to keep an eye on his wife; she was the most likely to lead them to him.

Cory flopped onto the couch. What a mess, and it was because of Tower. What had hardened the lawyer, making him so unfeeling? How could someone be so evil?

50

BLACK CARRIED A BAG OF LAUNDRY INTO THE LAUNDROMAT. The only person inside was a gray-haired woman reading a book. He went to the rear of the store and put his clothes into a dryer. Black slipped a bill in a coin card machine and started the dryer. He sat on the bench watching the door.

As the clothes began tumbling, a wiry man in a wool cap walked in. He loaded the machine next to Black, and after it began cycling, sat on the bench next to Black. He said, "Man, the hawk is out today."

Black said, "Yeah, the wind is blowing."

He looked around, reaching into his jacket. "Here's the info on the bailiff."

Black nodded. "How do you know this guy?"

"He's from the neighborhood."

"Is he solid?"

"Rock-solid."

"You told him I wanna talk to him?"

"Uh-huh. I told him you'd meet him at O'Brien's on Forty-Sixth Street at three."

Black nodded and got up. A rush of dry heat hit him as he

pulled open the dryer. Pulling out a tee shirt, he said, "Dry as a bone."

He loaded the clothes into his bag and walked out. Black hailed a cab and got out on Thirty-Ninth Street. After walking two blocks, he tossed the laundry into a trash can and headed to his meeting.

Black walked into O'Brien's Irish Bar. Sitting at the bar, two men were hunched over their drinks in the narrow room. Black walked along the brick-faced wall to a handful of high-top tables in the back.

He sat at the last one, next to a wall decorated with shamrocks. The bartender took a couple of steps toward him. "What'll it be?"

Eyes on the door, Black said, "Jack, on the rocks."

As he placed a glass full of amber liquid in front of Black, a beefy man lumbered in. He glanced at the two drunks at the bar and headed to the rear. Dressed in jeans and a bomber jacket, the man nodded at the bartender. "Gimme a Bud and a shot of rye."

Black examined the Hispanic man as he raised himself on the barstool. He was carrying as much extra weight as his age and said, "So, you wanna know about Ledger."

"Mostly what you know about him and Tower."

Black held up a hand as the bartender approached with the beer and shot. He nodded as the server left.

"Like I told Hernandez, I seen Tower handing over a chunk of cash to Judge Ledger."

"When was this?"

"Like a week before the McCarron trial started."

"And you think that's why he excluded the recording from the trial?"

"Yeah, I mean, he's done it before."

"You saw him accept cash before?"

"No, but I know Tower must have paid Ledger off on the Boler case. He wouldn't let the knife into evidence while everybody knew he used it to kill his wife."

"I didn't know that one. How'd he rule it was inadmissible?"

"Some bullshit about the chain of custody. The DA went nuts, and even the *New York Times* said Ledger overstepped."

"Going back to McCarron, now, how sure are you that Tower was paying off the judge?"

"Sure as I'm sitting here. I didn't know he was in his chambers, and Charlene, she's the court clerk, had some papers she needed signed, so I was gonna put them on the judge's desk, and they were right there. Tower had a briefcase with stacks of cash in it. What else was he doing with it?"

"I'm not interested in the judge, it's Tower I'm after."

"That's okay with me. I mean, I don't think the judge is doing right, but I'm just trying to earn a little, you know?"

"You know anything about the Cory Lupinski case?"

"The music guy?"

"Yeah."

"I see it on TV, but that's it. Why?"

"Tower's his attorney."

"Who's the judge?"

"Waterstone."

"He's all right. I only had him a couple of times. He's a quiet guy."

"I'm going to need an affidavit from you—"

"I don't know."

"It won't go anywhere. We're just going to use it to force Tower to back off."

He shook his head.

"The only person that's gonna see it is Tower. I'm going

to tell him if he doesn't stop screwing with my client that I'll go public with it."

"I can't have that getting out. Ledger would come after me. He's nasty."

"Don't worry. It'll never get that far. Tower's going to cave."

"How do you know?"

"It's the last thing he wants out. Plus, I got some other stuff on him."

"Who you working for?"

"That's confidential."

"Confidential? That's bullshit. You want me to put this in writing, and you won't tell me who it's for?"

"I'm sure Hernandez told you we're willing to pay good money for the information."

"How much?"

"Ten grand, cash."

"Make it twenty and we got a deal."

"Done. It's going to have to be notarized."

"No problem. How fast can you get it?"

"Give me two days. Meet you here, same time?"

"Not here. The Playwright Bar on Thirty-Fifth Street."

"Been there. Good place to watch the game. They've got screens all over the place."

"See you then."

Black placed two twenties on the bar and walked out.

He walked a block before putting his jacket on. He needed a clear mind and didn't want the drink to cloud his thinking.

Black thought about how Tower would react when he was shown the incriminating document. Any way it went, he was sure Tower would deny it. Though Black was developing a strong dislike for the lawyer, his job was to get Cory off the hook.

He tried to calculate the odds Tower would cave without a fight. But the more he considered it, the less likely he thought it would be. Black knew he'd have to be careful or risk having the attorney strike back if he was backed into a corner.

51

BLACK MADE A COPY OF THE AFFIDAVIT THAT RUIZ GAVE HIM. It was short, but the bailiff had put the day he witnessed the bribe in it. The operative had two choices: go to Tower directly with it, or use an intermediary.

Black knew Tower, not well, but well enough. He considered a scheme of approaching the lawyer, telling him he'd come upon a potential problem for the attorney. He knew Tower would demand details. Black felt he could concoct a believable story.

It was a good plan, but two things worried the investigator. Tower was a world-class schemer and would organically suspect Black's involvement. Black believed he could defend the claim and remove the suspicion.

But his main worry was revealing his involvement in any capacity. Based on what the lawyer was doing to Cory, Black wanted to avoid the crosshairs as long as possible.

Black could send the document by mail or use a messenger. The post office would provide the most cover. If he used Express Mail, it'd arrive overnight. The operative didn't want an employee reading the affidavit, as it would add a level of unpredictability.

If he put it inside a second envelope marked Personal and Confidential, it would guarantee Tower would personally eyeball the inflammatory document. He also could call Tower, telling him about the affidavit. He could use a burner phone with a voice distorter to disguise his voice.

It was too late to mail it, and Black was too disciplined to default to calling. It had to be a conscious decision. Black would sleep on it.

CORY LOOKED OUT THE WINDOW. Tire tracks cut through the snow dusting the streets. His eyes followed the roof of a police car as it headed toward his building. Cory held his breath as he backed away from the window.

Had he blown it? Black had told him to throw his trash down the chute in the hallway once a week. He specifically said to do it in the middle of the night to crush any chance of being seen.

After he ate last night, Cory tied the top of the garbage and put it by the front door. He brushed his teeth and did a set of push-ups. It was just before seven. He had several hours to kill before going to bed.

Cory sat on the couch and put the TV on. He scrolled through the free movie section and chose *Lawrence of Arabia*. He wasn't sure if he'd like it, but he'd heard the score, composed by the famous Maurice Jarre, was exceptional and featured two themes: one to show the British side and another the Eastern.

Cory clicked play, knowing there was the added benefit of it being a long movie. He was enjoying the orchestral score more than the movie when the screen announced an intermission. Cory couldn't remember the last movie he'd seen a film with a break.

As the orchestra played the overture, Cory took the opportunity to go to the bathroom. Washing his hands, he spied the bag of trash by the door. It was a quarter to nine. He looked through the peephole. No one was in the hallway.

He grabbed the bag and cracked open the door. No sign of life. Cory grabbed a hat off the hook and put on his fake glasses before clicking the latch. He kept the dead bolt open and stepped into the hallway. Cory walked to the door housing the trash chute and recycling room.

Approaching the elevator bank, Cory froze. A ding sounded an arriving car. He looked over his shoulder; his apartment was at the end of the hall. While making a dash for the refuse area, the doors of an elevator opened.

Cory nodded at a man with a closely cropped beard and boots. The man said, "Hey, you must be the guy who moved into Fourteen F, right?"

"Uh, yeah."

"I was wondering if somebody was hiding out in there."

"Funny."

He stuck his hand out. "Marty, Marty Kelly. Nice to finally meet you."

"Uh, Cor—John Cochran."

"Like the guy who was OJ's lawyer?"

"Uh, yeah."

"So, where'd you move from?"

"Br—Baltimore."

"Never been there. You move for work?"

"Yeah."

"What do you do?"

"Tech."

"Cool. Man, I could use some help with my Wi-Fi hookups. Maybe you can take a look at it for me."

"I don't know much about that. I do, like, web design stuff."

"Neat. Must be busy."

"It's been crazy, that's why I never leave the apartment."

"That sucks, man."

Cory shrugged. "Look, I'm working on something right now, so I gotta go."

"Okay, I'll see you around."

Cory dumped his trash. Marty was standing outside his door. He lived across the hall. Cory waved and went to push his door open. His neighbor said, "Hey, tomorrow I'm having some people over. A couple of the guys from the station live in the building, you'll love them. Why don't you come over around seven and say hello?"

"Uh, I don't know. I got a project I'm trying to finish up."

"You got to take a break. Come over, have a brew and say hello."

"Thanks. I'll see how the day goes."

Cory closed the door behind him and sank to the floor. The guy said station. Was he a cop and he was having more cops come tomorrow? Cory wagged his head. He'd been so good. Why couldn't he have just waited a few more hours?

Cory got up and turned off the TV. He knew Black would want to know. But did he really have to tell him? If the guy was a cop, he should advise Black. The operative would know what to do. If he wasn't a police officer, what was the harm of avoiding him going forward?

The neighbor could be a fireman, Cory thought. They work at stations. Cory recalled what Marty looked like. It was hard to tell until he remembered his last name, Kelly. It was

Irish, and a lot of police officers were of Irish descent. Maybe he was a cop.

Like it or not, Cory would have to tell Black what had happened. He'd let his guard down, and now he needed Black to tell him what to do.

52

———

CORY STAYED UP, ALTERNATING BETWEEN LOOKING OUT THE window and peering through the peephole. He was nervous over telling Black about his encounter. The operative would pepper him with questions, and Cory tried to predict what he'd ask.

He looked at the time on the day's burner phone. It was minutes before six a.m. He hit dial.

The call was answered, but no one spoke. Cory said, "Hello, it's me."

"What's wrong?"

"I wanted to tell you something that happened."

"Spit it out."

"I was taking the trash to the chute and a guy came off the elevator. His name's Marty Kelly—"

"You spoke to him?"

"Yeah, but I didn't tell him anything. He wanted to know if I was the new neighbor. He lives right across the hall—"

"What time was this?"

"Uh, a couple of hours ago. I was waiting to call you."

"He say anything unusual?"

"I'm worried he might be a cop."

"Why?"

"He said he was having some guys over from the station and wanted me to come over."

"Station?"

"Yeah."

Black went silent.

"You think he's a cop?"

"I'll find out. Meanwhile, sit tight."

"What'll I do if he is?"

"I don't do hypothetical."

"Come on, man. I'm just trying to be prepared."

The phone went dead. Cory said, "Bastard!"

Three hours later, the burner vibrated. "Hello."

"How old was this Kelly guy?"

"About forty, why?"

"There's three Martin Kelly cops in the Boston Metro area."

"Any of them live in my building?"

"Addresses aren't made public."

"Let me describe him to you: my neighbor is about—"

"Photos aren't published either."

"What are we going to do?"

"I'll do more checking, but keep an eye out for him. You said he's across the hall, so watch when he leaves, see if he's in a uniform. It's the fastest way to find out."

"I can't believe this. I'm screwed."

"Get a hold of yourself. Nothing's happened at this point."

"Okay, what happened with that crooked judge Tower was working with?"

"We got something interesting yesterday. It might be enough."

"Oh my God. Really?"

"Keep your eyes on Kelly and call me with any developments."

Cory went to the door and looked through the peephole. It was quiet. He pulled his eye away and thought about what Black had said. They were close to getting the goods on Tower. Cory wondered exactly what he had.

Had Black been able to turn someone? If it was the judge, it would be huge. The media would be all over it, giving Cory a chance to clear his name.

Once the story broke, he'd reach out to Worth. He didn't know much about the law, but if Tower was implicated in a bribery scheme, they could ask the court to postpone the trial as he'd need a new attorney.

Cory realized he hadn't asked Black if he got a message to Linda. His wife was entitled to know he was okay. He took another look across the hall knowing that Black played things too safe. He'd never reach out to Linda.

She must be going crazy on her own, and she had to deal with the kids. He regretted leaving without telling her. It was selfish, and he hoped she'd forgive him. If his plan worked out—and with what Black said, it looked like it was about to —she'd get over it.

Things were developing much faster than he, or Black for that matter, had figured. Was he finally getting a break? Was the universe evening things out?

Linda needed a lift; she needed to know he was safe and on the cusp of exposing Tower for the evil man he was. He grabbed the phone off the couch and dialed Linda's number.

Cory whispered, "Linda, it's me."

"Cory? Oh my God. Are you okay?"

"I'm fine. How are you and the kids?"

"We're good. Where are you?"

"I can't say. Did Black call you?"

"Who?"

"Never mind."

"I can't hear you. Why are you whispering?"

Cory spoke in his normal voice, "Everything is all right. I'm doing good but miss you and the kids."

"We miss you too. When can you come home?"

"I'm not sure, but we got some dirt on Tower that should let me come home and straighten everything out."

"Oh, I hope so. We miss you so much. I'm worried sick about you."

"I know. I'm sorry, but it was the only way. How's Ava?"

"Ava is Ava. She's put up a wall, but it's a low one."

"Tell her I'm okay and I love her. What about Tommy?"

"He's doing good. He accepts what I tell him. When he asks for you, I tell him a little longer and we listen to the songs you wrote for us. They're wonderful."

"It was my way of saying something."

"I'm wearing mine out. Are you in Mexico?"

"Can't say."

"The police took your laptop, and the detectives grilled me about Mexico, trying to get information out of me. They don't believe I don't know anything. But I don't. They even talked to the kids."

"What? Who told them they could do that?"

"Don't worry, I was there, and the police were good with them. It wasn't more than fifteen minutes or so."

"That's bullshit—"

"What did you expect they would do? They're doing everything they can to find you."

"They'll never find me."

"Be careful."

"Don't worry. I got everything under control."

There was a knock on the door. He tiptoed over as Linda said, "Are you sure?"

Before he looked through the peephole, he said, "Uh, I think so."

"It's so good to hear your—"

"I gotta go. See you later."

Cory jammed the phone in his pocket. He was trapped. He didn't want to answer, but he was sure his voice had carried. He fished his clear glasses out of his pocket and put a Boston Red Sox cap on.

He said, "I'm coming." Cory took a deep breath and opened the door.

53

IT WAS HIS NEIGHBOR. "HEY, I KNOW IT'S EARLY, BUT I heard you talking as I was leaving for work."

"You're a police officer?"

"Yeah, got out of the academy a little over two years ago."

"Oh. You like it?"

"Love it. Never a dull moment."

"I'll bet. What's up?"

"Just wanted to remind you about tonight."

"I don't know, I got a deadline for this project—"

"Stop in for five minutes. You're new to Boston, you need to meet people our age."

"What time?"

"Seven. I'm counting on seeing you later."

"I'll try, but I'm overloaded with work."

"I'm expecting you, don't let me down now."

Cory threw his head back as Marty walked away. What was he going to do? He couldn't walk into an apartment full of cops. Why had he been impatient? It was the damn trash. What had been the rush?

Cory grabbed the day's phone out of the box and dialed Black's number. "What?"

"The guy across the hall is a cop."

"You sure?"

"He had his uniform on and I asked him."

"Okay."

"What should I do? He invited me over, kept pressing me. You think he knows who I am?"

"Stop panicking and focus."

"Okay, I just want to know if there's a plan B or something. Should I hit the road?"

"Stay put until I tell you otherwise."

"Should I go to the get-together?"

"Of course not."

"What should I tell him?"

"If he pushes it, say you're sick. That's it. Upset stomach from Mexican food you ordered for lunch."

"Okay. Makes sense."

Cory felt confident when he hung up, but five minutes later he was concerned about lying to his neighbor. The guy was a cop, wouldn't he know Cory was making it up? He probably would, but people lied all the time when they wanted out of social situations.

He told himself, instead of worrying, to do something constructive. Relying on Black to solve every problem was childish, and if something went wrong, he'd regret sitting on his hands. Besides, last time he was the one who came up with the plan to stop Tower from extorting him.

Cory thought about Tower. There was plenty of information on the web about the lawyer's legal triumphs but almost nothing about him personally. He'd read gossip pieces covering three of Tower's love interests, but it seemed he'd never been married or had children.

Cory felt sorry for the lawyer. He had plenty of money and was high profile in the legal world, but Cory knew he was lonely. He envisioned the attorney walking into a dark Park Avenue penthouse after a long day at the office.

He remembered Tower saying he was a transactional person. He popped the term into a private browser.

A couple of definitions came up. What had Tower meant when he described himself as transactional? Cory's idea was along the traditional sense of the word: an exchange of money and services. It wasn't emotional. If it served both parties, you'd do it. That seemed like Tower, Cory thought.

Cory read a list of synonyms. Words like negotiable and flexible gave him some hope that whatever information Black had on the dirty judge would cause Tower to end the framing. Tower would decide that killing the bribery story was an exchange that he'd make.

He looked at the time. It wasn't nine a.m. yet. He had hours to kill before Black would have any feedback from Tower. It was wishful thinking, he knew, but Cory still hoped to hear Tower agreed to stop framing him before he had to deal with his neighbor.

Cory wondered what kind of childhood Tower had. Was he the youngest in the family and had to compete with older brothers? That made a lot of people competitive and could answer one of the questions about the lawyer.

He started digging in and was able to trace Tower back to Fordham Law School. There was nothing on what high school he'd attended. Was he from out of state? Cory went back to the needs-based scholarship Fordham awarded Tower.

He scanned the grantor's website. The home page featured a half dozen winners of last year's awards. Cory clicked on the Meet the Recipients page. He opened the bio link for a smiling girl with red hair. The opening line said she was from the Bronx.

Cory went to the background information on a Hispanic young man. The line that caught his attention was a reference to the abundance of promise in the local community that reinforced the organization's policy to award grants only to New York residents.

As the dishwater sky further darkened, Cory set the tablet aside. He rubbed his eyes and lay back on the couch.

Cory woke up with a start. The bell was ringing. It was dark. He went to the door as it rang again. It was Marty. He donned a hat and glasses and opened the door.

"Sorry, man, I fell asleep."

"No problem. Hey, I'm sorry. The get-together is off tonight. I gotta work a double."

"Oh. Crime never takes a day off."

"And how. A fugitive from New York is in the area, and it's all hands on deck."

Cory swallowed. "Oh."

"Maybe we'll do it next week, after we catch this guy. But be careful out there. This guy is dangerous."

"What he do?"

"Killed someone."

"Oh my God."

"All right, I'll see you around."

54

———

Cory closed the door. Was he the fugitive they were after? It seemed crazy. If so, it wouldn't be long before Marty was given a picture of the suspect. He thought about the amateur disguise he'd been using. A trained police officer would see right through it.

Why hadn't Cory been disciplined enough to supplement that hat and glasses with the teeth, stomach bladder, and limp-inducing pebble? He wasn't cut out for a life on the run. He was a musician, not an intelligence agent.

Cory's head moved between the cabinet holding the phones and the tablet. He needed to tell Black they might be onto him but didn't want to appear panicked. He grabbed the tablet and plugged his name in the search bar.

A rattling sound caught his attention as he scanned the page of results. He realized it was one of the phones. Cory pulled the box out and picked up the lit one.

"Hello?"

"They're onto you."

"The police?"

"Who'd you call?"

"Nobody."

"Bullshit. Who'd you call, your wife?"

"I just wanted to—"

"What did I tell you? Huh? To keep your damn mouth shut!"

"I'm sorry—"

"Don't give me that sorry bullshit. I'm busting my ass to save yours, and you go fuck it all up."

"I didn't—"

"You get the hell out of there and now."

"Where do I go?"

"Half of me wants to tell you to figure it out on your own, but I'm close to closing this up for you."

"You are?"

"I expect to hear from Tower before the day is over."

"Oh, man. Please let this be over."

"I'll call you right back, but get your shit together. You're out of there as soon as I tell you."

Cory stared at the phone for a full five seconds. Under his breath he said "Oh man" and ran into the bedroom. He grabbed his backpack and started jamming in his clothes.

He opened two cans of sliced peaches and ate both. Cory took a handful of nutrition bars and canned foods and slipped them into his bag. He spread the cell phones over his pockets and set the backpack by the door.

Cory went to the window. Traffic was thick, but there were no police cars in sight. He put on his fake stomach, teeth, and coat. He grabbed a handful of coffee pods and stuffed them in a coat pocket.

Peering into the hallway, the day's cell vibrated. He answered. The instructions from Black were short. Cory put his hat and glasses on. He took another look.

It was clear. Cory slipped the pebble in his shoe and

stepped into the hallway. Heart pounding, he looked both ways and headed for the stairwell.

Out of breath, Cory paused outside the door to the lobby. He inhaled deeply and pulled open the door. He headed to the right, away from the main entrance, toward the mail and package area.

Keeping his head down, Cory slipped out the back entrance into a stream of commuters heading to North Station. He joined the stream but took the doors into the parking garage for TD Garden.

He walked up the ramp into a cold, gray New England morning. Cory recalled what Black said and headed toward Mass General Hospital. Crossing the Longfellow Bridge into Cambridge, Cory pulled out the cell phones. Black said to throw them into the water. One by one, he watched them kick up a splash.

He held the last two over the railing but pulled back. Black said to keep the Wednesday phone. He stuffed it and the Friday one and a charger into a pocket. Cory walked over the rest of the bridge. He felt a surge of relief. Realizing crossing the Charles River meant nothing, he picked up the pace.

Walking on Prospect Street, Cory opened the buttons of his jacket. He wriggled the backpack off and fished inside with his hand. "Damn it." He'd forgotten water. Cory zipped the backpack and kept walking.

The bottom of his foot hurt. He needed a break. Cory leaned against the back of a building housing a Star Supermarket. With a trailer blocking the view, he swapped the pebble from one shoe to the other.

Sweat ran down Cory's face as he turned onto Lexington Avenue. Tightly packed houses lined both sides of the

Somerville street. The clapboard homes were separated by driveways running to the rear of their small lots.

Cory looked ahead. Number fifteen was a washed-out blue home with a porch that tilted toward the sidewalk. He darted down the driveway and climbed three stairs to a landing. He lifted up a corner of the welcome mat and snatched the key.

Cory looked around and entered the ground-floor apartment. The wooden floors creaked as he went from room to room. Cory filled a glass with water as he surveyed the high ceilings and ornate moldings in the hundred-year-old home.

Blinds shut, the place was dark, but Cory didn't like that windows lined three sides of the place. Would keeping the blinds down all the time raise suspicion with the neighbors?

Cory pulled open the fridge and sighed. A bottle of Coke and a half-empty jar of mustard. The pantry was half full with boxes of pasta, cereal, and canned foods. His stomach turned when he saw a stack of Spam. He pushed them to the rear and took a can of tuna.

Stuffing a forkful of albacore into his mouth, Cory heard footsteps on the rear porch. He hugged the wall. There was a knock on the door.

55

Cory heard someone go down the steps. Lifting the edge of the blinds, he saw a Fresh Direct truck at the curb. A second later a man appeared, jumping onto the driver's seat of the van.

His regard for Black had risen as he took two bags of groceries in and put them away. He would have to do exactly what the operative said. Cory hoped he'd forgive him for calling his wife.

Cory took the tablet out. He located the cable box and entered the pass code to get on Wi-Fi. When he put his name in, he groaned. What popped up was a *New York Post* piece titled, "Police Hunt Down Grammy Winner."

It was right there, in the first sentence. The cops had a lead on Cory. An unnamed source in the NYC Police Department said they'd traced a call he'd made. They were confident he was in the Boston metro area and were working with the FBI to narrow down the location. Cory cringed at the thought that G-men were involved.

The second paragraph was more depressing. It stated that an all-points bulletin had been issued and that both the

Boston Police and Massachusetts State Police were on high alert. If that wasn't enough, it quoted the police commissioner saying the public should exercise extreme caution because he was considered armed and dangerous.

Cory threw his head back. How can they say that? He was harmless. They were spreading lies about him. What would his kids think with someone in uniform saying that about their father?

He returned to the piece and read the next paragraph. Cory flung the tablet aside and got up, muttering, "What does the Bonner thing have to do with anything?" How long was he going to have to keep paying for his mistake?

Cory went into the kitchen and started opening the cabinet doors. There wasn't a drop of booze in the house. He gave a thought to trying to order something online before deciding to take a shower instead.

Sitting on the couch after a steaming shower, Cory held the tablet and searched Spotify for something to listen to. He wanted something classical and selected the Beethoven channel. As the violins faded and a cello solo began, he kicked off his shoes and closed his eyes.

A screeching car woke Cory. An advertisement for auto insurance was playing. He shut the music app and went to the bathroom. He heard someone walking around in the apartment above him. Who lived upstairs? Was it an associate of Black's?

Cory was hungry and went into the kitchen. The linoleum floor was cold. He picked out a can of Progresso lentil soup. Pouring the contents into a bowl, the cell on the counter started dancing.

He picked it up wondering if it was a trick call from the police. The calling number didn't have the same exchange that Black used.

"Hello?"

"Got bad news."

"I got to move again?"

"Soon enough, but Tower didn't bite."

"What do you mean?"

"He told me to fuck off, is what he did."

"He's not worried about the bribery thing going public?"

"He said it'd be my word against his."

"But what about the guy you mentioned?"

"He's recanting."

"How the hell can he do that? We paid him twenty thousand."

"How do you think? Tower probably threatened him or paid him triple what we did."

"We can pay more. We need—"

"It won't matter. Tower got to him."

"What are we going to do now?"

"I hate to tell you, but I'm done with this."

"What? How can you do that?"

"Look, Tower's got too much firepower."

"You're going to let me go down? Just like that?"

"I'm sorry, but he said he'd come after me, and I got a few things in my past that can't get out or I'm going away for a long time."

"Come on, man. I got kids—"

"I'd like to help, but it's just too much for me to get involved with."

"What am I supposed to do? Where can I go?"

"You can stay there, say, two weeks."

"And do what? How am I going to find what I need on Tower? I got no contacts in your world."

"Look, I wish I could fix this one, but I can't."

"But I don't even know where to start."

"Start with his past. There's got to be something in it. He changed his name as soon as he turned eighteen."

"You think he's hiding something?"

"Has to be. Just don't know if it's something you can use to get him to drop it."

"Okay, okay. But what about the police? They're tracking me down."

"I told you not to call anyone."

"I know, but what am I going to do?"

"You got to lie low, be smart."

"Can't I get more time?"

"I don't know if that's a good idea. If the phone you used to call your wife is pinging, they're going to track you."

"I'll get rid of that phone. Take the SIM card out—"

"You gotta dump it. The faster the better."

"I will. It's just that, without you, I feel like, I got no chance. I'm going to end up in jail."

"Get a hold of yourself, you can do it."

"Can't you help for a little while longer?"

"I gotta go."

The call disconnected and Cory said, "God damn it!"

Cory dug out the other phone and pulled the SIM card out. He watched it spin as he flushed the toilet. What the hell was he going to do?

He was pissed at Black. How could Black just dump him like that? He tried to push the anger out of his head so he could concentrate on what to do. The cops were on his tail.

Cory knew he had to stay invisible if he was to avoid capture. He poured the bowl of soup into the sink. His heart sank at the thought of Linda finding out there wasn't a solution around the corner.

He cursed Tower and crushed the soup can. "Ouch." Cory dropped the can. Blood poured out from a cut below his thumb. Cory ran the faucet and put his hand under. The water turned red as it hit his hand.

He examined the slice. It was deep and two inches long. Cory wrapped a dish towel around it. Seconds later, the blood ran through it. He took it off and tossed it into the sink. He put another one on and held his hand over his head.

He felt a warm liquid running down his arm. He needed stitches. Now what?

56

———

Cory Googled for a hospital or urgent care facility nearby. A Care Well Urgent Clinic was five blocks away on Broadway. He didn't have insurance. He didn't want to pay cash but would have to.

He wrapped a new towel around it and gingerly put his coat on. Cory had his hand on the doorknob and turned around. He put his hat, teeth, and glasses on and stuck the pebble in his shoe. The bottom of his foot hurt like hell and his hand throbbed.

By the time he got to the strip mall, the towel around his hand was soaked in blood. Cory pushed the clinic's door open and those in the waiting room trained their eyes on him.

Exaggerating his limp, he held his arm up. "I need help. I can't stop the bleeding."

"Calm down, sir. We need you to fill out some paperwork—"

"How do you expect me to write anything with this hand?"

"I understand. Can we have your insurance card?"

"I left my wallet home. Take care of my hand! I need stitches."

"Follow me."

Cory was shown into a closet-sized exam room. A nurse came in, introduced herself, and unwrapped the towel. "That's some cut. It's deep. How did you do that?"

"On a can of soup."

"When was your last tetanus shot?

"I have no idea."

"You'll need one, and this will require stitches. Let me get the doctor."

An hour later and four hundred dollars lighter, Cory put a shoulder to the door and stepped outside. His hand and wrist had enough gauze wrapping it to fill a pillow.

The doctor had given him a prescription for an antibiotic. Cory was considering the risk when he saw them.

Two police cars had entered the shopping center's parking lot. Cory turned away from them and limped his way into a 7-Eleven.

Cory grabbed a bag of pretzels wondering if someone in the clinic had noticed him. They had plenty of time to check on him. He remembered the nurse coming in but leaving immediately. Had she been checking his face?

Trying to look as casual as he could, Cory looked out the window and dropped the snack. A police officer was headed for the store's door.

"Hey, let me get that for you."

An older man reached for the pretzels. Cory said, "Thanks."

He handed the bag to him. "Do we know each other?"

Cory shook his head. "No."

"You look familiar. Did you go to Somerville High? I taught there for twenty years."

"No, I'm from Brook . . . Brookfield."

"Oh yeah? My sister lives up there."

Cory watched the cop. He was by the door, surveying the store. "Haven't been there in a long while. I moved to Baltimore as a kid."

"Boy, I know you from somewhere."

"They say everybody has a double." Cory looked at his hand. A smidgen of blood was peeking through. "I got to go and get a prescription filled."

"Have a good day."

The cop was talking to the clerk at the counter. Cory headed to the back. He made it look like he was mulling over soft drinks but was trying to follow the police officer in the reflection off the fridge's glass door.

Cory debated how long would be too long to stare at sodas. He had to do something or risk drawing attention. He pulled the door open, propping it with his shoulder and grabbed a Coke.

He went to the checkout area. The officer was talking to the clerk. Cory put his items down and smiled at the cop, who said, "What happened?"

As the clerk rang up his items, he replied, "If you can believe it, I cut it on a can of soup."

"I did that years ago. The edges are too sharp."

"Yeah, I needed stitches."

Cory paid and left. "Have a good one."

He was tempted to look to see if the police officer was coming after him but kept walking. He began to relax a little as he passed the halfway point. His shoulder was hurting from keeping his arm up, and the shot they'd given him before sewing the cut closed had started to fade.

The thought of needing aspirin hit him. The doctor had wanted him on antibiotics for five days. Going to a pharmacy was risky. You had to hang around waiting for your pills to be ready. Someone could recognize him. He decided not to chance it. Besides, he needed to conserve the money he had.

Cold and hurting, Cory couldn't wait to get back. He rounded the corner onto Lexington Avenue and stopped. A police car was heading down the street. It was moving too slow, Cory thought as he exaggerated his limp.

He'd slipped up at the clinic giving the Lexington Avenue apartment as his address. Were they onto him? He was only a couple of houses away.

Cory nodded at the cop behind the wheel, but the officer didn't acknowledge him as he passed. Cory turned around. The police car was finishing a turn down the street Cory had come up. Cory hustled to his place.

He locked the door, kicked off his shoes, and went to the front window. The street was empty. Cory checked the medicine cabinet. A bottle of Tylenol was half full. He spilled two out and sucked the faucet.

Cory was hungry. He eyed the canned food and opted for two energy bars. As he tore the wrapping off with his teeth, he heard a strange sound.

It was coming from the front of the house. With visions of a SWAT team emptying out of vans, Cory lifted the edge of the blinds off the window and sighed.

A neighbor was dragging two trash cans to the curb. Cory relaxed. He took his bars to the couch and clicked on the TV. Scrolling through channels, Cory paused and went back one station.

He stood up. A newscaster was standing in front of the Boston building he'd hidden in. The screen read, "Boston Police Close in on Fugitive Musician."

57

———

Cory listened to the reporter. The way he talked, it was only a matter of time before they caught him.

He had to go. But where? He grabbed the tablet and pulled up a map of the area. He zoomed out. Vermont and New Hampshire were so sparsely populated, he'd stand out. Rhode Island might work, he thought, as he scanned the map. What about Canada?

He had a fake passport, but did they use facial recognition software at the border? Since he'd fled north, he figured the authorities on both sides of the crossing would be on the lookout, and he put the idea of Canada aside.

Cory paced the room. No matter where he went, he'd have two problems: how to get there, and where to stay. He stared at the tablet. A memory came to him. It was worth a shot.

He made a call. "Donny, it's me."

"Cory? Holy shit. Where are you, man?"

"Have the police been in contact about me?"

"Some detective came when you first took off, but that was it."

"I need help, bro."

"Anything, man."

"You remember that horse farm your uncle had?"

"Oh, man, I think about that place a lot. We had such good times working there. What about it?"

"He still have it?"

"Yeah, but my uncle is in his eighties and never gets up there. My cousin kind of runs it for him, but they're getting ready to sell it."

"The cops are on my ass. Is anybody staying in the room we used over the carriage house?"

"I doubt it. They moved the horses out of there because he couldn't take care of them anymore."

"Can I stay there?"

"Sure. I'll set it up."

"Thanks, man. I hate to hassle you—"

"It's not a hassle. You're gonna need food and stuff."

"Yeah, and a phone I can use, and a hot spot to get Wi-Fi for the internet. I got a lead I got to follow to end this mess."

"Give me a day."

"I can't wait. The cops are breathing down my neck. I have to take the next train out."

"Okay, man. I'll get on it now. Call me later."

Cory wanted to tell him to let Linda know he was okay. "Hold on."

"What else?"

What Black had said about keeping his plans secret flooded his head. "Nothing. Just wanted to say thanks, brother."

"Hey man, you know, you'd do it for me."

Cory hung up wondering if he would actually put himself in jeopardy to help a friend. Saying it was one thing, but doing it, especially something as serious as this, was another. Did Donny know helping a fugitive was a crime?

He looked around the apartment. It was hard to believe he was moving on already. He remembered one of the people on the run had said next to leaving your family behind, constantly being on the move was the worst part of trying to hide.

Cory dismissed letting Black know he was moving. Tower had his claws in a lot of people, and though he couldn't see the operative double-crossing him, he couldn't take the chance.

He carefully opened two cans of chicken. Having the use of one hand made the simplest things tough. Cory spooned both down and put a couple in his backpack. He remembered how parched he was on his last move, added two bottles of water, and zipped it up.

He put his fake belly, glasses, and teeth on. He surveyed the room, peeked out the front window and switched a light on for good measure.

Cory bent down and put the stone in his shoe. He needed to fade into the background, but with his hand bandaged it would be difficult. Cory told himself it was okay, and as he stepped onto the porch, he actually believed it.

The train station was finally in sight. Cory couldn't walk much more; both his feet were sore. A handful of people were on the platform. Climbing the stairs, he heard a distant whistle.

Cory hoped the nearly perfect timing was an omen. He decided to avoid the ticket office and buy one on board. He got on an empty car, took a window seat, and tried to nap.

The train slowed, waking Cory. A sign read Stamford. Cory straightened up. He'd been asleep for two hours. He remembered the next stop was Greenwich and looked around the car. Only two men in their twenties.

The train lumbered forward and before it reached its normal speed, slowed again. Greenwich was in sight. Besides the green in the pockets of its residents, Connecticut's wealthiest town was brown. Founded in 1640, the old town's farms had slowly been bought by hedge fund managers and turned into estates.

Cory walked into downtown Greenwich and took a cab by an office building. Using broken English, he told the driver to drop him at the Stanwich Golf Club.

The small farm was just west of the golf course. It was cold and it started to drizzle. Cory brushed off the thought it was a bad sign, reminding himself rainbows appeared when it rained.

He saw the turnoff to Pacer Lane and smiled, recalling when Donny and he rode his uncle's tractor into a drainage ditch near the farm's entrance. One of the hinges of the gate was broken, and it was clear the place had fallen into disrepair.

It was sad, but Cory hoped it was the perfect place to hide out. The pain in his foot ran up to his knee. He couldn't chance taking the pebble out and slowed his pace, though the rain picked up.

The main house was dark. A solitary light next to the door was on. Cory remembered playing countless games of Uno on the porch. The wicker set was gone, but the smoke curling from the wood stove in the carriage house was almost as good as seeing his kids.

58

CORY STAMPED HIS FEET AND WRIGGLED OFF THE BACKPACK. The room was smoky but warm. He headed straight for the stove. He eyed the pizza box on the knotty pine table as he warmed his hands. Swinging open the stove door, his stomach growled.

Donny had left a note that he'd turned the water on in the main house and that the phone was his personal one. He left a number for Cory to call, using it for any messages for Donny. His friend had gone all out.

Cory took a piece of pizza out. It was cold but tasted good. He took a bite of a second piece as he placed the box on the stove.

Cory pulled two chairs close to the heat. He took his jacket off, hung it on one, and sat in the other. Exhausted, he kicked his shoes off and held his bandaged hand near the heat. He was groggy.

Both feet hurt. Cory dragged the platform that served as a bed close to the stove and reclined. He looked at the exposed beams, remembering the time Donny had thrown his sneakers up there. It had taken him an hour to get them down.

Cory's eyes were closing. He reached for his backpack, and positioning it as a pillow, felt something. He probed with the tip of his finger. It was a carving. Cory had cut Linda and his initials into the bed.

He shined the light from Donny's phone onto the deep cuts he'd made with a knife. He'd been in love with Linda since he first saw her. He traced the carving with his finger and vowed to do whatever was necessary to be reunited with his family.

Cory woke up cold and stiff. His hand throbbed and his back hurt as he got off the bed. The fire in the stove had been reduced to embers. He put firewood in and stoked it.

He massaged his feet and thought about Tower. Black mentioned he had changed his name. That fit with his inability to trace much of Tower's history before law school. He took the tablet out and turned Donny's phone into a hot spot.

Cory pecked a question in. He was surprised how easy it seemed to be to find out if someone had changed their name. He read through two blog pieces on the subject. Both said that in order to change your name, you had to go to the court in the county you resided in.

That meant to locate someone who had changed their name, you'd search the records in that county for the relevant documents they needed to make the change. Tower was always referred to as a New Yorker, but that didn't mean he was one when a name-change request was filed.

Cory thought about that until realizing the law school scholarship. You had to be a local. He Googled New York name changes and went to the link, nycourts.gov. A bolt of adrenaline coursed through him as he read. The official site led off with the statement that name change applications were public.

The privacy tab mentioned being able to have the records sealed to prevent anyone from seeing them. However, the court would only grant those if your safety was in danger.

Cory grabbed a slice of pizza. Biting into the crust, Cory noticed a link for Adult Name Change Petitions. The page helped you complete the documents necessary to request a name change. He couldn't understand why they'd make it easy to change your name. There were exclusions for those in prison or on probation, but it didn't make sense.

Maybe it had something to do with most women changing their last name when they married. He read that name-change records were filed in the clerk's office in the county where the person lived.

Cory began his search, hoping the results were organized alphabetically and not chronologically. He got up after an hour, stretched his back and put another piece of wood in the stove before resuming his search.

He almost missed it and scrolled back up. There it was. He leaned in: Barney Tower was formerly known as Richard Sullivan. The address listed at the time was 39 Bank Street.

It was now an expensive neighborhood, but what was it like in 1990? Dinkins was mayor, and the crime-ridden city was crumbling.

Cory didn't know what to do first. If Tower was eighteen at the time, he was born in 1972. It was about right, figuring Tower to be about fifty. He remembered Linda saying something about Ancestry.com having birth records for anyone born in New York City.

He input Richard Sullivan and 1972 and two records appeared. Cory wanted to call Black and ask him what to do next. He decided to wait until he really needed help.

Cory paced the room. Why would an eighteen-year-old change his name? He could have committed a crime as a minor and wanted to distance himself. He'd read the courts wouldn't allow a name change for someone still on probation or parole. It couldn't be that then, he reasoned.

The only explanation that made sense was to get away from his family. Maybe he grew up in a dysfunctional household or possibly his father or mother committed a heinous crime. He Googled how to find out if someone had a record.

After clicking through a number of sites claiming to be free but then asking for a fee, he realized even if he paid, he'd need the first name and date of birth. Cory had neither. He'd have to dig into the neighborhood Tower grew up in. But would what he might find be enough to force Tower to retreat?

59

Cory needed people who knew the family, someone who could tell him what Tower was like as a kid and find out what was in Tower's past that he wanted kept secret. Cory wondered if Tower had a brother or sister.

He Googled several variations on finding if someone had a sibling but kept coming up empty. If he could find a neighbor, they'd not only be able to provide background on Tower, but also reveal if he had siblings.

Cory knew Tower was born in 1972 as Richard Sullivan and had been living in the West Village in 1990. He also knew the power of social media had no equal when trying to connect with someone.

He was certain the police were watching his social media accounts and created a new email account with Google. Cory took that email address and opened an account on Facebook, under the name Dan Saturn.

Cory used a picture of a fiftyish man from the web as his profile picture. He created a couple of posts with images of cats and seascapes. Though he thought the chances were slim, he searched for people named Sullivan. A list in the thousands confirmed his suspicion.

He scrolled through the list wondering how to sort through it. He could look for people around Tower's age or for anyone living in the city, but the work to narrow down the possibilities did nothing to ensure he'd find a relative.

Cory thought about calling Black or Donny to ask them to canvas the Bank Street neighborhood. Thirty years had passed, but maybe someone still lived there who knew Tower. Cory began posing different questions looking for a way to find someone who knew Tower as a child.

Searching for histories of families living in New York City on Facebook, a couple of worthless results came up. One, a group named Staten Island in Days Gone By, gave Cory an idea. He typed Greenwich Village in the search bar and smiled.

There were groups called the West Village Neighbors, Neighborhood Church of Greenwich Village, and the Greenwich Village Society for Historic Preservation. Cory applied for membership in each of them. The only condition was asking if you lived or had worked in the Village.

Acceptance came quickly, and Cory began combing their member lists, hoping for a Sullivan. There was one, an Elroy Sullivan, but he was black, causing Cory to discount a connection. He started reading through the posts in the West Village group.

They varied from crime-related to gossip. Cory's spirits were lifted by two items: 'whatever happened to' a couple of residents who were briefly famous, and 'has anyone heard from' this person.

Cory decided to post something: "Thanks for adding me to the group. I lived in the area a long time ago. Was actually thinking of moving back, but I see it's gotten expensive. Good for those who stuck around!

"I was wondering if anyone knew what happened to my friend Richard Sullivan. The family lived on Bank Street. It would be wonderful to catch up with him after all these years. If anyone remembers him or his family, I'd appreciate a DM. Also, does anyone remember the waitress at the Waverly Inn with the red hair?"

Cory posted similar messages in the other groups and went back to reading posts. Even though a notification alert wasn't showing, he checked every five minutes to see if a response had come in. He knew it would take time if someone were to answer.

He tried to calculate the odds. They were long. Somebody would have to see it in their constantly changing feed. They'd have to know Richard Sullivan and reach out to a new, unknown member.

Cory got up and went to the dormer window. A flurry of snow was morphing into thickening snowfall. He couldn't sit around waiting for someone from a group to contact him. He had Tower's original name. How could he learn about his earlier life?

He paced the small room, stoking the fire and wracking his brain for ideas. Cory went to see what he could make to eat when he saw Donny's phone sitting on the pine table. He grabbed it and punched in a number.

Cory left a message. He took out a can of chicken noodle soup, carefully pulling the top back. As he set it on top of the stove, Donny's cell rang.

"Hello."

"It's me." It was Mr. Black. "Hey, thanks for calling me back."

"You okay?"

"Yeah, doing good."

"Where'd you go?"

"Greenwich. Up in Connecticut. My friend Donny, his uncle has a horse farm we used to go to as kids."

"It's quiet?"

"Oh yeah, no one lives on it anymore."

"Keep your head down."

"I am. I know you said you were out, but I could use some help."

"What's going on?"

"I did what you said and started with the name change. Tower's real name is Richard Sullivan."

"Interesting."

"He lived on Bank Street in the West Village. But that's all I came up with. I don't know what to do next."

"You want my help?"

"Oh, man, if you could. I'd be so grateful."

"I said I was out—"

"Come on, man, I need a little help with this."

"All right. I'll check into Sullivan."

"Thanks so much."

"You got to do me a favor. Stay put. Don't talk to anyone and don't go anywhere."

"I won't, don't worry."

"Anything changes, or feels off, call me right away."

60

Cory hung up and pumped his fist. Black was back on the case. He looked at the phone in his hand. He wanted to tell Linda everything was going to work out. He shook his head. Black said not to talk to anyone.

Cory felt too close to nailing Tower to take a chance. Linda would understand. The more he thought about it, he realized it was the kids, especially Ava, he was concerned about. Tommy would ask questions, but Linda would smooth things over.

He could see the dead-face look on Ava. Cory would work as hard as he could to repair the damage his arrest caused his daughter. But he had to get home first.

This mess wasn't his fault, it was Tower's, he thought. And Stein. His old manager not only screwed him out of money but got himself murdered. He cursed Stein and replayed the confrontation he'd had with him.

Cory admitted to himself going to see his manager with a knife was not only stupid but a major reason he was hiding out in a drafty carriage house. He took the soup off the stove, vowing not to act like an idiot again.

Eating the soup, Cory checked the Facebook groups for activity. There was nothing. He looked at news sites for anything about himself, but that was quiet as well. He finished snacking and sat on the bed.

Cory unwrapped the gauze around his hand. The wound was red. Wrapping it back up, he hoped it wasn't getting infected. He was exhausted. He stretched out and drifted off to sleep.

CORY OPENED HIS EYES, squinting against the sun rays slicing through the little window. He rolled over, groaning at the stiffness throughout his body. He heard a muffled sound and tiptoed to the window. He didn't see anything.

He arched his back, wondering what time it was. Cory grabbed the tablet and shook his head. He'd been sleeping for ten hours. Hungry, he opened a box of Special K. Scooping handfuls into his mouth, he opened the Facebook app.

There were two notifications. He tapped on the first one. It was from a member in the historical Village. The reply to his message was nothing but a simple welcome to the group. Cory said thanks and went to the next message.

This one was from the West Village Neighbors group. He clicked. It was a reply to his post from a Gavin Hill. Cory's pulse quickened as he read:

"Hello Dan, Nice meeting you and welcome. I remember Richard Sullivan, he lived across the street. I'm in the middle of something, but I'll send you a direct message. Best Regards, Gavin."

Cory typed a response: "Thanks Gavin. I look forward to chatting with you. Richie and I lost contact when we were just kids but were good friends. It'd be nice to catch up after all these years. Have a good one, Dan."

Cory stood. Could it be? Had he really found someone who knew Tower as a kid? He went to the messenger app, but there were no messages. He refreshed the screen. Nothing. He tried to envision what this Gavin looked like and how old he was.

Cory wondered how well Gavin knew Tower. Was he finally going to have luck on his side? Cory tried to quell his optimism, but it was hard. As a complete novice, he had developed his own lead. Surely, an operative like Black would come up with a lot more.

He told himself that he'd been upbeat before and had his hopes crushed. But Cory felt this was different as he paced the room. Then he heard a sound like a bubble popping. It was the Messenger app.

He clicked and there it was, a private message from his new friend, Gavin Hill:

"Hello Dan, it's been a busy day. As I said, I knew Richard Sullivan. He lived on the other side of Bank Street many years ago. It has to be about 30 years now."

Cory replied, "Thanks Gavin. Do you know where he went after there?"

"Don't remember. He kept to himself back then."

"What about his family? Are they still there?"

"No, they moved out about ten years ago."

"Where'd they go?"

"The Leonardos went to New Jersey."

"The Leonardos?"

"Yes, they had taken Richard in after what happened."

"What happened? I don't know."

Hitting the send button, Cory heard people climbing the

stairs. Then a voice, "Police!" The door busted open. As officers rushed in, Cory glanced at the screen. It read that someone was typing a comment.

"Hands up, Lupinski!"

61

Cory froze as the police surrounded him. An officer grabbed his good wrist and slapped a cuff on. The cop pulled his bandaged hand behind him.

"Take it easy! My hand's cut up bad."

Cuffing it to his other wrist, the office snickered, "You'll get all the attention you need, at the prison infirmary."

As they marched Cory down the stairs, he noticed the cop cars were a combination of the Greenwich local force and the Connecticut State Police. He wondered how they'd tracked him down. Had Donny slipped up? It had to be. How else could they have known about the farm?

Every time the cop car bounced its way down the access road, a spike of pain hit Cory's wrists. He scooted forward from the back of the seat and tried to protect his injured hand. Something was gnawing at him, and he said, "How did you find me?"

"Keep quiet!"

"Oh, come on, man. You got me. All I want to know is how."

"New York said somebody called in a tip you were here."

Cory rolled it around. A tip? Donny would never turn him in. He traced his departure from Somerville. He was certain no one saw him. And if they did, he was wearing his disguise. Nobody knew he was in Greenwich.

"Shit!"

"Hey! Shut up."

Cory realized the only person, besides Donny, who knew his whereabouts was Mr. Black. He thought over why the operative would double-cross him. He knew the answer.

It was Tower. The lawyer had gotten to him. There was no other explanation. Cory had trusted Black with his life, and Black had delivered. Until now.

Cory regretted pushing Black to help him after he'd backed away. He could see it now; Black had been getting pressured by Tower and decided it was too dangerous to continue helping. Maybe Tower dangled money or had something on Black, and when Cory called, the operative decided to go for it.

What was he going to do? The upside was his wife and kids would know he was fine. But one of many downsides was the effect the coverage he was going to get would have on Ava. The press loved filming a handcuffed suspect being walked into a police station.

He'd need a lawyer, and the best choice would be Worth. Or would it be? Would Tower know he was onto him? Chances were Black told him or he'd found out another way. Tower was connected and formidable.

Worth was conservative, but Cory now had a connection between Tower and a witness. He also had a possible entree into Tower's past, lifting his spirits. They came crashing down when he realized his life was in the hands of a lawyer who never believed him, and Gavin, a so-called friend he'd never met.

It was a mess, and there was the threat he'd get charged with something for violating the terms of his bail. Would he have to forfeit any of the money he'd posted to guarantee he'd stay around to face the charges? Cory's head hurt. Wasn't dealing with being framed enough bullshit to deal with?

A CROWD of reporters was massed in front of Manhattan's Detention Complex. The prison on White Street, known as the Tombs, had housed some of the most notorious criminals in New York's history.

Each officer grabbed an arm and led Cory toward the jail's entrance. Cory kept his head down as reporters shouted questions.

"Where were you hiding, Mr. Loop?" "Why'd you run?" "What happened to your hand?" "How does it feel to go from a Grammy winner to a felon?"

Cory looked at the woman who asked the last question. "I'm innocent. I'm being framed for something I didn't do."

"Why'd you run then? Don't you have faith in the justice system to exonerate you?"

Cory turned his head as they were about to enter the building. "I believe in our system. I needed more time to state my case and the court said no."

Cory was ushered into the booking area. He was fingerprinted, probed, and shoved into a cold shower. After drying off with a threadbare towel, he put on an orange jumpsuit.

Cory was given the opportunity to make one call. His hands trembled as he dialed Linda's number. He felt tears welling up and hit disconnect. He called Worth, his old lawyer, instead.

The attorney wasn't in, but they promised to get the message to him and assured Cory he'd visit as soon as possible. Cory held the receiver even though the woman had hung up. He faked a few words before putting the phone down.

A guard shoved a pile of bedding with a mildew smell at him, and Cory was shown to his cell.

He surveyed the small space. A cement ledge served as a bed, and inches away was a stainless-steel toilet without a cover. A metal desk that looked like half of a picnic table was bolted to a wall.

The jail was noisy, but Cory jumped when the guards slammed his door shut. He put the linens on the slab and sat, wondering how long he'd have to stay. Cory shrunk away from the bars as two heavily tattooed inmates peered into his cell and laughed.

Relieved when they left, Cory realized how scared he was. He was a musician, a father. He'd made mistakes, but he wasn't a hardened criminal. He closed his eyes, trying to envision his family. He needed to see his wife, but when a granite slab of a prisoner began taunting him, he questioned whether he'd survive long enough.

62

BRIEFCASE IN HAND, WORTH WAS STANDING BESIDE A GRAY metal table as Cory was ushered into the room. A guard, belly hanging over his belt, stood in the far corner. Cory surveyed the soulless space as his lawyer asked, "How is your hand, Mr. Lupinski?"

"Getting better. They changed the dressing when I complained."

The escort cuffed Cory to the table, which was bolted to the floor. He eased his back against the steel chair, arching away from the cold.

Worth eased himself into the chair opposite Cory. He kept his valise in his lap, perching his butt on the front of the seat.

Cory said, "I know I seem crazy with changing lawyers and all, but I want you to defend me, okay?"

"I'm agreeable to representing you. The terms will be the same as the original engagement."

"How soon can you get me out of here?"

"That's going to be difficult. You're a proven flight risk."

"But I only took off because I didn't have enough time. They wouldn't give me a postponement."

"Let's take this one step by step. The first order of business will be to notify the court of the change in counsel for the murder case. As soon as it's granted, I'll petition to move the trial date."

"You think it will work?"

"I need time to prepare your defense, and I'm certain the court will grant it."

"Really?"

"Absolutely."

"Good." Cory leaned in. "I'm sure Tower is behind this. I found out he's in cahoots with the witnesses, and I'm digging in on his past. He changed his name when he turned eighteen. There has to be a reason, and when I find out, we'll use it to have him back off."

"An assertion like that must be ironclad. Accusations against officers of the court are a serious matter."

"I know, but I'm going to need you to find out what we can about Tower's connection to the witnesses. We show that, and it blows up their case."

"Let me remind you, the state is charging you, not Mr. Tower."

"But I can prove it's him, I got to get out of here."

"Unfortunately, house arrest is the only way I see the bail being granted. You'd have to agree to wear a monitoring device and pay for twenty-four-hour guards to ensure you don't flee."

"I can do that. How much is the guard thing going to cost?"

"It's difficult to estimate until the court, if the court, allows it. They'll set the parameters, such as whether multiple guards are required."

"I don't care what you have to do, just please get it done.

I want to see my wife and kids. I haven't talked to them in a long time."

"You'll be allowed to call them. The new law allows for free domestic calls for up to twenty-one minutes every three hours. But no call can be longer than fifteen minutes."

"I didn't know that."

"And you should be given a tablet to use. You can't go on the internet, but you can use it to access educational material, read books and newspapers, and email those on your approved contact list."

"What? That sounds crazy, but I'm happy to hear it. How do I get somebody on the contact list?"

"Give me a list. I'll make sure it gets in the right hands." Worth took a pad and pen out of his briefcase and slid it across the table.

Cory started writing. "Of course, I want Linda and the kids on the list. And my buddy Donny."

As he wrote, he wondered if he should let Worth know about Gavin Hill. Was it safe asking the lawyer to contact him? Tower was a concern but a small one, the larger one was having Worth screw up the relationship. Who knew what Hill would do if he knew he was in jail? But he ultimately needed to be on the approved list.

Cory said, "This is going to sound off, but a friend of mine, I don't know his email address because I always talk to him on Facebook. He was helping me with some information on Tower. Can you get in touch with him?"

"If you provide a means of contact, yes."

"But you have to be careful. This guy finds out I'm in jail, he'll probably shut down."

"I'll be discreet."

"And he thinks my name is Dan Saturn."

"This is all very clandestine, isn't it?"

"I know, it seems crazy, but you got to trust me. Do you believe that Tower is framing me?"

"I understand how it appears if a witness met with him, but there could be a valid reason."

"But you said there wasn't any reason right after I saw him."

"I'll grant that it's unusual, but we're going to need more, much more. Putting eyewitnesses on the side for a moment, we have the history between you and the deceased that needs to be addressed, but the most problematic is your blood at the scene."

"Tower had somebody plant it there."

"That may be, but we can't simply discount it, we need to prove it or present a compelling narrative to how your blood ended up in Mr. Stein's home."

"I could say I had a nosebleed."

"That would put you in his house. You've denied being there."

"I wasn't."

"How did your blood get there?"

"I don't know."

"As I've stated from the beginning, if we can't address the evidence, we have to consider a plea. Allow me to get to work on the change in representation and talk to the DA on what they'll want for your release."

"Okay. And don't forget to get a hold of Gavin Hill. He's going to be key."

"I'll reach out. Now, you should already know this, but you're a celebrity, and that means the inmates and guards will be gunning for you."

Cory shrugged. "At least the media can't touch me in here."

"No, but they can add pressure to those who make public decisions. Therefore, you must avoid confrontations and disturbances. If you get into trouble, it'll weigh on my ability to get you out of here."

63

Cory resisted the urge to hold his nose. The smell of body odor was making him sick. After a twenty-minute wait, Cory made it to the head of the line. A guard with a scar running down his cheek said, "Lupinski! You're up. Number nine."

Cory rushed to the open telephone hanging on the white-tiled wall. He tapped a number in. It rang twice.

"Linda? It's me."

"Oh my God, Cory. Are you okay?"

"Yeah, it's not the Hilton, but I'm all right. When can you come and see me?"

"Mr. Worth said next week. He said we can start emailing tomorrow."

"Yeah, I'm going to get a tablet after I finish my calls. Can you believe it? I can call every day, and they give me a computer?"

"I miss you so much."

"Me too. How are the kids?"

"They're all right. Tommy still accepts what I tell him,

but Ava . . . you know, she's having a tough time with all this. She won't go to school."

"It's all my fault."

"Stop blaming yourself, Cory. That bastard Tower, it's all his fault."

"We're going to get him, you'll see. Bring the kids next week."

"I was thinking to see what it looked like myself. You know, see if it's okay for them."

"I need to see them . . . but, uh, okay. See what it's like first. Worth is working on getting me out of here. Maybe I'll be out before you even get here."

"Really?"

"Yep."

"Oh, please God."

"Don't get your hopes up too high."

"How's your hand? I saw on the news—"

"It's better. I cut it on a can when I got to Somerville."

"Somerville? In Massachusetts?"

"Yeah, I had to leave Boston—"

"You went to Boston?"

"At first, and then when I called you that time, they traced my call."

"Oh my God."

"It's okay. From there I went to Somerville and then I had to go to Greenwich. Where they found me."

"How did they know you were there?"

"I'm pretty sure Black double-crossed me. I think Tower got to him."

"But he was helping you."

"I know. You can't trust anybody. I'm going to get what I need on my own."

"On your own? You're scaring me, Cory. You need a lawyer, a good one."

"I'm working with Worth. I think he's coming around a little about me being framed."

A recorded voice broke into the call. 'You're approaching the end of your allotted time. You have thirty seconds before the call will disconnect.'

"Lin?"

"You got to go."

"We'll talk tomorrow. I love you. Tell the kids I love them and will see them soon."

"I hope—"

The line went dead.

Cory trudged to a holding area. He'd have to wait an hour before getting back in line for the phone again. It was okay. He had the time and needed to talk to Donny.

———

A BANG on the bars snapped Cory out of mentally rolling around his conversation with Donny. He was convinced his friend hadn't leaked his whereabouts. It had to be Black.

"Move it! You want this or not?"

A guard was holding a tablet through the bars. Cory went to grab the computer, but it was pulled out of reach.

"You don't play by the rules, we'll take it back. No contact with anyone unauthorized. You can read, research legal stuff, and get educated, but if you're one of those nerdy types, don't even think of trying to surf the web or anything."

"I won't."

"You do anything close to it, and we'll revoke privileges. You understand?"

"Don't worry, you won't get any trouble from me."

The guard looked him up and down. "You're that musician, right?"

"Yeah, used to be known as Cory Loop."

"What do you play?"

"Guitar."

"Me too. Mostly blues."

"The blues are the root of jazz and rock. It always comes back to the blues."

"That's what they say. But I'm just a hack."

"I'd be happy to give you some lessons. I taught a lot of adults."

"Maybe I'll take you up on that."

He held up his bandaged hand. "I need to get back to playing. My hand is all stiff."

"It's getting better?"

"Yeah, this bandage is nothing compared to what was on it before."

"All right. Maybe I can get you some space in the library to loosen up. They got a couple acoustic guitars in the rec room. They're crap, but better than not playing."

"Yeah. I had this teacher when I was starting out, he said to pick up your instrument every day, even for just five minutes, if that's all you got."

"Sounds like the guy at the music store I was taking lessons from, he said not to put your ax in the case. He said leave it on a stand where you can see it. Said you'd pick it up more often."

"He's right. When I was a kid, I basically slept with my first Gibson. And I still got her."

"It's weird, sometimes, I get so mad, so frustrated practicing, can't seem to make any progress."

"I know it's hard, but you can't get frustrated. You think you're not making progress, but if you're practicing the right things, you're definitely improving, even if you can't see it."

"That's the thing, what to practice?"

"I love noodling around on my ax as much as the next guy. And it's not a bad thing, you have to have fun, but you need to work on the stuff that's hard to play. Slow it down, get it under your fingers."

"That's what my guy says, stop glossing over the tough stuff and get it right."

Cory shook his head. "Some things just take longer. Break it down into small pieces and get one part of it down. Then move to something else."

"You mean like one phrase in something hard to play?"

"Sometimes not even that much. Just one bar. Get down one bar as good as you can and move on to a new thing. You'll accomplish something and avoid getting frustrated."

"Makes sense. Hey, what's the deal with tuning to a G?"

As Cory started explaining it, another guard shouted, "Franklin, get moving. They need you in laundry."

"Got to go."

"Nice to talk music, man."

Cory did feel good talking about music as he fired up the tablet. He hoped Franklin would take him up on his offer. Cory signed into his Gmail account. The in-box had over three hundred messages.

He bypassed them, going to one his lawyer sent. He noted the email address he provided and sent a message to Gavin Hill:

"Hi Gavin, Sorry I've been out of touch. I didn't know what was wrong, but it seems my Facebook account was hacked. Ugh! Let's use email to chat until I get it squared away. Your last message was about the family that took Richard in. I'd love to hear all about it."

Cory hit send and went to his in-box. There was an email from Linda, but what caught his eye was the one below it.

His heart raced. Cory's finger hovered over the open button as he considered the possible implications.

64

The EMAIL WAS FROM THE KRAVIS CHILDREN'S HOSPITAL AT Mt. Sinai. Cory received regular communications related to his volunteer work, but this was different. The subject line was "Blood Supply Critically Low - Please Donate Today".

Cory's eyes scanned the body of the message, but he wasn't reading. He was trying to place the faces and names in the blood donation center. Who was it?

Cory composed a message to Worth: "I think I know where the blood came from. I've been donating blood for years at Mount Sinai. Somebody must have taken some of mine and planted it. We need to find out who works there that's connected to Tower."

After alerting his lawyer, Cory read Linda's message. He told her about the Mt. Sinai link and that he was waiting on the West Village Facebook connection. Cory ended his reply on an upbeat note, mentioning he was giving a guard music lessons.

There was another message from Linda. She had cut and pasted a couple of notes his musician friends had sent her. They wished him luck in evading capture. He smiled at how

Americans loved an underdog, especially one who could outwit the authorities.

Cory explored the tablet, checking out the library and legal and educational resources he could access.

He wondered what he'd be able to find if Worth couldn't get him out, when an email came in. It was from Gavin Hill. Cory took a deep breath and opened it.

"Hello Dan, Sorry about the Facebook troubles. About a year ago, the censors there put me in Facebook jail when I kept posting about how terrible the mayor was. He's running the city into the ground. Maybe you posted something they didn't like."

Cory read the email again. He didn't say a word about Tower. This was crazy, he thought. Cory took a second and wrote back: "Hi Gavin, I don't think I posted anything political, but these days the weather will offend somebody. I requested an account review and expect they'll reverse it. You were starting to tell me about Richard Sullivan and the family he lived with. Want to hear more . . . Dan."

Cory paced the small cell. This emailing back and forth was wasting time he didn't have. He wondered whether he should ask Gavin for his telephone number. It would speed things up. He grabbed the tablet and typed out a message. Before hitting send, he rolled it around.

Would Gavin think he was being too forward? What if Gavin asked for Cory's number?

Cory discarded the email. He needed to clear his mind. He navigated to the music app and pulled up Jim Hall and Pat Metheny. They were two of his favorite jazz guitarists. Cory appreciated their technical skills and incredibly different styles.

He sat on the bed and closed his eyes. The music washed over him, inspiring him to get back to playing. A lick Jim

Hall played in a duo with Bill Evans caught his attention. He paused the player and internalized the three-bar phrase, mimicking what he thought were the chords and notes with his fingers.

Cory's bad hand was tight. He couldn't wait to hold a guitar again. Couldn't wait to get back to his family and life.

Cory said, "You're still hanging over into the next measure, just before the bridge. Cut off the note on the upbeat of four."

Franklin said, "I thought I had it that time."

"You're almost there. You're doing great. I'm just picky."

"Let me try again."

"All right. One, two—"

The door swung open. A bald-headed guard stepped into the rec room. "Lupinski, your lawyer's here."

Worth was standing in a cinder block-walled room. The canary yellow walls did nothing to diminish the space's drabness. It matched the somber look on his lawyer's face, alarming Cory.

"I didn't know you were coming. Everything all right?"

"Please take a seat."

"No. Just tell me."

"Getting you released is going to take some time. We're not going to have the bail hearing."

"Why not?"

"The DA objected, claiming that the fake passport you had was evidence you were planning to leave the country."

"I wasn't—"

"They mentioned the activity on your laptop supported their fears."

"Oh, man."

"New York courts are inclined to allow bail, but the feedback was concerning. I felt it best to pull the petition rather than risk a denial."

"You pulled it?"

"I had no choice. We'll wait until the atmosphere is more forgiving. Additionally, it'll give you time to build a clean record while you're in here. That will help."

"How long do I have to wait?"

"A minimum of thirty days."

"A month?"

"It may be sooner. The court is going to put the trial on the calendar soon."

"What will the date be?"

"I asked for six months to prepare. The DA objected. I expect we'll meet in the middle. Approximately ninety days from now."

"That's right around the corner."

"We need to get to work. Is there any information from the Facebook contact?"

"I'm working on it. He was supposed to email me. What about the blood bank at Mount Sinai? That's definitely where it came from."

"I spoke to the head of the department, a Mrs. Murray. She assured me they have the strictest of protocols governing the collection and storage process."

"Everybody says that bullshit. Meanwhile, people hack into everything."

"If you can identify the person you believe responsible, I could attempt threatening them with a subpoena."

"I have good contacts there from the volunteering I did. They're still getting money from the foundation I set up, so, I hate to say it, they owe me. Get Mount Sinai on the contact list."

65

Cory dialed Mt. Sinai, reaching Jane Santo. The head of the hospital's public relations for the children's division said, "Cory? Is that you?"

"Yep, it's me. How are you?"

"Aren't you, uh, in—"

"Yeah, I'm calling from the Tombs."

"Oh my God. Are you all right?"

"I'm doing okay. Look, I need some help. I'm being framed for murder, and they say my blood was found at the scene."

"I don't understand how this involves me."

"Not you directly, but you know I've been donating blood for the kids for years now."

"Yes. We're very appreciative."

"My lawyer spoke to Mrs. Murray, and she gave him the line about how secure everything is regarding the donation and collection process."

"I have to agree. Though I don't know the specific procedures, the hospital has SOPs on everything. Something as important as the blood bank has some of the most stringent ones."

"Can you do me a favor?"

"That would depend."

"Usually, Jeff or Caroline takes my blood, and there's an old guy, Jerry, who shuttles the bags and stuff."

"I know them, not well, but what about them?"

"They're all still there?"

"Yes. As far as I know."

"Can you find out who else could get to a bag of blood after someone donates?"

"Access is limited. The blood supply is a precious resource."

"I know that. But can you just check? All I need are their names. There can't be many since you said access is limited."

"That's a human resources issue. I don't—"

"Come on, Jane. I'm not asking for a lot. My life is on the line! I did a lot for you. All I want to know is who can touch the blood I've been donating and whether they had a record or something in their background."

"Okay, okay. I'll check and get back . . . oh, how will I let you know?"

"I'll call you tomorrow."

CORY WASHED away the medicinal taste of the powdered eggs they were fed for breakfast with a cup of burnt coffee. He put his tray away and lined up against the wall. It was only 7:20 a.m. He'd have to wait until at least 2 p.m. to see what Santo had on the blood bank employees.

He saw Franklin stepping in between two inmates who

were getting in each other's faces. Cory couldn't imagine working in such an environment. Franklin walked one of them to the back of the line and inserted the other near the front.

The guard walked over to Cory. "How you doing this morning?"

"All right. You practice that lick?"

"Soon as I got home."

"In all twelve keys?"

"I did five or six of them."

"Nice. Play 'em every day for a week, and you'll own it."

"I really like the way it sounds."

"I have a couple of variances on it. I'll show you later."

"Great. See you at four."

"Okay. I'm going for my shift in laundry."

"Wish I could get you out of it."

"It's okay, man. I need to burn some time."

Cory got back to his cell after working and checked the tablet for any emails. His heart leapt at the sight of one from Gavin Hill. He swallowed and clicked it:

"Hello Dan, Hope you're having a good day. Sorry I got sidetracked. My wife gets dialysis twice a week. Betty just got onto the transplant list. We're hoping she doesn't get worse until a kidney becomes available, but we have faith it will all work out.

"Getting back to Richard Sullivan. The family he lived with was a foster one. The Leonardos were special people. They'd taken in many troubled children over the years. I believe Richard was with them for about five years or so. Like a lot of things, it's hard to remember these days.

"Best regards, Gavin."

Cory reread the message. He'd glossed over the transplant

part the first time. Here was another family getting upended by the need for an organ. Moving on to the part about Tower, he was living with a foster family. Why? Had there been abuse? Is that what drove Tower to be a vindictive, controlling person?

Who were the Leonardos? Were they still alive and living in the Village? Cory composed a reply:

"Hi Gavin,

"So sorry to hear about your wife's transplant needs. I'm familiar with it as my mother-in-law needed one. It's super important to get to the right hospital. I know NYC has some great places, like Columbia and Weill Cornell, but I did a lot of research, and the shortest wait times were always at Nebraska Medicine in Omaha.

"I know it's far, but it's something to consider. Time is the enemy in this battle. Good luck!

"Thanks for the info on Richard. Do you know what happened that led him to leave his family? I wonder if the Leonardos are still around. If so, do you know a way to contact them?

"Thanks for trying to help me, Dan."

Cory typed another email out, this one to Linda, asking her to see if she could come up with anyone named Leonardo that lived in the city. He also sent a message to Worth letting him know that Tower had a troubled past and had lived with a foster family in the West Village with the surname of Leonardo. He asked the lawyer whether he could get a private investigator to hunt down the family.

Cory didn't know what to do next. If he wasn't locked up, he'd have taken a ride to the Village and gone door-to-door looking for information.

He got down on the floor and did some push-ups to drain the adrenaline.

In the lunchroom, Cory kept to himself, pushing around the mystery chuck meat. After the midday meal, prisoners were allowed to use the phones. Cory was poised to bolt out of his seat as soon as the guards allowed lining up. He wanted to be among the first ten in line.

66

Cory picked up the receiver and plugged in Mt. Sinai's phone number. It was a good hour earlier than he wanted to call, but he couldn't wait any longer. He crossed his fingers.

"Jane Santo. How can I assist you?"

"Jane, it's Cory. What did you find out?"

"Oh, hi Cory. I checked with HR. I'm sorry, but very few people have access to the blood supply, and no one raises suspicion. Everyone who works there has been with the hospital a minimum of eight years."

"Are you sure?"

"Yes. I couldn't let anyone know what I was doing, so I looked over the records myself, telling them I was looking for some employees to highlight in a PR campaign."

"And there wasn't anything even a little suspicious?"

"No. I wish I could help you but . . ."

"Okay. Thanks."

Cory was supposed to call his wife but didn't feel like talking. He just couldn't fake being upbeat. He went back to his cell wondering for the millionth time why Tower was doing what he was.

He knew he'd pissed the lawyer off by outsmarting him to stop the extortion. If Tower wanted to sue him or send one of his goons to intimidate him, he'd get the knee-jerk reaction, but to frame him? For murder?

Tower had to be some kind of genius nutjob. There was no doubt he was highly intelligent, but he had a dark side, one that let him cross ethical and moral boundaries without remorse. What made him like that?

Cory used the tablet to access educational resources and found himself reading articles on personality types and disorders. There were a surprising number of disorders, and they were confusing.

The most likely fit, Cory thought, was Tower was a narcissist. Cory understood them to be control freaks with a strong desire to be admired. It sounded like the lawyer, but the information wasn't useful. He x'd out of the program and went to his email box.

WALKING DOWN A DIMLY LIT CORRIDOR, Cory got back to trying to figure out who had planted his blood. Did Mt. Sinai sell or trade with other hospitals? Maybe they had too much of type A and needed AB, or perhaps they exchanged it for medicines they needed.

Approaching the rec room, he discounted another institution being involved. Cory had a common blood type; it couldn't be in demand. He pushed through the door as an idea hit him.

Franklin was holding a guitar. "Hey, Cory. How you doing?"

"Pretty good. Look, I hate to ask, but can I use your phone to make a call?"

"I could lose my job."

"I know it's a lot to ask, but I'll be fast. I need to ask someone a quick question."

"I don't know . . ."

"My ass is on the line."

"All right." Franklin opened up the door and looked both ways. He closed it and retreated to a corner of the room, waving for Cory to follow him. He handed him his phone. "Stay here. The cameras don't catch here. Hurry up."

"Thanks, man."

Cory dialed a number. "Mount Sinai. How may I direct your call?"

"Jeff Corbin. In the blood bank, please."

"This is Jeff."

"Hey Jeff, it's Cory. Cory Loop."

"Cory? Is that really you?"

"Yeah."

"Oh my God. How you doing?"

"Okay, I guess. Look, I don't have much time. You know I donated blood all the time—"

"Yeah, you were here, like, once a month."

"I need to know who else would have access to a bag I donated."

"What do you mean?"

"Say you take my blood. What do you do with it after I'm done?"

"It gets inventoried and goes into the refrigeration unit."

"And then what? What happens to it? Who can get to it?"

"It stays there until it's requisitioned and pulled from inventory for a transfusion."

"So, a nurse would have access?"

"Yeah, and sometimes a tech or aide."

"Let me ask you, do you know of anyone with access who might have had a record?"

"A record?"

"Yeah, someone who committed a crime."

"Not that I know of, but I don't know everybody who works here. The place is massive."

"I know, but just the people in contact with the blood. Is there anybody new or was new?"

"Not that I remember."

"You're sure?"

"Sorry."

"It's okay, man. Thanks."

"Hey, wait a minute. Now that I think of it, there was this guy, his name was Brian Cliff. I'm not saying he did anything, but he was here for a pretty short period."

"How short?"

"I don't know, maybe a month or so."

"What kind of a guy was he?"

"He kept to himself. Seemed like a regular guy."

"What was his job?"

"He was a records clerk."

"And he had access to the blood?"

"He wouldn't be handling it or anything, but they'd be doing inventory, stuff like that."

"His name was Brian Cliff?"

"Yeah, that's it."

"Thanks, man. I gotta run."

Cory hung up and Franklin said, "Everything all right?"

"Can I squeeze in one more quick call? It's to my lawyer. I got to get it off my mind, or I won't be worth anything trying to show you licks."

Franklin took another look in the hallway. "Hurry up."

Cory dialed as fast as he could and was connected to Worth.

"Mr. Worth, listen, I just found out there was this guy, Brian Cliff, he worked at Mount Sinai for a couple of weeks, right before I was framed. He had access to my blood. It's got to be him."

"Where did you obtain this information?"

"From Jeff Corbin, he works in blood collection. He's been drawing my blood for years."

"In what capacity was Brian Cliff employed?"

"Records clerk, he was doing the blood inventory. Can you do something, like, bring him in?"

"We'll run a background check first. Determine if there is evidence of criminal activity in his past."

"I'll bet there is."

"I'm not a gambler, Mr. Lupinski. I'll be in touch."

"Hold on. Did you see my email about the Leonardo family? Tower lived with them right before he changed his name."

"I've been in court all morning. Just started going through my communications. Allow me some time—"

"I don't have time; the trial is coming up. You said so yourself."

"I'm well aware of the date, Mr. Lupinski. Please be assured that your case is a priority for this office."

"All right, but I want you to get me out of here."

"It's my belief that not enough time—"

"I don't care. Just file for a bail hearing. Ankle bracelet or whatever, I don't care, get me out of here."

"The petition was already prepared. I'll submit it immediately."

Cory hung up and handed the phone back. "Thanks, man. You're a lifesaver."

He took a deep breath. "Okay, let's get to work. Play me that blues lick, but start it on the third. It's my favorite way to play it."

67

It wasn't the cement bed that kept Cory up. It was his fear that every lead seemed to be dying. He'd asked Linda to search the web on Brian Cliff, but she was unable to find anything linking the man to a crime.

Gavin had also gone silent on him. He never responded about the Leonardo family, and Cory had played ping-pong with sending another email. The poor guy's wife was sick, and he didn't want to push him. It wasn't right, and Gavin might get upset and cut off communications.

Cory sent a quick message saying he was thinking about him and his wife and that he hoped she was doing well. He also told him not to forget that Nebraska Medicine was a good option if time was becoming an issue.

Cory read the email from Worth for the tenth time. The subject line was Brian Cliff. He recalled hesitating before opening it. But the body of the message was nothing more than the lawyer asking him to call his office that afternoon.

Was it bad news? If it was something positive, wouldn't the attorney want to tell him in person? That way they could go over what strategy to use. Cory had met with Worth a bunch of times but still couldn't get a read on something like this.

Cory tossed the tablet onto his pillow, recalling how Worth was when he first represented him. The lawyer didn't play it soft with him. He told him he was in deep trouble and had tried to convince him to take a deal.

Worth didn't sugarcoat, he decided. Either way, there wasn't a person on earth who wouldn't opt to deliver bad news by phone. Besides receiving a tip, which was unlikely, Cory couldn't think of another way to find who'd planted his blood at Stein's house.

He needed another Mr. Black, one who wouldn't turn on him. How was he going to get one sitting in jail? He thought how much easier it was with Black around.

He was secretive but effective. Cory remembered what he had said about keeping a secret. He was right. Black had made him a victim by telling him he was in Greenwich.

He wondered about asking the inmates if they knew an operative. Cory killed the idea, thinking the more people that knew, the likelier it was it would get back to Tower.

He thought about Tower and the blood. He had to keep a tight circle, or it would leak out. As he considered it, he became convinced Tower would have used one of the witnesses who put him at Stein's home.

It made sense; the witnesses were already either paid by Tower or indebted to the lawyer. Why bring someone else into the conspiracy? Cory's anger grew as he considered just how much they may have been paid to plant his blood at the scene of the crime.

Cory headed for lunch, fantasizing about getting revenge

on the men who'd testified against him. They deserved to pay for what they were doing to him and his family.

Who was going to even the score if not him? It was risky, but he didn't care if he died trying to get revenge.

As he held his tray out, Cory ran through ideas on torturing the men. As an inmate spooned a plop of potatoes on his dish, Cory smiled. The server said, "You like this shit?"

"Nah, just thinking of something." He didn't want to reveal it was the thought of them begging for their lives that made him smile.

Cory dropped his tray on a table away from the section Franklin was responsible for. He didn't want to talk, and he didn't want to eat. Linda was visiting after lunch, and he didn't want to see her either.

Cory lined up as soon as allowed. As the line grew, Franklin came over.

"Hey, Cory. Why'd you sit all the way over there?"

Cory shrugged.

"You all right?"

"Not feeling so good."

"Sorry."

"I'll be all right. But, uh, I gotta pass on the lesson today."

"No problem. Feel better."

Cory mumbled, "I'll feel better when those bastards are dead."

"I couldn't hear you."

As the inmates began filing out, he said, "Nothing. Forget it."

Cory waited in the pen outside the visitor room. He looked at the other men. They were joking around with each other. Most were heavily tattooed and missing teeth.

As the doors opened, Cory vowed to get revenge on Tower and his accomplices. He thought about turning around, claiming he was sick, and tried to catch a guard's attention as they filed in.

He looked around the man in front of him and caught a glimpse of Linda. Sitting at the table with her was Ava. His eyes welled up. Cory hadn't seen his daughter since he'd run. He wiped a tear away, and a smile burst out on his face.

Cory embraced his sobbing daughter. A guard warned them there was no contact permitted, and Cory held on a second longer. "It's okay, honey. I'm getting out of here, don't you worry."

"Are you sure?"

"A hundred percent."

"When?"

"We're getting really close. Mr. Worth is working on a lead on someone who planted my blood at the scene."

"Wow. Really?"

Given the way he felt about the phone call request from his lawyer, Cory said, "Yeah, but even better is that I'm waiting to hear back from someone who knew Tower before he changed his name. He was in foster care with a family called the Leonardos."

"What is that going to do?"

"Well, we need to understand more about Tower. There's no doubt something happened when he was a kid, and we think we can use it to pressure him. It's hard to do research stuck in here but—"

"Tell me what to do. I want to help."

"I don't want you mixed up in this. My lawyer and me have everything under control. I want to know how you're doing. How is school?"

The hour-long visit flew by. Cory kissed his daughter and

wife and left the room looking over his shoulder. He felt like a different person than the one who walked in. His spirits were as high as his hopes. Ava was not only sympathetic but wanted to help.

Cory felt a tinge of embarrassment at the lust he felt for revenge. He realized he was acting no better than the people who framed him.

68

———

Standing in front of phone number eight, Cory took a deep breath. He grabbed the receiver and punched his lawyer's number in.

"Hi, Mr. Worth."

"Mr. Lupinski. How are you?"

"Okay. I guess."

"You're going to improve, because I heard from the court. Your bail hearing is tomorrow."

"Really?"

"Yes, but remember there's no assurance you'll be released. Understood?"

"Yeah. So, I guess you didn't get anywhere with the guy at the hospital."

"Quite the contrary. I'm not stating he had a role in planting evidence, but Brian Cliff has a criminal record."

"He does?"

"Yes, two vandalism charges, a burglary, and an arson charge. Interestingly, Barney Tower represented Mr. Cliff in three of the four cases."

"It's got to be him."

"We can't jump to conclusions, but I'm encouraged by the connections."

"I told you. Oh, man. I can't believe we've got him."

"We're not there yet."

"Why can't you bring him in? Question him under oath."

"Deposition is an option. However, I'm unsure what we'll learn. People like Mr. Cliff tend to lie or take the Fifth."

"But at least we'll know it's him."

"I'm aware of that. I was considering approaching the DA. We can inform him of the circumstances surrounding Mr. Cliff and the witness Mr. Ruiz."

"You think he'll drop the charges?"

"No, but I believe he'd be amenable to allowing for your release."

"Tower will find out. He'll go on offense and pressure these guys. He might even have them killed."

"Hold on, Mr. Lupinski. Mr. Tower cannot act with impunity."

"You don't know him. I told you from the beginning about him. I want to wait until we have everything we need. So much against Tower, that he has to back down."

"I understand your apprehension, but we don't have the time."

"Can't you get me a postponement?"

"Not without revealing what we discovered."

"Damn. I still want to wait. Just a little longer, okay?"

"If you wish, but what about Mr. Cliff?"

"Don't depose him yet. I mean, get everything ready, but I don't want to tip Tower off."

"I understand your fears, but my legal advice is to bring what we've uncovered about the possible collusion to the DA."

"No, it'll backfire. I need you to hold off."

"Though it's against my better judgment, I'll hold off notifying the DA. However, I must warn you, time is running out to mount a proper defense."

"Can't we bring this up at the trial?"

"This amounts to hearsay, which is inadmissible. If the judge even allows it, the prosecutor will tear it to shreds."

"I need a little more time."

"You're not planning anything dangerous if you're released, are you?"

BACK IN HIS CELL, Cory checked his email. There was nothing from Gavin. He didn't know what to do. He needed information on Tower as a kid but was constrained by the inability to search the entire web for clues.

An inmate, pushing a cart by his cell, said, "Hey, Music Man! You want a paper or book?"

"No thanks."

As the inmate moved away, Cory had an idea. He calculated the year as 1985. It was when Tower would have moved in with the Leonardos. Now, where to begin?

Cory knew searching the archives of New York City's newspapers would take a ton of time, but he had nothing better to do. Cory figured the *Daily News*, which liked to play it sensational, would be the place to start.

He navigated to their archives tab. Cory wasn't sure what he was looking for but would search for something disturbing involving a kid or family.

The screen was a thumbnail of the front pages of the day's paper. He sat back; the task was daunting. He wondered whether if what had happened was so heinous it would make front-page news.

It was possible but worth the try. He scrolled through headlines: President Reagan pressuring the Russians; the introduction of New Coke; a devastating earthquake in Mexico City; the hijacking of TWA flight 847; and terrorists commandeering a ship named the *Achille Lauro*. He paused looking at the front-page image of the famine in Ethiopia.

The hopelessness of the situation in Africa made him think. Was his search futile, or should he not be deterred by what seemed desperate but in comparison wasn't?

69

———

Cory blinked his eyes several times before standing. He stretched his back. He'd been scanning old newspapers for two hours and was only in the middle of the year. Whatever he was searching for, if there was anything, could have happened any time before Tower was taken into the Leonardo home.

Cory had heard of kids being shuttled from one foster home to another. Something could have happened when he was five and he was put into another family's home at that time before transferring to the Leonardos.

Taking two hours to go through half a year, he calculated it would take forty hours to go through just the headlines of the morning and late editions. Cory shook his head and picked up the tablet. An email had come in. It was from Gavin:

"Thanks for your concern about Betty. She's doing better today.

"I forgot to tell you about Richard. You know my memory ain't what it used to be!

"It really was a very sad situation for the young man. He

was the victim of abuse, by his own father, if you can believe it, and the state took over. They had good intentions, but the system failed him.

"The first family they put him with ended up being the same situation he was rescued from. It's incredible. I don't blame him for taking matters into his own hands.

"I remember watching the Gandhi assassination on TV when Betty told me about Richard. Of course, we didn't know him at the time, but we felt bad for any kid having to go through that.

"I don't recall where the Leonardos moved to, but Betty says they moved to Staten Island. She said she remembered the street was Dawson Circle because it reminded her of the TV show *Dawson's Creek*.

"Thanks for the tip on Nebraska Medical. Let's hope we don't have to take the trip.

"Best regards, Gavin."

Cory reread the email. He tried to read between the lines. What had happened to Tower? Was Gavin cryptic on purpose? Tower had been abused. Not only by his father but by another family.

Cory circled the cell. How could the people in charge of protecting children put him into an abusive household? Gavin had said Tower took matters into his own hands. What did he do?

He read the message again. Gavin mentioned Gandhi being killed. All that Cory knew about Gandhi was that he was a leader in India who preached nonviolent resistance. He recalled a movie he'd seen about him, but it was set decades before Tower was born.

Cory Googled the leader. The summary said he'd been assassinated in 1948. What the heck was Gavin talking about? Was he getting dementia? He scrolled down. Gandhi must have been a popular name, he thought, especially for leaders.

He clicked on a woman, Indira Gandhi. He looked at the summary of the former prime minister. Bingo. She was killed on October 31st in 1984.

Cory had a date stamp. He wouldn't have to page through years of reporting. He looked at the *Daily News* from October 30th, the day before Gandhi was killed. The front-page headline was about a New York congressman suspected of corruption.

He went page by page. Cory saw an article on page nine whose headline read, "Father Arrested." Cory read the piece: a man was taken into custody for chaining his son to the car door while he drank in a Flatbush bar. The kid was five. It didn't fit.

Cory went to the paper for the 31st. He expected to see a headline about the killing of the Indian leader. But the morning edition featured a story about a woman involved in a scam of the telephone company. He opened the late edition. The headline screamed, "Gandhi Shot Eight Times."

He paged through the paper. The first eight pages were coverage of the assassination. Cory swiped to page nine. A headline halfway down caught his eye: Eleven-year-old Fatally Stabs Man.

Cory held his breath as he read the article:

In a late-breaking story, police were summoned to a Hell's Kitchen apartment at two this morning. Upon entering the home, they found the body of forty-two-year-old Edward Rosen in one of the home's bedrooms.

Mr. Rosen's wife told police she had been sleeping and that sounds of a struggle woke her up. She went to investigate and found her husband had been stabbed multiple times. Mrs. Rosen informed police she believed an eleven-year-old child they were foster parenting had stabbed her husband to death.

The minor, whose name is being withheld, was taken into custody and is being held in a juvenile detention center pending an investigation.

Cory reread the article, doing mental math to see if the age fit how old Tower would have been in 1984. It did. Why had Tower killed his foster father?

Cory's mind raced. Had Tower served time for the murder? If so, he was living with the Leonardos in 1985; how could he have gotten out so soon?

The killing was what Gavin had referred to. He had mentioned abuse by his biological father. Had the abuse damaged Tower so badly as a child that he snapped and stabbed his foster father?

Cory had heard of situations where someone went into a trance, mistaking a person for someone else. Had Tower thought Mr. Rosen was his father and stabbed him? Then he recalled Gavin's message.

Cory pulled it up. He said that Tower was subjected to abuse again and that Child Protective Services had failed. Had Mr. Rosen abused Tower as well? It was hard to believe.

Envisioning Tower as a helpless child, Cory felt a surge of sympathy for the lawyer. What a terrible thing for a child to experience.

Cory felt the need to reinforce protection against any inappropriate contact or speech his kids were subjected to. It had to be reported, no matter who did it. He'd tell Linda to say something to Tommy and Ava immediately.

Cory's thoughts went back to Tower. What next? He had to look into the Rosen family and knew they had lived in an area of Manhattan known as Hell's Kitchen.

70

Cory was ferried with eight other inmates in a van to
the Centre Street Court House. Legs shackled and hands
cuffed, the nine of them snaked their way up a beige stairway
to a small cell.

As the men sat on metal benches, a guard unlocked the
door. "Lupinski. You're up."

Cory was taken outside and his legs unshackled. He was
led into the courtroom. He scanned the audience, spotting
Linda in the first row. She smiled and waved.

Cory's legs quivered. He had to get out. Worth stepped
over and showed Cory to one of two chairs behind a table.
Cory turned around, mouthing, 'I Love you' to his wife.
Worth said, "Don't say anything. Regardless of how it goes.
If they deny bail and there's an outburst, it'll be
remembered."

"I got it. You think I'll get out?"

"These proceedings are difficult to predict."

"All rise, this court is now in session."

Everyone stood as a bald man in black robes made his

way to his seat. He adjusted his glasses as the bailiff announced Cory's case.

After both sides staked out their positions, the judge asked them to approach the bench. Cory concentrated on hearing what was being said. Leaning forward, he worked his ears as if he were at a jam session playing a tune he didn't know.

The assistant district attorney was objecting to what Worth was saying, telling the judge that Cory had run once. Worth assured the judge with a monitoring device and the amount of money at risk, his client wouldn't run.

The judge looked at Worth. Cory stretched his neck, picking up the question posed: "Will you take responsibility for your client? Guaranteeing his appearance in this court?"

Worth nodded. Was this going to be successful? Cory wanted to signal Linda but kept his eyes glued on the discussion. The prosecutor shook his head. Cory heard him beg the judge, repeat that he'd run before and had means to do it again.

The judge acknowledged the concern and thanked them. The lawyers retreated to their stations. Cory studied Worth. He'd make a great poker player. Cory leaned in but the attorney put a finger to his lips.

The judge moved the mic back in place. "The court will grant the release of Mr. Lupinski to afford him an opportunity to mount a defense for his upcoming trial. The release will be subject to maintaining the monetary bail posted, require Mr. Lipinski to wear an ankle monitoring device, and bear the expense of a twenty-four-hour guard."

Cory turned to Linda, and the judge said, "Mr. Lupinski, let me warn you that this release is conditional. The slightest violation will land you back in prison."

"I understand, Your Honor. Thank you so much."

The judge pounded his gavel, and Worth led Cory out. He was going to be free, for a while.

OUTFITTED WITH AN ANKLE DEVICE, Cory bounded up the stairs, leaving the six-foot guard at his building's entrance. The door to his apartment was open, and Linda and the kids rushed to embrace him.

A tearful reunion was broken up by Tommy. "Let Daddy see the banner. Look, did you see it?"

"That's super! You made that?"

Tommy beamed, "Yeah. Ava helped too."

Arms around both kids, Cory said, "You don't know how good it feels to be home with you."

Ava said, "We're glad you're home, Dad."

He kissed both of them and walked around the apartment. He stepped into his studio.

"Dad, you must have missed playing."

"You bet I did. I played a little with this guard, Franklin, gave him a couple of lessons. He was a good guy."

"You can play all you want now."

Before Cory could respond, Linda said, "How about a home-cooked meal?"

"Music to my ears."

IT WAS 10 P.M. Cory read two books to Tommy and stopped in Ava's room. He sat on the edge of the bed. "You all right?"

"Yeah, why?"

"I know it's been hard on you."

"I'm okay."

"Kids giving you a hard time at school?"

She shrugged. "It's okay."

"No, it's not."

"Don't worry, Dad. I don't let it bother me anymore. They don't know what they're talking about."

"I promise, this will be over soon. We're close to exposing the plot against me, and now that I'm home, I can really move things along."

"I can help."

"Thanks. Right now, concentrate on your schoolwork. You'll need good grades to get into college. If I need you, I'll let you know. Sleep well, princess."

Cory plopped on the couch next to Linda. He put his legs on the table. "It's going to take some getting used to this." He tugged his pants up, revealing the ankle device.

"It's a small price to pay."

"And the guard. But I don't care. You can't imagine what it was like in there."

"I'm sure it was scary."

Cory shrugged. "Yeah, I'm not going back, I can tell you that."

"God forbid."

"Don't worry." Cory nestled into his wife.

She put her arms around him. "I missed you so much."

Cory put his hands under her sweater. "You feel so good. Let's go to the bedroom inside."

The warmth of Linda's silky skin felt good. Cory didn't want to slip out of bed, but there was work to be done. He slid his arm out from under her neck. Linda stirred but didn't awaken.

Cory scooped up his clothes, dressing by the door. He left the bedroom and closed the studio door behind him. He now had unfettered access to the information on the web.

He'd start with the Rosen family. Cory had located their address in Hell's Kitchen, an area next to the Theater District, but the wife had moved shortly after the scandal had broken.

Cory empathized with the woman. Unless she'd turned a blind eye to her husband's perversion, she'd been drawn into something evil through no fault of her own.

71

———

Cory searched the *Daily News* for information on the
Rosens. The first name of the man Tower had killed as a child
was Jack. He couldn't find his wife's name. He tried the *New
York Post* archives. A picture on page four caught his
attention.

A kid was being led down the stairs by a police officer.
His face had been blocked out with a black bar. In the
doorway was a woman in a housecoat. The caption read, "At
the murder scene, Jody Rosen watches her foster child taken
into custody".

Cory leaned in. The black-and-white picture was grainy,
but Cory could feel the anguish on her face. It was a mess, he
thought. He studied the little boy. It was Tower as a kid. He
looked so small. He was just a bit older than his own son.

He wondered what state of mind Tower was in. Was he
crying? Did he realize what he'd done? He envisioned Tower
methodically planning the attack. He could see the lawyer
unemotionally stabbing his stepfather.

In Cory's mind, the man deserved his fate, but it was still
a chilling act. He considered the series of events that led to

Tower taking a man's life. Tower lost his mother early, and his father, instead of caring for him, abused him.

Compounding the damage, a government agency responsible for protecting kids failed to protect Tower. The agency not only ordered him back into the house with his father but failed to vet the foster parents they placed him with.

It was inexcusable. Cory felt for Tower as a kid, forced to fight abuse. No wonder he changed his name. Tower was looking to put distance between him and his past.

He knew the lawyer was irreparably damaged, and it was understandable. But why frame Cory? Was it the revenge thing, a controlling obsession, what?

Cory stared at the newspaper photo wondering how many other kids were being destroyed. He shook his head and hit the print button.

He went back to searching. Cory needed to verify the circumstances. He needed background and tried to track down Jody Rosen. She'd know what happened, but would she be willing to talk?

No matter where he searched, he couldn't find her. He checked the obituary pages, and bingo, there was a Judith Rosen who died a dozen years ago. The woman, a resident of Queens, fit as Tower's foster mother.

Cory tried to clear his mind. One door had shut. Should he tell Worth to depose Brian Cliff over the blood? Maybe Gavin could provide more background.

He opened the email conversation he'd had with the Facebook contact from the West Village. Reading through, he decided to follow the lead to the one thing Child Protection Services had seemingly done right, placing Tower into the Leonardo home.

Gavin had mentioned Staten Island as the place the Leonardos had moved to. Cory navigated to New York City's property tax site. He checked the street Gavin's wife mentioned and crossed himself.

He went back twenty years and plugged it in the portal. He scrolled through all the listings on the street and came up empty.

He went to the next year and the following one until finding the Leonardo tax bill. Jumping to the year ahead, he found the names of the people who'd bought the Leonardo home.

He Googled for a phone number and checked the time. It was 11:20 p.m. Not a time to call if you wanted cooperation.

THE NEXT MORNING, Cory made waffles and said, "I'll be right back. Gotta make a quick call."

He slid into the studio and called the people who'd bought the Leonardo home. They were helpful, giving him the address and telephone number they had. Cory checked it on Google Maps. They were living in Bensonhurst.

Cory called the Leonardo home. Cory held his breath as it rang. "Hello?"

"Mr. Leonardo?"

"Yes, who is this?"

"You don't know me, sir. But I—"

"I'm hanging up. Goodbye."

The phone clicked off. Cory hit redial. "Is that you again?"

"Yes but—"

"I'm blocking your number. Goodbye, don't call again."

"Please." Cory heard a dial tone. "Damn it." He called back but it went straight to voice mail. He left a message saying he needed to talk about Richard Sullivan.

72

───────────

Cory left a dozen messages for Leonardo but never received a call back. He had to talk to him. Leonardo could be the only person who knew the entire story.

He wanted to go to Bensonhurst, but there was the ankle bracelet and a guard outside. Evading the guard was doable, but the GPS monitor would set off an alarm as soon as he was a hundred yards away.

He fingered the bracelet. Was there a way to get it off without destroying it? The guy who fitted it warned if he cut it off, a digital alarm would be sent.

Cory popped a question into Google: *How to take an ankle monitoring bracelet off.* He couldn't believe what came up. He scanned a set of four videos, clicking on one titled "Man Shows How to Remove a GPS Tracking Ankle Monitoring Device."

He watched the three-minute video. The man showed step-by-step how to safely remove one without triggering an alarm. He rewatched it. Nothing magical was involved and only required a screwdriver and a butter knife.

Cory pulled up his pant leg and compared his device to

the one in the video. They were close. It was risky, because if he damaged it, they'd know. Chances were he'd end up behind bars again.

He watched another video. This one took under three minutes to get free. It just seemed too easy. Didn't law enforcement realize these instructions were out there?

Cory called Leonardo again, but it went to voice mail. He left another message and went into the kitchen. Opening the junk drawer, he fished around, pulling out a butter knife he'd used as a scraper and a screwdriver.

He checked the time. He had almost four hours until Linda came back from her part-time job. Cory took his laptop into the living room and sat on the floor. He played the video, imitating the way the man jammed the knife in between two parts of the device.

After wriggling it for half a minute, a cap popped off on the inside and slipped to the floor. The next part was more difficult. The now exposed inside of the bracelet had two screws that needed undoing.

Reaching the screws was hard. He pretzeled himself and worked both free. It took five minutes and strained his neck, but the device came off. He checked it. The red light was still on.

Cory grabbed his jacket. He looked out the window. The guard was parked in front of the entrance. Cory slipped out of the apartment. He made his way to the basement and up the cellar stairs.

Heart pounding, Cory hopped over the fence and headed to the subway station. He wondered whether he was on the way to ending his nightmare or setting himself up for jail.

73

Cory turned off Nineteenth Avenue and headed down Seventy-First Street. He checked the addresses and crossed the road. The house he was looking for was a brick-faced, two-story home. He walked up the driveway to the door. A man was singing opera. He rang the bell.

The door opened as far as a chain allowed. A white-haired man said, "The Buratos live upstairs."

"Mr. Leonardo?"

"And you are?"

"Cory Lupinski. You don't know me, but I need to talk to you."

"I'm sorry, son, but with the senior scams, I don't talk to strangers."

"That's smart but—"

"Goodbye."

As the door started closing, Cory said, "Please, hold on a second."

Leonardo peered out. Cory said, "Look, I'm going to be straight with you. Just being here could get me put back behind bars."

Leonardo leaned back.

"Don't be afraid. I'm not going to do anything. I just want to talk about Richard Sullivan."

"Richard Sullivan?"

"Yes, he was one of your foster children, right?"

Leonardo wagged his head. "Yes, I'd never forget him. He hasn't done anything, has he?"

"It's very complicated, but he changed his name to Barney Tower."

"Oh, right. I remember that."

"Do you mind if we could talk inside?"

Leonardo eyed Cory. "I guess that would be all right." He took the chain off. "Come in."

"Thanks. I really appreciate this."

Cory followed the old man into a room. A recliner was centered in front of a TV.

Cory said, "Ah, Pavarotti. Is this the PBS special?

"Yes. It's one of my favorites."

"What a voice, what a personality. Pavarotti was larger than life. I wish he was still around."

Leonardo shut off the TV, saying, "Men like him only come around every hundred years or so."

"I guess so."

"Before him, it was Caruso."

"He had a powerful voice, but I think Pavarotti could finesse the emotion."

"I don't disagree, but when Caruso was around, opera singers didn't really act."

"You're right. I never thought of it that way."

Leonardo flashed a smile. "Sit. You want some tea?"

"No, no. Look, thanks for talking to me. I know this came out of nowhere, but I need your help."

Leonardo lowered himself into the recliner. "If I can help, I will. What's this about Richard?"

"This is going to sound crazy, but someone is framing me for murder, and that person is Richard Sullivan, now known as Barney Tower."

"Really? That's serious."

"I realize that. Let me tell you the whole story." Cory told him everything that happened.

"That's a lot to absorb. But I still don't understand what you want from me."

"I'm trying to understand what happened to Richard. It could explain a lot and maybe something will help. Tell me about his past. How did he come to live with you?"

"Well, Jenny, my wife, she passed eight years ago—"

"I'm sorry."

"That's okay. Anyway, we got married late and never had kids, so we decided to become foster parents. It was challenging, but we enjoyed it. But most of all, we helped a few kids along the way. One time, we had two very troubled kids. They were abused. I still have a hard time talking about it."

"Was that Richard?"

"No. He came after. You see, it was good like I said, but it took a toll on us, and we decided it was time to stop taking kids in. A couple of years after we did, a social worker we knew at Child Protection came to us about Richard. I mean, we knew about what happened before she approached us."

"What happened?"

"I'm not saying we were perfect foster parents, but we provided a stable, loving home for all the children, and the two troubled kids did especially well while they were with Jenny and me. It was why they asked us to help with Richard."

"He was troubled?"

Leonardo nodded. "If losing his mother in a car crash when he was only five wasn't traumatic enough, his father abused him."

"Sexually?"

"Yes, I'm afraid so."

"How'd it come out?"

"Richard had gotten really quiet and wouldn't eat. He'd lost ten pounds and looked terrible. A mother of one of his playmates was concerned and pulled it out of him. She called Child Protection Services and reported the abuse, refusing to allow Richard to go home."

"Good for her. Then what happened?"

"The agency screwed up, is what happened. They put Richard back with the father, and it got worse. The kid ran away and was found by a cop walking around Union Square, I think it was."

"He could've been kidnapped."

"I know. Then, CPS put him into a foster home with a first-timer."

"The Rosen bastard?"

"Yep."

"How the hell did that happen?"

"I'm not making excuses, but the system is frankly over-whelmed. There's no way they should have placed Richard in a foster home with no experience."

"When Richard stabbed the Rosen man to death, was it a mental thing where he confused Rosen for his father?"

Leonardo shook his head. "No. I didn't see the medical files but was told an examination showed beyond doubt that he'd undergone recent abuse."

"Bastard."

"It's heartbreaking."

"Did he have to go to trial or anything?"

"No. Once he was examined, it was pretty much over. The kid was just trying to protect himself."

"What happened to the father?"

"After Richard ran away, they finally arrested the father for abuse, and he was beaten to death in jail."

"Got what he deserved."

"It was all very tragic."

"How was Richard when you had him?"

"You know, the funny thing is, he was pretty much okay. He kept to himself and dived into his schoolwork. We took him to therapy. Twice a week in the beginning, then weekly for about three years."

"No problems?"

"He'd have bad nightmares, but who wouldn't?"

"You know, he became a super successful lawyer."

"I'm not surprised, he was a smart young man."

"What was he like?"

"Quiet and kind of a loner. And controlling, very controlling."

"He didn't trust anyone, I'd guess."

"That's true."

"Tell me more about the controlling thing."

"I don't know if competitive is the right word, but Richard, he wanted to be in control, to run things."

"What do you mean by that?"

"He was particular about the way he wanted things. I guess these days, they'd call him obsessive."

74

———————

CORY COLORED A RUBBER BAND WITH A BLACK MARKER, using it to keep the bracelet around his ankle. He wanted to tell Linda what he'd done, but she'd be mad, not excited like he was.

He replayed the conversation with Leonardo. What he learned about Tower's past was tragic, but was it enough to make the lawyer back off?

Worth wanted to go to the district attorney with what they knew about the man they believed planted the blood and Tower's connection with one witness. Cory felt it wasn't enough and worried Tower would find a way to turn it against him.

Cory considered telling Worth about Tower's past, but it wouldn't mean anything to the DA. Cory would keep the disturbing information to himself.

He couldn't get the image of Tower as a kid being abused out of his head. He was about Tommy's age. You couldn't get more vulnerable. He was brave enough to say something, and instead of saving the kid, the child agency put him right back with his father, who was abusing him.

The father probably retaliated against Tower for saying something. Cory wondered about the ramped-up abuse. Tower couldn't get back at his father, who was killed in jail, like he did the foster parent he stabbed to death.

But that didn't stop Cory from speculating what the lawyer would have done. Considering revenge raised a question in his mind.

He tapped his cell. Leonardo's number was still blocked, and the call went to voice mail. "Hi, this is Cory. I came to see you about Richard Sullivan. I wanted—"

"Hello. Sorry about that."

"No problem. I was wondering about the social worker who put Richard back with his father and then with the Rosens. Was it the same person?"

"Well, there are a couple of people involved in every case, but Richard's case manager was Lily Martinez."

"Is there a way to get in touch with her?"

"I'm afraid not. She committed suicide, or at least that was what it was called."

"Why do you say that?"

"They say she jumped off a building. But there were witnesses who saw her being led by a man into the building where it happened."

"When was this?"

"Not long after Richard moved out."

"Didn't the police investigate?"

"Yes, and there was no doubt that Martinez was depressed. She felt responsible for what happened to Richard and left the agency right after he came to live with us."

"Did Richard ever mention her?"

"He didn't like her for obvious reasons. She tried several times to reach him, but he wanted no part of her."

Cory finished the call and tried to make sense of what he was told. Had the social worker committed suicide, or had Tower somehow killed her?

He paced the apartment. Tower had killed his foster father in retaliation for being sexually abused. But planning and killing a social worker who'd made a mistake was a completely different matter. Was Tower someone who could premeditate the murder of a caseworker? Years later? Cory needed more on the social worker and was about to Google her when his phone rang. It was Worth.

"Mr. Worth."

"Mr. Lupinski. I hope you're well."

"All is good. What's up?"

"I'm following up regarding the information on Mr. Tower's possible collusion."

"What about it?"

"My recommendation is to go to the District Attorney. While the data is not legally compelling, I believe it'll persuade them to delay the trial."

"Okay, but give me a week, okay?"

"That'll put us close into the period we need to prep for the trial."

"But you said once you go to them, they'll postpone it."

"That's my belief, but you can't face a charge like this without proper preparation."

"I understand, but that's what I want to do."

As soon as Linda left the apartment, Cory looked out the window. He watched his wife wave to the guard as she got into an Uber. As it drove away, he let go of the drapes.

Cory took the ankle device off and stuck it in his night-stand. He dug to the bottom of his underwear drawer and took an envelope out. He put his coat and a wool cap on and stepped into the hallway. It was empty. He scampered down the stairs into the basement.

Cory emerged from the Lexington Avenue subway station, keeping his head down as he walked. It was now or never, he thought, following a woman into Tower's office building.

He waited for an empty elevator and took it. As the doors slid open, Cory heard voices in a panic. The reception area was empty, but down the hall two women were leaning over a man lying on the floor.

"Mr. Tower, Mr. Tower! Are you all right?"

"Maggie, call an ambulance."

Cory ran down the corridor. "What's going on?"

"He collapsed, just like that."

"I told him to go to the doctor, he was complaining about pain in his chest."

"It could be a heart attack." Cory bent down. Tower was unconscious. "Is he breathing?"

"I don't know."

Cory put his hand by the lawyer's nose. "I don't feel anything! You know how to do CPR?"

The woman nodded. She pinched Tower's nose as the other woman said, "An ambulance is on the way."

Cory stepped back as they tried to revive Tower, saying, "Is it working? Is he breathing?"

"No."

"Keep doing it. He can't die. Come on, Tower, breathe. Breathe, damn it, breathe!"

As the sirens got louder, Cory pressed the elevator button.

He had to leave. A ding sounded. Cory said, "Is he breathing yet?"

"No."

Cory stepped into the elevator wondering if his luck could get any worse.

75

—————

Cory said, "Do me a favor and read to Tommy tonight."

"What's the matter?"

"Nothing."

"Don't tell me that. You didn't say anything the whole time we ate. Ava said you kept making calls. She's worried. She thinks something is going on with the trial."

"I'll tell her not to worry. I got everything under control."

"It doesn't feel like you do."

"I'm just worried a little. It's natural."

"You sure?"

"Go read to Tommy. I gotta pick up my guitar and play to clear my head."

As soon as he closed the door to the studio, he pulled his phone out and called the attorney's office. Tower was in stable condition. Cory would go see the lawyer tomorrow.

—————

"You're not going to work?"

"My stomach is bothering me."

"Didn't you take anything?"

"Yeah, but it's not working. I gotta go to the toilet, again."

Linda trotted to the bathroom and Cory went to the bedroom. He unhooked the monitoring device and put on a jacket. He opened the underwear drawer, pulling an envelope out. He stuffed it inside his coat and peeked out the window. Confirming the guard was sitting in his car, he headed to the door.

Linda came out of the bathroom. "Where are you going?"

"To end this nightmare."

As he put his hand on the doorknob, she said, "No! You can't leave. They'll know—"

Cory lifted his pants leg.

"You took it off? What, are you crazy?"

"Don't worry—"

"Don't worry? They're going to put you back in jail. Is that what you want?"

"It's going to be okay."

"I swear, you go to jail, I'm not visiting, you hear?" Linda ran to the bathroom.

Cory slipped into the hallway and tiptoed down the stairs. He took the basement exit and hopped the rear fence.

***

CORNELL WEILL'S lobby was bustling. The reception line was long. Cory went into the coffee shop, poured a cup of java, and headed to the elevator bank. His phone rang. It was Linda. He swiped it away.

The cardiology unit was on the third floor. Tower was in 301 W. It was several doors down from the nurses' station.

Cory smiled at a nurse sitting behind the counter as he walked by.

The door to the lawyer's room was open. Cory paused before going in. The TV was on. Cory walked into the private room.

The lawyer was sleeping. He crept to his bedside.

Tower's skin had a gray cast to it. A tube fed a supply of oxygen to his nose. It was the first time Cory had seen stubble on the attorney.

Cory looked at the man who had torn him from his family. The man who'd double-crossed him and was planning to send him to prison for the rest of his life.

Cory eyed the chair on the other side of the bed. A stack of pillows sat on it. Cory could use one to smother the evil lawyer. It would be easy. Tower wouldn't put up much of a fight.

He was vulnerable. It'd be over before the attorney would know what was happening. Cory heard footsteps and turned to the door. It was a nurse hurrying to another room.

Cory's stomach dropped as he circled the bed. Standing over Tower, Cory now had a view of the door.

76

Cory moved his hand slowly toward the lawyer. He nudged him gently. Tower was completely out of it. Cory hesitated for a long moment. He asked himself if it would all work out.

He grabbed Tower's shoulder and jostled him. "Barney, wake up. Come on, open your eyes."

The lawyer stirred, but his eyes remained shut.

Cory lifted the attorney's arm and dropped it onto his abdomen. Tower grumbled, opening his eyes. "Hey, take it easy."

Cory hovered over his nemesis. "It's me. Look at me."

Blinking, the lawyer focused his eyes. "Lupinski. What are you doing here?"

Tower's hand crept toward the call button. Cory snatched it away. "If I wanted to kill you, I would have done it already. But I'm not like you."

"What do you want?"

"You got to stop framing me."

"I have no idea what you're referring to."

"Stop the bullshit. I'm telling you, you better stop setting me up for the Stein murder."

"Or what? You'll kill me?"

"No." Cory reached into his pocket, pulling the newspaper photo out. He held it in front of Tower's face.

Tower lifted his head off the pillow. "What is that?"

"It's you. I know all about you, Richard Sullivan."

Tower blinked rapidly. "Who?"

"You know damn well that's your name."

Tower batted Cory's hand away. "Get out of my room."

"If you don't get those witnesses and Brian Cliff to tell the truth, I'll go public with this. The whole world will know about you and your father."

Tower's face didn't reveal anything.

"And I won't stop there. I'll tell them about what you did to Martinez, the social worker."

"I didn't do anything to her. It was ruled a suicide."

Cory held up a hand. "That's bullshit, and you know it."

Tower said nothing.

"Look, I can't imagine how difficult it was for you. I feel for you, man. But I'm warning you, the truth about you has been buried for a long time, and it can stay that way. If you don't end this madness, I'll go to the press. You'll have to live through it all over again."

Tower's eyes narrowed. "Just who do you think you're playing with?"

"Who? Richard Sullivan, that's who. And this ain't no game."

Hand shaking, Cory put the article on the lawyer's chest and walked out.

Tower closed his eyes, contemplating his next move. He was exhausted but steeled himself. What had seemed perfect —revenge on Lupinski while getting O'Rourke out of a jam —was on the verge of exploding.

He admonished himself for failing to take the time to think things through. The connection between Stein and Lupinski had proved too tempting. Even with a body to deal with, he shouldn't have rushed.

He never took risks, especially when it came to thugs like O'Rourke. The gangster compared himself to old-time mafia bosses who put layers between their instructions and the goons carrying them out. But after defending him a couple of times, he knew O'Rourke was nothing more than a hoodlum. One with an explosive temper.

Tower smiled, recalling O'Rourke's bravado, volunteering his punks as witnesses and to plant the blood. He wondered who was stupider, the gangster or Lupinski, who had suddenly grown a pair of balls.

He'd have to play it carefully, but he saw two paths out of the mess.

Cory slipped back into his apartment and collapsed on the sofa. Linda came in. "You're crazy. Somebody had to see you."

"No. Everything is cool."

"Where did you go?"

"To see Tower."

"Have you lost your mind?" She went to the window saying, "The police are probably on their way."

"It's going to be okay."

"Okay? You went to see the guy you say is framing you—"

"He is."

"And you don't think he's going to tell the cops you were there? The hospital has cameras all over the place to back him up."

Cory went into the bedroom to get the ankle bracelet. Linda followed behind, saying, "I won't have the kids see you getting arrested. They've been through enough."

He paused before reaching into the drawer. "If you're worried, I get it. Take the kids out to dinner. They haven't been out in a while."

"So, I'm supposed to have a grand old time eating in some restaurant when my husband is getting arrested?"

"Nothing is going to happen. Trust me on this, okay?"

Linda threw up her hands and walked away.

Exhausted, Cory headed into the studio. He passed the empty stand his favorite Gibson usually sat on and picked up his Martin DC. Cory strapped it on and fished a pick off a tray.

He noodled around, playing parts of a Jeff Beck solo he'd transcribed as a teenager before playing Led Zeppelin's "Stairway to Heaven." He felt himself smiling that he'd remembered Jimmy Page's solo.

He reached to cue up a backup track, realizing his exhaustion had been replaced with energy. It was something he felt every time he played. He might get frustrated trying to learn something, but he never tired of playing.

Cory chose a blues track in the key of E and swapped out his acoustic for a pearl-white Fender. He plugged it in and put headphones on. He ran a couple of scales before turning the track on.

Cory let a bar go by, closed his eyes and began improvising. Before he knew it, the ten-minute track ended. He hit replay and worked out a lick he stumbled upon. Halfway in, he owned it.

He played for an hour longer. Cory smiled as he hung his guitar up. Once again, music had given him a place to retreat to. He hoped he wouldn't have to use it to escape from a jail cell.

77

Linda said, "I can't believe Tower didn't report you."

"It's been almost two days." Cory laughed. "He still can, so I'll hold off saying I told you so."

She frowned. "It was still stupid."

Cory shrugged.

"I've got to pick up Tommy from tae kwon do."

Linda left, and Cory went into the studio. He sat at the keyboard toying with chord progressions for the bridge of one of the songs he had penned behind bars.

He changed a dark minor chord to a bright major as his phone rang. It was Worth.

"Hello."

"Mr. Lupinski, I have great news!"

"You do?"

"Yes. The district attorney just phoned. They're going to drop the charges against you."

"Finally! What happened?"

"As I understand it, evidence surfaced proving William O'Rourke was responsible for the murder."

Cory looked out the window. The guard was gone. "So, that's it, it's over?"

"Yes. There are formalities that need to be executed—"

"What about the money we put up for bail?"

"It'll take a week or so to get it released, but I'll handle that."

"Can I ask you something?"

"Absolutely."

"You never believed me, did you?"

Worth hesitated. "Your case was extraordinarily—"

"Yes or no?"

"Initially, no. The evidence was overwhelming, and you had nothing to support your conspiracy claim."

"I didn't think so. That's why I changed lawyers."

"You were determined and correct in your assertion."

"I couldn't have done it without your help. I appreciate everything you've done for me."

"Sometimes obtaining justice can be messy. But your case reminds me why I became a lawyer in the first place."

"I'm glad you did."

"As you can imagine, there's substantial paperwork that needs to be filed. I'll be in touch."

Cory hung up and screamed, "Yes." He took off the ankle device and grabbed his jacket. He ran down the stairs and trotted toward the studio his son was taking classes at.

When Linda saw him coming at them, she stopped in her tracks and looked around. Cory raised his arms. "It's over. It's over."

<hr>

"WHO WANTS PANCAKES?"

"Me, Daddy."

"How about you, Ava?"

"Sure, Dad. But only one."

Linda put a pod into the coffee maker. As the java dripped out, she said, "Look what's on."

Everyone turned their attention to the TV. The newscaster said, "In a stunning turn of events, William Dublin O'Rourke, known as the Monk, was indited for the murder of Lew Stein. Authorities originally arrested Grammy-winning artist Cory Lupinski, whose stage name was Cory Loop, for the killing."

A picture of Cory onstage filled the screen. "Stein had been the performer's manager until a dispute over missing funds ended the relationship."

Cory's image was replaced by one of Billy O'Rourke. The anchor continued, "The district attorney believes that Mr. Stein, a known gambler, was indebted to Mr. O'Rourke, who allegedly heads a gambling ring."

Ava said, "That's the guy who did it?"

"That's what it looks like. I'm just glad it's over."

The doorbell rang. Linda looked at her husband. "Who's at the door at this hour?"

Cory said, "Keep your eyes on the pancakes."

He opened the door. It was Donny.

"Hey, bro, figured you wanted this back as soon as possible." He handed the guitar case to Cory.

"Thanks, man. It's good to have my Gibby back."

78

———————

Cory took his Gibson out of the case and was placing it on its stand when Linda came in.

"How was the session?"

"Good. Felt really good playing with Rocky again."

"Been a long time."

"Looks like the blackballing is over. I'm back in the rotation."

"Good. You get the mail?"

"No. I'll run down."

Cory put his key in the mailbox and took out a handful of mail. Walking up the stairs, he sorted it. A bill from Con Edison, a life insurance offer, a sales piece from Visa, and a letter.

It was from Tower Law Offices. He stepped inside his apartment. Cory opened the envelope.

"Holy shit."

"What's the matter?"

"Look what we got. Tower's office sent a check for a hundred thousand."

"What for?"

"There's no explanation, but the stub says refund. It's got to be the transplant money we gave him."

"But he said we weren't getting it back."

"I heard he may need a heart transplant himself. Now he can empathize with everyone waiting."

"He does? How do you know?"

"Worth called me on the way to the session to tell me the bail money is being released tomorrow. I asked him if he knew how Tower was doing after the heart attack, and he said he'd heard he needed a transplant."

"Poor man."

Cory wanted to say karma was a bitch, but said, "I wish him luck."

The next book in this series is, Cory's Shift: Cutting a New Track. Find it in eBook & Paperback.

I hope you enjoyed reading this book as much as I enjoyed

writing it. If you did, I'd appreciate it if you would write a quick review on Amazon or your favorite book site. Reviews are an author's best friend and even a quick line or two is helpful. Thanks, Dan

OTHER BOOKS BY DAN

Complicit Witness

Push Back

Ambition Cliff

You can keep abreast of my writing and have access to books that are free of discounting by joining my newsletter. It normally is out once a month and also contains notes on self- esteem, motivational pieces and wine articles.

It's free. See bottom of my website: www.danpetrosini.com

ABOUT THE AUTHOR

Dan is a USA Today and Amazon best-selling author who wrote his first story at the age of ten and enjoys telling a story or joke.

Dan gets his story ideas by exploring the question; What if?

In almost every situation he finds himself in, Dan explores what if this or that happened? What if this person died or did something unusual or illegal?

Dan's non-stop mind spin provides him with plenty of material to weave into interesting stories.

A fan of books and films that have twists and are difficult to predict, Dan crafts his stories to prevent readers from guessing correctly. He writes every day, forcing the words out when necessary and has written over twenty-five novels to date.

It's not a matter of wanting to write, Dan simply has to.

Dan passionately believes people can realize their dreams if they focus and act, and he encourages just that.

His favorite saying is – "The price of discipline is always less than the cost of regret"

Dan reminds people to get the negativity out of their lives. He believes it is contagious and advises people to steer clear of negative people. He knows having a true, positive mind set makes it feel like life is rigged in your favor. When he gets off base, he tells himself, 'You can't have a good day with a bad attitude.'

Married with two daughters and a needy Maltese, Dan lives in Southwest Florida. A New York native, Dan has taught at local colleges, writes novels, and plays tenor saxophone in several jazz bands. He also drinks way too much wine and never, ever takes himself too seriously.

He puts out a twice-a-month newsletter featuring articles, his writing and special deals and steals.

Sign up at www.danpetrosini.com